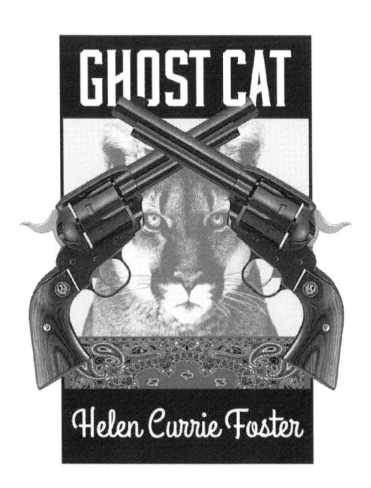

GHOST CAT

Helen Currie Foster

Alice MacDonald Greer Mystery Series

This is a work of fiction. All incidents, dialogue and characters, with the exception of some well-known public figures, are products of the author's imagination and not to be construed as real. Where real-life historical or public figures appear, the situations, incidents and dialogues concerning those persons are used fictitiously and are not intended to depict actual events or to change the entirely fictional nature of the work. Any legal issues and analyses are fictional and not intended or to be taken as legal analysis or advice. Coffee County and Coffee Creek exist solely in the author's imagination, where they are located somewhere in the Texas Hill Country between Dripping Springs and Fredericksburg.

Copyright 2020 Helen Currie Foster. All Rights Reserved.
Published by Stuart's Creek Press, LLC
Dripping Springs, Texas

SCP Stuart's Creek Press

Design by Bill Carson Design
Library of Congress Control Number: 2020906466
ISBN 9781732722903

For the Sibs!

KUDOS FOR THE ALICE MACDONALD
GREER MYSTERY SERIES

"The fifth title in Helen Currie Foster's simply outstanding 'Alice
MacDonald Greer' series, *Ghost Next Door* is a deftly crafted legal
thriller with many an unexpected twist and turn from first page to last.
An impressively entertaining and inherently riveting read...."
Midwest Book Review

OTHER BOOKS BY
HELEN CURRIE FOSTER

Ghost Cave
Ghost Dog
Ghost Letter
Ghost Dagger
Ghost Next Door

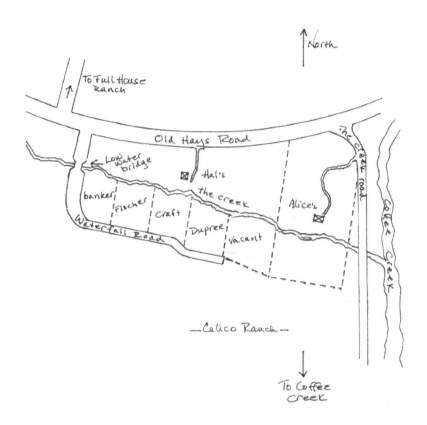

C h a p t e r O n e

A Moving
Black Quilt

Alice leaned motionless into the binoculars, scouting a bobcat. She'd seen the long grass move at the edge of the pasture, where her ranch dropped to the creek. But the cat had vanished. Might have smelled her, felt the weight of her eyes.

She'd stationed herself in her kids' old tree house with her dead husband's binoculars. Alice loved the living silence of the ancient live oak that held the tree house.

A bobcat would hunt until dusk, she'd heard. This time of year, early February, the setting sun shone straight down the creek, gilding the live oaks, turning the pasture gold.

The grass moved. Tawny ears materialized, then eyes. Whiskers. Bigger than she'd expected. Making the tiniest adjustment on the focal knob she leaned forward...and saw only brown movement.

Three burros blocked her view, standing in a tight knot at the cliff's edge.

No chance of cat ears now.

Later, she would think the story began then, but at the moment, she didn't know.

Dark came early this Sunday night, though the days were lengthening. New moon, no clouds: tonight would be clear, with bright stars. She climbed down the tree house ladder and hustled through the gate and into her ranch house.

*****

Alice woke at four, couldn't fall back asleep, got up, and made coffee. Just as she took the first grateful sip she heard a rifle shot somewhere down the valley—she couldn't tell which direction. Out in the Texas Hill Country it wasn't unusual to hear occasional shooting. She found it distinctly odd, though, to hear a shot before the sun came up.

Her phone vibrated—Tonio Ramos. Yes, said his text. He'd come. She'd asked him to walk the fence line with her this morning before work, an annual chore to see what posts needed replacing, what wire needed tightening.

Tonio worked long days at the concrete plant, but he came once a week to help her keep the ranch running: changed filters on the rainwater system, kept fences tight, insulated outdoor faucets before the first vicious norther hit the Hill Country. She knew she couldn't keep the place going without him.

They were formal with each other. Always *usted*, never *tu*. She fixed him big lunches, which he ate privately, on the porch or in his truck. He didn't like to come into the house. He always cleaned the dishes before bringing them back. Alice wasn't sure how old he was or where he lived, but she thought it was with other single guys in a trailer near the concrete plant. She'd gradually met some of his family, helped one cousin deal with insurance after a wreck, helped another cousin find an immigration lawyer. She suspected his parents might not be legal.

At seven-thirty Tonio's Ford Explorer rolled down the drive. Alice tugged on waterproof boots, zipped up her fleece jacket. She found her hiking sticks and walked outside.

Tonio stood by the Ford, squinting at the sky.

"Hola!" she called.

"Hola."

She looked up at the sky, where he pointed. *"Zopilotes,"* he said. Vultures circling down toward a point on her property across the creek.

She couldn't count how many. More were still coming across the sky to join the gyre.

"Something big?" she asked.

He nodded. *"Un venado?"*

A deer. Yeah, maybe so, she thought. A big one, though, not a fawn.

"Any word on Elena?"

"No," he said. "It's nearly a week." He seemed quietly frantic.

Alice frowned. Tonio's little sister, barely nineteen, had won a scholarship to Austin Community College. A counselor had called her parents, saying Elena was missing classes and hadn't emailed her professors. She wasn't answering her phone either.

"Have you contacted the police?"

His eyes widened in fear. "No," he said.

Alice turned up her collar against the cold, studying Tonio. His face, usually a ruddy bronze, had a gray cast. Time to get going. *"Que piensa?*" she asked. "Want to aim for the northwest corner, then walk south, cross the creek, and circle back up here?" She estimated that was at least half a mile. "We can do the other half next weekend."

He nodded.

"For the creek, I'm bringing my hiking sticks."

She and Tonio parked his Ford by her north property line. They hiked west along the fence. Tonio ran his fingers along the top wire from time to time, checking tension.

At the northwest corner, after Tonio checked the fence braces, they turned south. As they started down the long slope to the creek that bisected her property, Tonio tied bright pink survey tape to tree branches encroaching on the fence. He'd return later with the chain saw. He and Alice climbed through the fence that bordered the creek, designed to keep the donkeys from escaping upstream or down, and picked their way across the drifts of shattered limestone that lay like sandbars—rock bars—in the clear blue-green water.

Once across the creek, they climbed up the bank, aiming for the southwest corner of the ranch. Alice looked up, noticing the empty sky.

The vultures were gone.

Was that good?

* * * * *

"Time to cut cedar again," Alice said, dodging the trees along the fence line.

Tonio nodded. Baby cedars looked charming, like miniature Christmas trees, but quickly burgeoned into impassable thickets. They fought their way through one such thicket, trying to avoid the branches' sharp prongs. Alice walked ahead while Tonio tied pink tape to the top fence wire.

A vulture lifted into the air ahead. The ground quivered. Alice stared. A moving black quilt blanketed the straw-colored grass on both sides of the fence. She counted at least sixteen vultures.

Must be a big buck.

She walked slowly forward. Two of the closest vultures took an impatient step away from her and the quilt shifted, the birds grumbling. She moved closer.

On her side of the fence, she saw fingers, a forearm, a small gold bracelet. A slim body lay splayed beneath the lowest fence wire, face in the grass, hands clawed into the ground. Someone had tried to crawl under the fence. Alice found her voice.

"Tonio!"

He ran toward her. One vulture lifted, shifted, dropped back to the far side of the quilt. Tonio's mouth fell open. "Elena?" he whispered. He pointed at the forearm. "The bracelet!"

Alice charged toward the vultures, wildly waving her hiking sticks. The birds lumbered into the air. Tonio stooped close to the body. He dropped to his knees, tears streaming down his face. Alice tried to keep her eyes away. She'd already seen the bright blood on the ripped flesh of the legs. The skirt up over the thighs. Tears in the blue shirt, revealing dried blood on the back. Furiously she whacked at the vultures. One rose, so full it couldn't take off. It vomited flesh out onto the ground and lifted, airborne, above Alice and Tonio.

She turned. "Is it Elena?"

Tonio looked up, face full of pain. *"Mira!* Look at her! Was she—look at her leg!"

He pointed. Alice walked closer, sticks held high in the air. One thigh was covered with blood, some dried, some still oozing red. A round black hole in the bloody flesh of that thigh.

She'd been shot.

The vultures circled, some waddling back toward Tonio and Alice, eager for the main course after the hors d'oeuvres. Tonio took off his coat, laid it over the bare legs. He stood and flailed at the birds.

Alice handed him the sticks. She pulled out her phone and with shaking fingers dialed 911. "Emergency," she heard herself gasp, rattling off the details. Then she called George Files at the Coffee Creek Sheriff's Department and left a message. As she hung up she concluded she'd better meet the Coffee County officers so she could guide them to the body. She couldn't make Tonio do that. They'd be demanding ID, squinting at him with suspicion.

"I will stay," Tonio said. He stood guard, gripping the sticks.

"Don't move her," Alice said. "Don't touch anything." She studied his face. *"Si?* Touch nothing at all!"

He nodded.

She hurried through the thicket, cedar twigs slapping her face, and headed for the house.

C h a p t e r   T w o

Blood in Her Mind's Eye

At noon that Monday, with the last sheriff's department car gone, Alice escaped the ranch to her law office, a small limestone cottage on Live Oak Street, west of the Coffee County Courthouse. Her secretary had already heard. Silent, shaking her head, red ponytail swaying, Silla handed Alice a sympathetic cup of coffee and a stack of messages.

At six Alice drove home and showered for a long time. She couldn't contaminate tonight's book group with the day's horrors. I get it, Lady Macbeth, I finally get it, she thought, closing her eyes as water poured down her face. She soaped her hands again and again, rubbing suds over her face, neck, armpits, chest, crotch, legs, feet, trying to wash away the memory of Elena's body under the fence. Cameras zooming in on blood stains in the grass, unending questions from the crime scene team, an ambulance bouncing across the pasture to the edge of the bluff above the creek, grim-faced men finally toiling back uphill with the body. "Bullet went through the thigh," she heard one man say. So far as Alice could see, they'd searched the surrounding area fruitlessly. No one had bagged anything.

At book group tonight they were supposed to discuss poems. She hadn't the heart to choose one. Clean and damp, still with blood in her mind's eye, Alice drove back to Coffee Creek and pulled into Miranda's drive. Miranda, tall, tart, elegant, managed the local branch of Madrone Bank. Miranda had befriended her when Alice first moved her law practice to Coffee Creek. Alice punched the doorbell, automatically rereading the plaque on the elegant little house: "1876. Coffee Creek Historical Society."

Miranda opened the door, white wine in one hand, and hugged Alice with the other. "I heard," she said in a low voice.

She ushered Alice to the living room. Vintage Miranda: cool blues and whites, with vintage photographs and bright folk art on the walls.

"Alice," Red Griffin said, Alice's best friend, her blue eyes worried. Another hug. "Hey, Alice," Jane Ann Olson said, her voice warm, comforting. Red ran a horse rescue ranch; Jane Ann ran a title company.

On the couch sat a fifth woman, a dark-haired pretty stranger with thick round-framed glasses. "Alice, meet our guest tonight," Miranda said. "This is Holly Dougal. You remember, we read one volume of her trilogy, *Tales of the Road*, about the old roads and cattle trails that ran through the Hill Country?"

"Oh yes!" Alice said. She'd raced through the first volume of *Tales of the Road* three straight nights in her evening tub, then ordered the next two volumes. She stuck out her hand to Holly. "I loved your books, loved every mile. How much was history, how much did you imagine?"

"Great question." Holly lifted her face toward Alice, her eyes huge behind the lenses, wavering as she tried to focus on Alice

"Holly and I met this week at the bank," Miranda said. "Since we've already read her book I asked her to come discuss it."

Alice was relieved to learn that Miranda hadn't invited Holly to join the group. The book group's entry rules were rigorous. Alice, Jane Ann, Red, and Miranda—all currently single, mid-forties, energetic—worked hard at their careers in Coffee Creek, and they'd vowed never to ask clients to join the group. "We can't mix business with our frank assessments," Jane Ann had said. "And I don't just mean about books."

Brutal honesty was permitted at book group. "Tell the truth," Red had said. "Can that be our motto?" They'd all voted yes. "What do you *really* think?" required real answers. Alice didn't want to worry whether her opinions offended a potential client. Miranda didn't want her own acerbic comments to put off her bank clients. Book group was their refuge from the often hilarious mismatch between ideals and reality they saw in Coffee Creek. In book group they'd learned unvarnished truths about each other. They drank wine, shared confidences, tried out ideas in total safety. Their other motto: "What's said in book group stays in book group."

"We'll talk about the book after supper." Miranda waved them toward the dining room buffet. Napkins, silver, crystal wine glasses. Crawfish étouffée and rice in chafing dishes. Salad. Red grinned at Alice, then said to Holly, "We don't always eat like this."

Alice picked up a serving spoon and a crimson napkin. Blood red. She had an instant flashback of a body soaked in blood, splayed beneath barbed wire. She stood stock-still.

Finally, Red's voice penetrated. "Alice?" Alice shook her head, stuck the serving spoon back in the étouffée, and moved on to the salad.

She'd eat nothing formerly alive. Even if crawfish had no blood. Did they? She took herself to a corner chair and stared at her plate.

That night she climbed into bed, closed her eyes to say a prayer for her two children off at college, for her beau, Ben Kinsear, and his children, and especially for Tonio and Elena's family. Pulling up the sheet she realized she recollected only fragments of Holly's talk about her book. She did remember the shock of hearing Holly say that she was losing her sight to fast-moving macular degeneration and could no longer read the fine print in the tomes she researched for her historical fiction. "I've decided to start writing screenplays," she'd said.

Bravo, Alice thought. Holly had made a name for herself as a novelist but now had to shift gears. That took guts.

At the end of the evening, when Miranda was retrieving their coats, Holly had joined Alice, standing very close, and surprised her. "Do you have time to talk to me tomorrow at your office? I'd like your help on a few things." She smiled. "I'd like to get some things dealt with."

Alice had agreed without asking what things. There was something about Holly that made Alice want to say yes. Okay. Get ready. She shut her eyes and fell into uneasy sleep.

Chapter Three

Stay on Your Toes

The next morning at nine Alice glanced out the front window of her office as a dusty sedan pulled up. Holly climbed out of the passenger seat, oriented herself, and marched up the sidewalk toward the front door. The driver sped off.

Alice got Holly settled in the armchair at the tea table by the window. She usually conducted first interviews with clients not from one side of her old partner's desk, but in civilized armchairs at the antique Scottish tea table by the window framing the pecan tree in the back yard.

"So how do you handle getting around, if you can't drive?" she asked Holly.

"My gardener dropped me off. He's picking up plants for the ranch. He's reworking the beds by the main house."

Silla, font of all Coffee Creek knowledge, had told Alice that Holly and her new husband, Russ, had bought a small but famous ranch property near Coffee Creek, one Alice was eager to see. "We bought it because the author of *Holy Alamo* wrote it there," Holly had told the book group. "He typed it on his old Royal, out there in the cabin by the creek."

Now, sitting at the tea table, stirring coffee, Holly got to the point. "My younger sister, Marcy, was in an auto accident five years ago. The other driver T-boned her car. Marcy's head hit the driver's side window really hard." Holly took a breath. "She's never really recovered. You know what they say about prefrontal cortex injury? Messes with your executive function and can change your personality."

Alice nodded. She knew all too well from helping clients deal with lasting effects of wrecks and strokes.

"For the last two years she's been in an assisted living group home in Waxahachie. It's been great for her." Holly tilted her face toward the window, then back toward Alice. Alice couldn't tell how much Holly could see. "Marcy's happy, secure."

"And you're…?"

"I'm on the dotted line for the cost. I signed the long-term contract. Marcy needs this place. There's no one else to help."

"Your husband?"

Holly smiled. "Russ? He would in a heartbeat, if I asked. He knows

I'm committed to taking care of Marcy. But we got married in a hurry." She laughed at Alice's surprise. "No, I'm not pregnant. Russ has a son from a prior marriage. I have Marcy to support. We're not planning to have kids. It was romantic, though. He took me to Big Bend. I could *feel* the vastness, the beauty. We wound up getting married that weekend at the Gage Hotel in Marathon. The desk clerk was our witness." Holly stuck out her left hand, showing the slightly battered gold ring. "We found two old wedding rings in a pawnshop that day."

Alice felt herself smiling, charmed by Holly's warmth and her own memories. She and Kinsear had spent their first night together at the Gage Hotel, on a trip to Big Bend. He hadn't called last night; she wondered if things were awry with one of his daughters. The oldest was giving him fits.

Alice looked back down at her legal pad. "What about your parents?" she asked.

"They've pretty much used up their savings. Mom's in a memory care unit with advanced dementia. Dad's probably going into hospice soon. Not good."

"No other siblings?"

Holly shook her head no. "I see now that I need to be sure Marcy's life is…funded, no matter what happens to me. And this eyesight thing—well, look." She pushed aside the dark bangs, and Alice saw a fresh bruise at Holly's hairline.

"How'd that happen?" Alice asked sharply.

"We're doing some renovation out at the ranch, including a new office for Russ. It's taking forever. I went out to see the slab this morning and tripped over a bit of rubble. Didn't see it. In fact, Russ and I have talked about finding me another location, maybe in Coffee Creek, where I can write until we finish the renovations." She tilted her face toward Alice again. "I was on the gymnastics team in college. Balance beam was my best event. Now, tripping on a little speck of concrete? Unable to stay upright?" She shook her head. "I don't want to blow it out of proportion but that fall on the slab scared me. Life can be short, right?"

Alice nodded, thinking of her husband, Jordie, lost when his helicopter went down in the North Sea. Nothing he—or she—had expected. "Shorter than we dream."

"The fall this morning finally brought it home to me. I just had a sense of the…of my overconfidence, you know? And I've got to take care of Marcy."

More questions, more answers. Alice suggested she take out a life insurance policy with Marcy as beneficiary.

"Makes sense," Holly agreed. "But hopefully she won't need to collect on my death for a long time. Meanwhile, I've got to take care of the long-term costs."

Tales had already made Holly some money and drawn some movie and TV offers. "I'm holding out for a Netflix deal. I'm winding up negotiations with a company in LA called Media Central. I need a big chunk, and I want to put it where it will support Marcy. I've hired a secretary, Sandra Sechrest. That's a help; she seems to be very efficient. I need to squeeze everything I can get out of anything I can still produce." She paused. "I haven't told people about my secret project. You're the first to hear about it."

Alice looked up, waiting.

"In case *Tales* doesn't hit big, I've got three other pieces squirreled away. I finished the third just before Russ and I got married. It's a trilogy, in screenplay format. Part history, part fantasy. War, romance, sex." She grinned. *"Dark Song Trilogy."*

"Oooh." Alice felt immediately drawn to the name, instantly susceptible to Holly's powers of literary enchantment.

"It's not bad." Holly's soft eyes focused somewhere near, but not quite on, Alice's face.

"So what provisions do you envision for Marcy? Is what you're after a trust that can manage her costs, no matter what?" She didn't specify the what. "Does she have a trust?"

"There's not one yet. That's why I need you. I need to be sure Marcy can stay in that group home for the rest of her life if that's the place she needs. Can you help?"

"Yes." But Alice was already fretting over knowledge gaps: she'd need much more information, on Holly's husband's assets, on ownership of the ranch, the new secretary's capabilities.

"You've got time to help me?" Holly went on. "I mean, can you start right away? I just want to get Marcy taken care of. Now."

Alice had watched clients procrastinate on decisions concerning their possible mortality. She understood why, once they finally made up their minds to take a step—will, trust—they were suddenly in an all-fired hurry to get it done. Her mind was already gnawing on the issues, weighing risks and remedies. She outlined a plan: first, a trust for Marcy, assets to include *Tales* and *Dark Song Trilogy* and a small account Holly had opened at Madrone Bank; second, a new will assuring the trust continued and was further funded on Holly's death. Holly nodded. "Sounds good."

"Okay, we'll get on it right away. I'll ask Silla to send you an engagement letter. There'll be a retainer." She liked Holly, but she'd learned: always require a retainer.

Holly nodded agreement. Alice stared again at the bruise, just visible at Holly's hairline. "Meanwhile, are you serious about a place downtown?"

"Definitely."

"Well, if you want to walk three doors down, you can see a house I've bought. It's small, only two bedrooms. Just an old limestone house like this one." Alice, the cautious investor, had found herself making an offer when she saw a "for sale by owner" on the nineteen-forties cottage. She liked the idea of investing in Live Oak Street.

"Like, now?" Holly sat up straight.

"If you want."

They walked together down the sidewalk and up the steps onto the porch of the rent house. "Reportedly John Coffee Hays slept here," Alice said, unlocking the front door, watching to be sure Holly didn't trip over the threshold. "But, of course, that's fantasy, since he died in 1883 and the house was built sixty years later."

"I expect he tented out all over Coffee County, maybe in this very spot," said Holly, the historian. She sniffed the air, took a few steps into the old front room. "Lots of light," she said, her face, with its thick lenses, turning slowly around the room. "That's helpful." The windows stood clean and bare above the old wooden floors, which Alice had had refinished. "I could put my desk over there." She pointed at the front window.

They walked into the kitchen, peered into the small bedrooms, smiled at the bath with its original pink and gray color scheme. "Perfect," said Holly. "I want to rent it. For, like three months. Would that work? Can I have it right now?"

Alice laughed. "You can."

"Hand me the lease! I'm moving in tomorrow!"

When they walked back up the sidewalk to Alice's office, the dusty sedan sat waiting for Holly at the curb.

*****

"Don't forget Eddie LaFarge's appointment," Silla said as Alice entered the office. "He emailed us copies of the vineyard LLC agreement and the buy-out agreement. He'll be here at one. You think I can get an autograph?" She slapped the folder on Alice's desk and spun out, red ponytail bouncing.

Alice felt the little thrill, not quickly suppressed, that Eddie's name evoked. The football pro turned vintner had returned home from California and was making prize-winning wines at his Hill Country vineyard. Now he wanted to buy out his partner in Raptor Cellars. The partner was balking.

At five until one Eddie climbed out of his battered red Ford 150. From her window, Alice saw him inspecting the office. She watched him pull off his ball cap and start up the sidewalk. He'd lost weight from his days as a center but still walked with the sailor's roll some players had. Bad knees, Alice assumed.

Silla was already planted at the open front door, eyes wide.

Eddie was used to hero worship. He smiled and shook Silla's hand, then stopped in Alice's office doorway, clearly curious. The blue eyes took in the tea table, the bookcase, and Alice's big partner's desk.

"My fort." Alice came out from behind the desk. "Like playing center." She wanted to see what was coming. Don't make Wild Bill Hickok's fatal error—sitting with his back to the door.

"Yeah," Eddie responded. "That's true. You gotta be able to read the defense, stay on your toes."

They grinned at each other. She pointed to the tea table. He carefully lowered his large frame into the armchair. Silla brought coffee.

"So why do you want your partner out?" Alice asked.

Eddie frowned a bit. "I can afford it now," he said. "I want to expand, produce more wines. Don't want to have to share the decision-making with him."

"Okay," Alice said. "Sounds like you don't really need his input?"

"True," Eddie said. "Ol' Brad's got plenty of money, but he's a little weak in some other areas."

Alice raised inquiring eyebrows.

"Like morality," Eddie said. "Or maybe judgment." She waited while he decided how much to tell. "We had a wine tasting last month. Brad invited himself, flew in from Palm Springs, trying to show he wanted to stay involved. He announced he'd hire the caterer. Didn't want to use my usual one, though. He bragged how he'd found one on the web for way less money."

Alice waited.

"Food was fine, same as we usually order, maybe not quite as good. But the servers…Alice, there were two bosses, two men. They brought in about twelve workers, spoke only Spanish to them. At the end of the event the bosses, the honchos, watched while they all piled back into two black SUVs. Doors slammed, and off they went. I asked partner boy if this outfit was legit. 'Hey, the price was right! Half the price of those people you use!' he said. I asked him where this outfit was located, had he gone by to check it out. 'No, did it all online! Gotta save time and energy, man!'"

"What was the name?"

"Something blah. Your Best Catering, maybe? But those people weren't normal. Usually servers enjoy my gigs, they smile, they listen to me talk about the wines, they serve like they're positive about the event, part of the event, you know what I mean? But these people—it was like they were ordered not to talk. They kept their heads down and seemed scared." He looked out the window, then back at Alice. "I started to call the sheriff, I swear. But what was I gonna say?"

Alice frowned. She wasn't sure what he'd have said either.

Eddie pointed at the documents on the tea table. "Anyway, I think I'm entitled to get rid of him after three years, right? Buy him out? He's made more than enough money."

"Per the agreement, yes."

"He's whining, doesn't want to be out of the deal. He's asking for a three-year renewal. I want to cut to the chase, with you in charge. Can you write one of those 'here's the deal' letters?"

"Yes," Alice said. "If he's got any sense he won't want to litigate this. Can you have the buyout funds ready to transfer?"

"Yep. Your buddy Miranda's got my accounts now."

He'd met Miranda when Alice and Miranda drove out for a wine tasting, the day before Eddie taught Alice some new evasive driving skills. It might work out for them. Eddie was magnetic, but in a different way from Kinsear. She had a sense Eddie was looking for teammates.

He stood, she stood. "Maybe we can do some more business, Alice. I'm looking forward to getting this guy out of my hair."

"Glad to help."

They shook hands. He turned to go, then turned back. "George Files told me some poor girl got shot, out near you. Was that your place where she was found?"

The scene flooded back. The fence. The body. "Yes," she said.

"Very sorry. They any closer to finding out what happened?"

"I don't know. Sounds like you've got some sort of inside line with George Files. What did he say?"

"We've known each other a long time." Eddie smiled. "George says he doesn't understand why you get all the luck, finding the bodies."

"Talk about the wrong kind of luck."

"That's true. Life's short. 'Gather ye rosebuds while ye may.' Roses, not bodies. I'll be around when you want to talk. About the letter. See you." He sketched a sort of salute and lumbered toward the door. Silla was already in the hall, waiting to tell him goodbye.

"Old time is still a-flying," Alice muttered to herself, watching Eddie stride down the sidewalk toward his truck. "And that same flower that smiles today'"—well, no need to repeat the next line, about dying.

She picked up the file and began drafting the letter to Eddie's partner, Brad Gorman. It had been fun to see Eddie, fun to be working with him. His catering tale came to mind. She searched online for

Your Best Catering. There it was: "Texas Hill Country's Finest." But no mention of an address or physical location. Just a phone number with a San Antonio area code. It seemed odd not to mention the kitchen; people did want to know where their food came from. She turned back to her draft letter, forgetting about the caterer. When she was satisfied with it, she emailed it to Eddie. He replied, "Do it."

Alice found Silla. "Let's email it to Gorman plus send it certified mail, return receipt requested, to this address in the LLC agreement. Copy to Eddie."

"Got it."

That should get things moving. She disliked the idea of Eddie, with his innovative ideas and passion for winemaking, chained to a partner like Gorman.

Alice's phone rang. It was Kinsear, sounding grim.

Chapter Four

Got to Have the Right Guns

"Are you okay?" she asked.

"Me, with my U.S. passport, I'm okay," Kinsear said over car noise. "Javier's dad got picked up by ICE last night in San Antonio. I've been down there with an immigration lawyer trying to get him out of jail." Javier managed Kinsear's ranch outside Fredericksburg. "He'd come across the border to see his baby granddaughter. God, those immigration laws are more complicated than any deal I ever worked on in New York. Javier's afraid he'll never see his dad again. Think about that. Javier's legal, lives here, but his dad can't come visit without winding up in jail. Made me sick seeing that white-haired old guy, so dignified, but so—I don't know. So humiliated. Those ICE guys…they're not old-style border patrol."

"Remember the old days, when people could just go back and forth to Mexico?"

"Yep. So sensible. Family could visit, go home. Now that's gone with the wind."

Then there was only road noise. "Ben? What else is going on?" Because there was something.

"It's Isabel. She's driving me batshit." Kinsear, a widower, was raising two teen-aged daughters, Isabel, in her sophomore year at UT Austin, and Carrie, a high school senior. "I finally saw her fall grades. Barely a 2.0. If she doesn't turn it around she'll flunk out. And apparently won't care. No matter what I say, she just goes off on me. 'You can't understand, Dad!'" he mimicked. "Well, she's right. I can't."

A parent is only as happy as his or her unhappiest child, right? Maybe this was a classic sophomore slump. "Does she have an adviser at UT, someone to talk to?" Alice asked.

"Oh yeah. We met. Disaster. Isabel treated all suggestions by the kindly adviser with studied indifference. The ice princess. Unreachable." Kinsear's voice bothered her. His usual confidence—gone.

"Where are you?"

"Nearly to San Marcos on I-35, trying to stay alive. Hoping you would say, 'What about dinner?'"

"You're on. We won't be alone, though." Her antiques dealer friend Bryce had invited a motley crew for one of his fabled potlucks. Kinsear admired the antique weapons collection on Bryce's walls.

"Okay. That'll improve my outlook. Now I've just got to survive to the next exit. I've got semis ahead of me, semis in my rearview, semis blowing past me. If I live long enough, I'll pick you up at your place."

Funny how if someone tells you his troubles, his load lightens and yours gets heavier. She racked her brain on her way home, trying to think of suggestions for Isabel. Gap year? Volunteer work? A job? She hadn't yet made any effort to meet Kinsear's daughters, partly because she didn't want to make invidious comparisons with her own children, off at college, making decent grades, treating their mother with kindness. She was trying to maintain neutrality on Isabel.

When Kinsear's old Land Cruiser crunched down her gravel drive, Alice walked out to meet him, carrying a baking dish swaddled in foil. "First let me get this stowed!" she ordered. Kinsear obliged. Then he enfolded Alice in a long hug, kissed her, kissed her again. Alice kissed him back, covertly sniffing to be sure he still smelled right. He did. Human animals, operating on a subliminal smell level. They stood a long moment in the twilight chill. Cool air, warm kisses.

"We could just stay here?" he suggested.

"Nope. I promised my mom's baked cheese-covered olive balls. Bryce assigned us to bring retro recipes, from the fifties. M.A.'s bringing her lemon icebox pie." Kinsear raised his eyebrows, grinned. He relentlessly pursued recipes from Alice's client and friend M.A. Ellison, a retired, shotgun-toting biology teacher. "But you'll stay tonight, right?" she added.

"Oh yes."

* * * * *

Bryce and his burly partner, John T, had built their house on a cliff downstream on Coffee Creek, several miles from Alice's place. Tall and impeccable in his violet gingham shirt and chef's apron, Bryce hustled Alice and Kinsear out onto the screened porch above the creek. "At last! The hors d'oeuvres have arrived!" Bryce announced to loud cheers, as Alice marched out onto the porch with her cheese balls.

John T was dispensing sidecars to a rowdy crew including Alice's friend Red, M.A. and her special friend Muddy Mackin, a retired rancher from Marathon, and Ham and Julie Dupree, who lived upstream from Alice. "My granddad's recipe!" warned John T. "Watch out!"

"Your creek looks beautiful," Red remarked. "Aquamarine water on a limestone bed. What could be prettier?"

"The water's low right now," John T said. "Of course, that could change in a heartbeat if we get one of those spring gullywashers."

"Our creek's low too," Ham said.

"We had a weird thing happen out at our place today," Julie said. "This malevolent dog jumped our fence and menaced our eight-year-old. Ham grabbed a gun and ran out just as a man in a black pickup roared up to our gate and jumped out and whistled."

"The man said, 'Don't shoot the dog. He's valuable,'" Ham said, voice tight. "I said, 'That dog's ever anywhere near me or my family, I'm shooting him. You wanna know what's valuable?' The guy gave me quite a look."

"He scared me," Julie said. "Creepy, with this tawny blond hair and pale eyes. He only cared about his dog—didn't give a damn about our kid. But Ham shut him down." She added, "And that dog was well trained. As soon as the man whistled, this one short whistle, the dog turned instantly and jumped over the fence and into the truck."

Alice didn't like the story. After the coming of the donkeys, she never saw coyotes or stray dogs on her place. Fox, yes; porcupine, skunks, armadillos, yes; apparently they got a pass. But her donkeys would make short work of that dog.

Bryce called them for dinner around the trestle table in the big room. John T announced the menu: "Beef stroganoff. My grandmother served it in Salado to her Ruskin Club. Very chic back then. Also avocado grapefruit salad with Helen Corbitt's poppyseed dressing." Everyone nodded, envisioning family tables from way back in the day.

Red passed a plate of puffy little pillows, toasted just so, saying, "These are my mom's split potato biscuits, from her own mother's recipe, but they're yeast rolls, not biscuits."

They dug in. After a moment Bryce said, "Okay, gang. Here's your chance to hear all about the hottest property in Coffee Creek. I mean, of course, Full House Ranch, which the writer Holly Dougal and her new husband, Russ Vay, just bought. And"—he lifted his fork like a scepter—"I've seen it! I got hired to appraise the furniture."

They demanded details.

"Built in the nineteen-twenties, incredible ironwork on the balconies, hand-made iron chandeliers, wrought-iron candlesticks as graceful as any Art Nouveau treasure in Europe. Floors covered with handmade tiles from a San Antonio tile works. Tall ceilings, eleven feet. Creaky wooden staircases to the bedroom wings upstairs." He stopped, looked at the ceiling. "A sense of space that's just right, somehow."

That's what Alice wanted her house to feel like. She wondered whether working for Holly included a tour of her ranch.

"What about the furniture?" John T demanded.

"Imagine a movie set from the late thirties, California ranch setting. Heavy wooden chairs with big cushions. Mission-style but heavier. Around doors, entrances, you don't find right angles, just curves, with heavy plaster, painted creamy white, on the walls. I felt like Cary Grant on one of his more glamorous sets. The house has a timeless style that makes you want to sit by the open doors looking out onto the garden, listen to the fountain, read a great book. Or write one, if you're Holly Dougal."

"Yeah, but what about the noise from that cowboy action place? Isn't that right next door?" John T asked.

"Cowboy action place? Where?" Kinsear inquired.

Bryce nodded. "The ranch property includes a corner parcel that the prior owner rented out to the Coffee Creek Cowboys. They run cowboy action events for single-action shooting. They've built wooden stages, like miniature movie sets, that can look like, oh, a rustler hideout or a saloon. Like a mash-up of the Hole in the Wall and old Dodge City. The lease is still in place, but I don't know what the new owners plan to do. I think Russ has shot some there."

"Cowboy action venues are hidden all over the Hill Country," Red said. "I've got a bunch of friends who've tried cowboy action. One partner at the Houston law firm I managed actually retired, bought a giant RV, and spends the year driving around the Southwest with his wife, competing in cowboy action events." She grinned. "If you're serious, you have to have great outfits, and under official rules you need a moniker, a shooting alias. His is Sidewinder Sam."

Good heavens, Alice thought. An alias? An outfit? Competitions?

Bryce jumped in. "And if any of you want to try your hand at single action shooting, I recently picked up a whole set of replica firearms for cowboy action. Two matching single-action revolvers, shotgun, lever-action rifle, plus leather chaps, and a very fancy tooled leather gun belt. Also leather wrist guards, from the widow of an enthusiast. Not my usual inventory, but I had to grab it."

"Yes," Red said. "You've got to have the right guns."

How did Red know so much about this? She'd never mentioned it to Alice.

Kinsear said, "When can I see them?"

Red said, "Me too!"

"Hang on, now!" John T said. "I might want first pick!"

"Oh my," Bryce said. "They're actually right here, locked up in the armory, down the hall. We'll have a tour after dinner." He looked at Kinsear's alarmed face. "But first, lemon icebox pie."

M.A. smiled sweetly. Kinsear sighed in relief. Under the table Alice furtively checked her phone messages and saw one from Holly: "Can you pls meet me at the ranch tomorrow a.m. to talk docs? Urgent."

"Yes. Ten okay?" Alice texted back.

"Perfect."

Also urgent: a night alone with Kinsear. He finished the lemon icebox pie and lavished praise on M.A. Under the dinner table he tapped Alice's boot with his. She read his expression, the raised eyebrows and the silent plea: "Can we leave?"

She stood, smiling. "It's been a long day. Bryce, John T, thanks!"

In the car she slid her hand around Kinsear's neck, leaned over.

"I'm about to run off the road, Alice."

She grinned to herself. "You are taking these turns with enthusiasm."

"That's what you call it?"

Chapter Five

A Full House

Holly had told Alice that the historic Full House ranch came to its next-to-last owner, a card-counting genius, in a late-night poker game. He never played poker again; the loser shot him, but his widow kept the ranch. The widow admired writers, which is how the author of *Holy Alamo* came to live in the creek cabin while he finished his book. Holly and Russ bought the ranch out of the widow's estate, outbidding others by a significant margin.

Alice had wanted to see Full House even before she came to Coffee Creek. In the fifties the widow had allowed a local brewery to photograph the rapids on the cypress creek. Many a bar in many a Texas roadhouse boasted a lighted beer sign featuring those rapids.

Armed with coffee Alice sped west out the Old Hays Road in her little green Discovery. She missed her old tan Toyota truck, relegated to hauling hay, but had to admit the sound system in her new ride made her voice sound better. Singing along to Sun Radio, she watched for the turnoff to Full House.

At the ranch gate she punched in the code Holly had texted. Pastures lay left and right; longhorn cattle, some speckled black and white, some burnt orange and white, peaceably raised their lethal horns toward her. Holly had said it was almost a mile to the house. Alice drove over a ridge and around a bend, then slowed, looking at the creek and the house beyond. Enormous cypress trees lined both sides of the creek, their limbs just hinting at feathery green spring foliage. Alice eased across the low-water bridge, stopping for a moment to look upstream and down. There's nothing like a cypress creek, with the magnificent trees, the spring-fed blue-green water, clear as glass. She rolled down the window, saw a quick silver flash, a bass, maybe. What a lucky fish, living here.

The drive continued toward two pecan groves. Between the groves sat Full House: red-tiled roof, two stories in the center, with one-story wings extending to each side. An English manor house with hacienda touches? Definitely movie material, Alice decided. She stopped her car in the drive, wanting to take it all in. Upstairs, the creamy stucco walls were broken by a series of tall French doors opening onto balconies with black wrought-iron railings. The porch roof protected imposing carved wooden entrance doors. Across from the entrance, built into the stucco wall of the stone-paved courtyard, stood an honest-to-God guardhouse.

Maybe it had been built for movie stars arriving in the thirties with chauffeurs and furs.

Alice turned just short of the courtyard into a gravel parking area on the near side of the house. She parked next to a beat-up blue Chevy truck with several bales of hay in the truck bed—the quintessential, indispensable ranch truck. According to her dashboard clock she was ten minutes early.

Out her rearview mirror she saw two riders trotting down the drive toward the courtyard—a big man with a gray buzzcut astride a tall palomino and Holly on a smaller bay. Alice watched as the two reached the courtyard, apparently oblivious to her car. Palomino man dismounted, gathered both sets of reins, and stood close to Holly. Holly swung her right leg over the saddle horn and slid down into his arms. He leaned over her, kissed her hair, said something. Holly tilted up her face, glasses glinting in morning sun, and the two kissed—for a long time. Fascinated, Alice concluded she might be watching love. She felt her own blood tingle.

A smiling young Mexican-American man emerged from the guardhouse and took charge of the horses. Holly and Palomino man disappeared into the house. Alice gathered up her briefcase, checked her lipstick, and headed the same way.

As she reached for the doorbell the front door popped open. She looked up into a good-humored face with sharp gray eyes, a gray buzz-cut, and a welcoming smile.

"You must be Alice. You're early! Five till nine. I'm Russ Vay."

"My dad always said five minutes early was on time," Alice said. "Drummed it into me!"

Then she was struck silent by the dark smooth tiles of the hallway floor, decades old, and by the high ceiling, the wagon-wheel chandelier, the wrought iron sconces on the walls. Russ followed her gaze. "It's pretty all right, isn't it?" he said. "A nightmare to renovate because we don't want to screw it up."

She liked his caution about messing with Full House.

"Holly will be just a minute. She knows you're here. Want to see the living room?"

Of course, she did. Again the creamy curved plastered walls, the black wrought iron chandeliers, and the massive stone fireplace, a fire crackling in the cool morning air. Mission oak furniture with heavy red print cushions. The rear of the living room was all French doors facing a stone courtyard with a fountain. She'd never envied anyone else's house, but this one…mm-hmm, she did.

"Who did the ironwork?" she asked.

"An old German from Fredericksburg. Made fences, made horseshoes, and then, when the widow got Full House, he made art. He also invented the Full House brand, which is part of the fireplace tools." He took Alice over to a set of handmade wrought-iron tools standing on the hearth and picked up a branding iron and held it up for her to see. "You know a full house is three of a kind and a pair?"

Alice nodded.

"He designed this ornate number three, with a wavy bar sticking out of the bottom of the three, off toward the right, and another sticking out of the middle toward the right, so it looks like the number three encompassing the number two. He put the same design on the iron gate to the parking area. Holly even got us some bumper stickers with this brand."

Russ looked toward the stairway. "My sweetie's here. She'll want to talk in her study."

Alice heard the light footfalls, then saw Holly enter the living room, running her hand along the wall. Alice hated that Holly needed help knowing where she was in her own house.

"Alice! Thank you so much. Come with me to the study. The workmen aren't here yet so we can hear ourselves think."

Holly's study, off the living room, looked out through French doors at the same courtyard. Her ceiling had a gaping hole, pipes visible in the darkness. White plaster dust had sifted over a mission oak desk by the French doors and a smaller desk by the hall door. "We're having to replace all the upstairs plumbing," Holly sighed. "Lead pipes, lots of leaks. And when the plumbers get here it sounds like the end of 'Sorcerer's Apprentice' in *Fantasia*. Bam bam bam!" She glanced toward the door. "It's closed, right?"

Alice nodded. "How do you write, now? Special computer screen?"

"Come see." She motioned Alice over to the desk by the French doors so Alice could see the business-like lamp with separate magnifier and the magnifying screen over the computer monitor. "So far I've managed. But no way can I do the research I used to. About this trust for Marcy's care. Here's the deal. She gets disability income from Social Security. That's not much. Right now her care costs me over a hundred thousand a year. The cost'll go up every year, of course. Marcy's just twenty-two. Ultimately I'll need—millions?"

Alice flinched. "Yikes. Will the royalties or other funds from *Tales* meet the current costs?" *Tales* was good, but—that good?

"It's why I'm shifting to screenplays. I got the idea because one producer wants to make *Tales* a series. I'm doing that myself, thank you. Remember I told you about my *Dark Song Trilogy*? Here are the scripts." She opened a desk drawer and pulled out a sealed thick brown envelope. She glanced again toward the door, then slipped it back in her desk drawer, behind other files.

"I don't think anyone knows they exist," Holly continued. "They're under wraps until the Media Central deal's complete. They're sending me the signed contract today. Then I can get my agent working on a really good deal for *Dark Song*."

"What exactly is in that envelope?"

"Three storylines, each with six separate episodes."

That sounded arduous. "How'd you do that?"

"Worked night and day after my ophthalmologist gave me the really bad news. Just before I met Russ."

"Russ knows about—about—what's happening to your eyes?"

"Oh, of course. Bless him. He says I can always see with my third eye. He's hilarious."

Alice hoped she was right—that Russ did want his sweetie both in sickness and in health.

"These new screenplays will also become trust assets, for Marcy's care, right?"

"Yes. *Tales* may not get us to the finish line but should at least give me a head start. If *Tales* works out, these screenplays should get more traction too. I'm also fiddling with the early stage of what might be a comic screenplay."

Bam! Plaster dust filtered down. Alice brushed dust off her face and shook it from her hair. Holly wiped dust off her glasses. Bam! Bam!

"See?" Holly said, pointing at the ceiling. "I definitely need another place to work! I wanted you to come out here to Full House so Russ could meet you. I also wanted another chance to talk to you—all by yourself."

"Of course. But you said no one knows about the screenplays. What about your secretary?"

Holly shook her head no.

"I always bring up this issue of client confidentiality, Holly, but it looms even larger when we're talking about significant intellectual property. If we communicate by email, can you read the emails?" Anyone could read her magnified computer screen from ten feet away.

"Yes." Holly held up her cell phone. "I've got a special screen on my phone."

"And your phone locks?"

"Yes, I have to use a code to open it."

"And your laptop? Is it private too? Can other people see your emails, your documents?"

"No, I don't think so. The computer requires a password. Of course, on any new writing I do, I can email that to my secretary so she can get it in shape."

"What about voicemail? Is yours private?" She looked at the phone on Holly's desk. "Is that a dedicated line or an extension?"

"Extension." Holly nodded. "There's another in the kitchen and another in our bedroom."

"We'll use the cell phone then." What else? Alice knew she was missing something. "If I send you drafts to review, can you read them? Print them?"

"Yes. I've got my magnifying glass." Holly sounded impatient.

"Okay," Alice said. "And when you're in Coffee Creek you can always walk down the street and talk to me."

"Right."

Alice heard voices outside the door, one low and rumbling with laughter, one female and breathless. Russ and—?

*****

Russ opened the study door and stood back. "Oh!" said a medium-tall woman in heels and pencil skirt. Perfectly made up face, horn-rimmed glasses, dark blond hair swept back with a clip. Late thirties, maybe.

"Good morning, Sandra," Holly said, smiling. "Alice, meet Sandra Sechrest. Sandra, meet Alice Greer, my lawyer and my new landlord in Coffee Creek."

Alice extended her hand. "Hello."

"Good morning," Sandra said, shoulders straight, eyes wide. She dusted the top of the small desk and placed her purse on it, then said, "Oops!" She'd knocked over several paint and fabric sample boards leaning against the side of the desk. "Aren't these charming!" Pale blue and pink chintz prints, pastel paint colors—not the same palette as the downstairs.

"We're renovating the old nursery upstairs. Or playroom, really," Holly said. "The previous owner turned it into a guest room, but it's big, with bookshelves, room for kids to play. We're going to restore it. Like we're doing with some of the other rooms."

Nursery? Though they weren't planning a baby? Alice saw Sandra's eyes blink rapidly, then gaze back at the lively prints on the sample boards. Sandra surreptitiously ran her hand across some pink miniature corduroy. "So soft," she said.

Russ didn't seem disturbed by the nursery plans. "It's a storybook house. We're having fun with it."

Sandra and Alice jumped at the sound of rapid gunfire, sustained, repeated.

"No worries, ladies," Russ said. "That's just the cowboy action shooting place, the Coffee Creek Cowboys. The previous owner rented out one corner of the ranch."

Holly heaved an exasperated sigh. "That's another reason I wanted an office in your Live Oak Street house, Alice. You can imagine what gunfire does to the writer's productivity." She looked longingly at her desk. "Just when I get rolling, rapid-fire shooting erupts. Plays hell with my plotting. Also, our favorite horse trail runs by the back of the cowboy action lease. You want to see a horse get spooked? Ride by when the shooting starts. I'm not kidding, I heard a shot go right over my head, Russ, the last time I went down there by myself. Miss Fancy reared up, snorting—took me five minutes to settle her."

"Wasn't that the last day of deer season? Probably a stray shot from some idiot. Anyway, the cowboy action lease runs out in sixty days," Russ said. "It's run by a group of enthusiasts, all volunteers. I kinda hate to boot them out; they built the sets themselves. But honey, we can tell them to find someplace else."

"I wanted to give a party here," Holly said. "A belated wedding reception. But that'll have to wait too."

"Well, I don't know," Russ said. "We could give a party at the cowboy action place!"

All three women stared at him, faces startled. Surely he wasn't serious?

"Never mind," he said. "Just call me the butler." He waved and left. Russ was one of those unconsciously attractive men who exudes the kind of good-humored warmth and, yes, comfortable sexuality that disarms most women. She'd felt herself smiling, hadn't she, when he greeted her? And Sandra seemed intensely aware of Russ. But Alice liked that he'd called Holly his sweetie.

Sandra put down the sample boards and straightened her already straight shoulders. "Well, I'm looking forward to getting the two of us moved into the Live Oak house!" she said.

"You won't have to be there the whole time, Sandra," Holly said. "Just part-time. I need a quiet place to write."

"Like Virginia Woolf?" Alice asked.

"Yes, exactly. A room of one's own."

Bam! From upstairs, followed by a string of not-quite-decipherable curses.

"But I don't mind a bit," Sandra said. Had she missed the point? "And you need someone to drive you."

"Oscar already does that. Our gardener," Holly responded.

"I really don't mind," Sandra said.

Alice looked at her phone. "Yikes! Holly, we still need to go over a couple of details, right?"

Holly turned toward Sandra. "We need a few more minutes, please."

Sandra didn't move for a second. "Of course." She swooped out the door, head high.

Holly sighed. "Russ is right. I need a secretary. But I need solitude too. I don't seem to have the right touch with her."

"Could she work part-time?" That seemed like a simple solution to Alice. "Or does she need full-time money?"

"The latter. She seems organized, so Russ thought she could also help keep track of my book events, drive me there, make our travel plans. He hired her full-time. She worked as a corporate paralegal at that Elder-something firm in Austin, then with another firm in Florida, where she grew up. Then she took a job in LA as the personal assistant for a movie producer. From a couple of comments she's made, I think she helps support her brother. He's a little undisciplined. That's the word she used."

Alice looked at her notepad. "Two more questions. If Russ has some interest in the trust assets, is he willing to disclaim those in writing?"

"Russ? Of course! We even have a prenup about that. My agent suggested it. Russ was fine with it."

"I'll want a copy of the prenup for the file. Also, what about trust executors?"

Holly nodded. "We need someone long-term."

"A bank with a trust department?" Alice suggested. "But you could have someone else you trust, excuse the pun. Does Marcy have a lawyer? A guardian?"

"Me," Holly said. "There's no one else. My parents right now— well, they can't."

"I'll think about this, get you some suggestions," Alice said. "Last question, for your will. What are the other assets?"

Holly opened the desk drawer and pulled out a stapled document, held it close to her eyes, then handed it to Alice. "Here's my old will. Bottom line, Alice, Russ wants to be sure he treats his son generously, and I want to be sure Marcy's covered. Otherwise, except for my writing, Russ and I both want other income that comes in to be community property."

"Does Russ already have a will?"

"Yes. He revised it before we got married." She dug out one more stapled document. "Here's last year's financial statement. What's not on there yet is the ranch itself. We own it together. Russ wanted to be sure I'd get it if he dies."

And vice versa, Alice thought, stowing Holly's papers in her briefcase. "Who do you want to be executor under your will?"

"Can you do it?" Holly's eyes were huge behind the lenses. "Alice, I'd really prefer for you to do it. My parents sure can't, and Marcy can't. Russ is fifty-five, I'm thirty-two. So"—her face lit up with that impish smile—"I expect to outlive him. Russ won't mind. And with moving to a new town and all—I'd really appreciate knowing you were watching out for me."

Alice paused. She usually preferred not to act as a client's executor. But Holly's circumstances weren't usual. "I think that could work."

"How fast can we do this? I have to be in town tomorrow afternoon. Any possibility the trust agreement could be ready for me to sign? I just…I want this taken care of."

Had she forgotten anything? Need anything more? She double-checked her notes. Nope. "I see no reason it can't be ready tomorrow afternoon. I'll get started. Meanwhile, here are the keys to your new Live Oak office." Alice laid the keyring, with its red tag reading "Live Oak," on Holly's desk, right next to her hand. "We'll be in touch."

Alice opened the study door. On the far side of the living room, Russ leaned back in a big armchair, Sandra hovering above. She heard Sandra ask, "Are you quite sure there's nothing else I can do for you? Any dry cleaning you need me to get to the cleaners? Anything at all?" So bright, so efficient. Organizes the dry cleaning too? Pretty useful. Alice noticed Sandra used a different tone of voice for Russ than for Holly.

Russ grinned up at Sandra. "Not now. Thanks."

His eyes met Alice's, and he heaved himself out of the chair. "Let me walk you to your car."

* * * * *

Russ and Alice started across the courtyard in chilly sunshine, Alice aware of Russ's bulk, warmth, good humor. She was shivering in her down vest; the cold didn't seem to bother him.

Two more vehicles sat parked near Alice's Discovery and the blue ranch truck. Alice assumed Sandra owned the cream and brown Mini Cooper. She peered in. Spotless. Beyond the Mini Cooper was a battered white van with ladders and pipes tied on top: "Waters' Plumbing."

"That's the bumper sticker Holly got us, with the Full House brand." Russ pointed to a faded mini sticker on the ranch truck.

Alice heard hoofbeats and turned to watch the palomino and the bay trot up to the wall by the parking area. Both gleamed in the sunshine. They must have just been brushed.

"Hey, girls," Russ said. He turned to Alice. "Holly and I ride early most mornings." He reached into his jeans and pulled out two horse treats.

"I saw you coming back. I'm glad she can ride," Alice said. "But I was going to ask you"—she stopped.

"Yeah, I was watching your face when she was talking about Miss Fancy. Don't worry, I make sure she doesn't ride by herself anymore. She still has some peripheral vision, but I go along to be sure she stays on a good trail. And not because of that wild shot she heard—you get that on ranches, some antsy deer hunter two miles away. Here you go, Miss Fancy." The bay extended a graceful neck and nuzzled the treat from his broad palm. "And I'm not forgetting you, Honey." The palomino lifted liquid brown eyes at him and delicately took the treat.

Russ went on, stroking Honey's neck. "Gotta tell you, Alice, I never dreamed I'd be this lucky. Living at Full House and riding with a woman like Holly." He snorted a happy laugh. "Not in that order. I mean, who'd have thought she'd pay attention to an old geezer like me?"

Alice watched the hands stroking Honey. Geezer? He seemed unaware of his appeal. Or the nursery.

"Take good care of my Holly," Russ said. She looked up, surprised. On one hand, of course she took good care of her clients. On the other hand, he seemed to have more than legal services on his mind. "I have to tell you, no offense, Alice, but I wasn't in favor of this separate office she's renting from you. I like having Holly where I can see her. She's—her eyes are getting worse and worse. She thinks I don't notice but it's getting hard for her to navigate across a room. I'm worried about her being by herself downtown. I'd rather she could be out here. When she needs to be alone, that's fine, and I still know she's close. But—" He looked at the Waters' Plumbing van. "It's just a three-month lease, right?" he asked. "That's about as long as we've been married."

Alice nodded. "No penalty if she wants to leave early. Is there no other place out here she could write?"

"Not really. That old writer's cabin by the creek has no heat, and she could break her neck on the trail getting to it. Cypress roots everywhere. Plus, these days she needs a secretary to clean up the writing. I know it frustrates the hell out of her." He took a deep breath, let it out.

Alice nodded, remembering Holly lightly tracing the wall with her hand. "I'll do my best."

Thoughts tumbling through her head—she needed the ranch deed, needed to think through the trust, needed to make the legal pieces fit—she left Full House and sped to town, feeling less peaceful than when she'd arrived. At least this new client distracted her from thoughts of Elena's body, lying under the fence. Again she thought of Tonio's grief-stricken face. Time to call George Files at the sheriff's department, see if he had any leads.

Instead Silla met her at the office door. "Get ready," she said. "You need to call a very angry guy named Brad about your letter concerning Raptor Cellars. Called an hour ago. Whooee! About melted my phone!"

C h a p t e r   S i x

Sufficient unto the Day

I rritated, Alice yanked Eddie's file from the corner of her desk. She reread her letter to Brad Gorman. She'd quoted the precise language from the agreement. It gave Eddie the clear right to buy out his partner after three years, no strings attached. What was Gorman's beef? She was reaching for the phone to call him back when a blur shot up the sidewalk outside her window, and a man shoved his way through the front door.

Silla was already there, feet planted, one hand on one hip, one hand on Alice's half-open office door, blocking his entry. "May I help you?" she asked.

The man stood five-ten, broad shoulders swaddled in an outdated Ultrasuede jacket. Ornate cowboy boots, new. Bulldog face, artificial tan. "I'm here to talk to Alice Macwhatever," he said. "You her?"

"No," Silla said. "You are?"

"Brad Gorman. She was supposed to call me back. I haven't heard a word."

"She does have other clients, Mr. Gorman." It was best not to make Silla mad. Alice left the safety of her partner's desk, took the door from Silla's firm grip, and told her, "Please take Mr. Gorman to the conference room."

Alice spun on her heels and retrieved Eddie's client folder. When she walked into the conference room Gorman was prowling around the polished oak table like a caged lion.

"Have a seat," she said, taking the chair at the head of the table.

Gorman had dark hair with a faintly reddish hue and white sideburns. Dyed, Alice concluded. Vain? Insecure? Both?

"Hey, I thought I'd get better treatment here in the sunny south," Gorman said. "Your famous hospitality and all."

"This is Texas," Alice said. "We're hospitable, but we also appreciate manners. I take it you got my letter?"

"That's why I'm here. Your letter won't work."

"You realize I don't represent you? Do you have counsel?" Alice needed to warn him of the ground rules.

"I'll get a lawyer if I need to," he growled. "But I came to see the lay of the land for myself." He leaned back in the chair, put his arms behind his head, assuming the "I'm totally comfortable" position. "I like it here. I'm thinking of moving my operations out here. Everyone tells me land's a good investment in this Hill Country, you call it. Furthermore, I can tell there's plenty of money to be made outta that vineyard. I'm good at that, let me just say. Let's build a wedding venue, host more events! Here I am, ready to work, and Eddie lays this buyout crap on me." He leaned forward, arms on the table, and narrowed his eyes at Alice. "Fuhgeddaboutit!"

Wow, he really said that, Alice thought.

"That ain't gonna happen! I like being a partner in that vineyard. Eddie can't just up and throw me out."

Alice shook her head. "Your agreement's quite clear. Eddie is entitled to pay your buyout fee and terminate the arrangement. Of course, you're free to look for business opportunities here, but you're out of the vineyard." She picked up her pen. "Did you bring the wiring instructions? We're ready to send your check."

"He can't use my money and then get rid of me!" he exploded.

Alice raised one eyebrow. "You made the deal, Mr. Gorman. This is the deal."

He tried another tack, leaning forward, arranging his face in a smile. Alice watched with interest as Mr. Hyde gave way to Dr. Jekyll.

"Let's talk turkey, hon." Whoops, bad bedside manner, Dr. Jekyll.

"Call me Ms. Greer or this talk's over."

"Oh, of course. Look, I've got great ideas for the vineyard, and I can make it up with Eddie. He needs me. He's missing the boat on what we could be doing. I've got great hospitality connections. We can run big events and rake in money, all for peanuts in costs."

"What 'connections' are you talking about? Eddie wasn't impressed with the people you hired for a recent event."

"Why not? They did great and for nearly nothing. Look, missy—"

Alice stood up. "This is going nowhere."

"Oh, sorry. Pretty touchy, aren't you? Lemme lay out the proposal."

She waited, standing.

"I take on the financial side entirely. I fund the events, I run that side. Eddie sticks to the wines."

"Eddie has given me instructions," she said. "I'd rather wire the money to you directly, but if you don't give me the bank information

I'll send a check today to the address you gave in the agreement."

He popped up, leaning on the table, his face a mask of rage.

"I won't accept that check! He's not getting rid of me! I'm in it and staying in it!"

"It doesn't matter whether you cash the check or not," Alice said, "because his only obligation is to send it. That letter and that check hit the post office and we're done." She was so angry her hands were shaking. She grabbed the folder tightly to remind herself to stay calm. "You and I are done too. If you've got counsel, I'm happy to talk to that person. Meanwhile I'll convey your response to Eddie. If he changes his mind I'll let you know, but my current instructions are to send you the final check."

"'I'll convey your response to Eddie,'" he mimicked. "Tell you what, I'll be conveying my response to him and his little vineyard, and maybe he'll figure out he can't mess with Brad Gorman."

"We don't take kindly to threats, Mr. Gorman." In her mind Alice saw the hillside of carefully planted vintage vines, an investment taking years to mature. Surely the man wouldn't attack vines. "You need to leave. Right now." She threw open the door. "Now!" she said again. Her temples throbbed; she could feel her blood pressure soaring.

Gorman stood, veins standing out in his throat, glowering at her. His voice changed. "By God, I know who's gonna be sorry. And it's not just Eddie." He thrust his way past her and past Silla, whose freckled face peered from the hallway. Silla gripped her cell phone in one hand and a large stapler in the other—the big one for stapling thick court filings. Gorman rushed out the front door and down the steps. He held his cellphone to his ear, talking furiously. He vaulted into the driver's seat of a black Jeep parked across the street, slammed the door, and roared off.

Mechanically Alice noted the vanity plate: "MYWAY."

"Lord!" Silla said. "That man gives me the creeps! What's he trying to do?"

"Take over Eddie's business," Alice said. She pointed at the stapler. "What were you going to do with that? Staple his mouth shut?"

"Yes," Silla snapped, "and anything else he's got."

Eddie, as predicted, dug his heels in. "I'm on my way to the bank for that check right now," he said on the phone. "I'll bring it by."

When he handed the certified check to Alice an hour later, Eddie's grim face startled her. He hadn't shaved; the grizzled two-day growth and the scowl on his face made her aware of the bull neck, the huge shoulders and hands of a former pro football center.

"You know, Eddie," she said, "I'd beef up security around the vineyard if I were you."

"Raptor Cellars has some armament." His voice was dry, level.

"But the vines don't," she said. She envisioned herbicide spray, fire attacking helpless vines wired in rows on the hillside, flames licking the leaves.

Eddie glanced at her, then out the window, his blue eyes looking left, then right, as if evaluating a defensive lineup. "He could damage my vines. That what you mean?"

"He may be capable of it."

Alice asked where he'd met Gorman.

"An old player buddy of mine recommended him. Gorman helped my buddy start a restaurant in Phoenix. That's Gorman's home base. But I found out he'd also funded a couple of vineyards in Sonoma. I thought he might work out on a one-shot deal. He's made a nice profit on his investment already. But we're done. You sending that check out today?"

Silla overheard him. "I'm on my way to the post office right this minute." She brandished the envelope.

Eddie thanked her. He turned back to Alice. "He didn't threaten you, did he?"

"Not directly." Was that truthful? She added, "I'll just say that Silla was standing outside the conference room with our biggest stapler in one hand and her cell phone in the other."

"Thanks, Alice. I didn't know this was gonna be so messy." He gave her one of those Eddie looks, unblinking blue eyes focused on her face. "You take care."

And he was out the door.

At this rate she should bill for hazard pay.

She realized she hadn't heard from Files and called him. There was no answer, so she left a message: "Any word on who shot Elena

Ramos?"

She looked around the office. Sufficient unto the day is the evil thereof. Maybe in work lay welcome distraction. She turned back to Holly's documents. Dry words on a page, yet words that could make things happen, like securing Marcy's place in the group home she loved. She plunged back into the trust agreement, spotting issues she needed to check with Holly. At sunset she was cross-eyed and made more coffee, then dived into the will.

Chapter Seven

Don't Know Exactly What's Going On

By seven on Thursday she was back at her desk reviewing Holly's drafts.

The phone interrupted. Ham and Julie: "We just left the HEB grocery, and we thought maybe we could lay a problem on you. Can we stop?"

Of course, she said yes.

Alice's law practice included wills, trusts, and real estate. People streamed west into the Hill Country, buying their dream property for water, for beauty, for the magnetic pull of the landscape. With Austin extending active tentacles toward Coffee Creek, she found herself dealing with long-time landowners selling part of the family ranch to developers, trying to keep enough for themselves, or turning the proceeds into a house in town and a smaller place for weekends in the country.

She hadn't yet confronted a problem quite like Ham and Julie's.

The couple sat before her, Ham running his hand through unruly brown curls, bulldog jaw set, brown eyes worried, and Julie, young face intent, wrinkles from days outdoors just beginning to frame her blue eyes. Both still wore jeans and boots from morning chores with their horses.

Ham began, "Like everyone who bought a little piece of the old Calico Ranch along our road, Waterfall Road, we're subject to the same covenants, the same land-use restrictions. No mobile homes and residential use only, except for ag use."

Alice nodded. Her ranch had similar restrictions.

"There are five lots on the creek side of Waterfall Road," Ham said. "The lots are ten acres and up. Calico Ranch kept the last downstream lot. That's the one that abuts your land, across the creek from your house."

Alice nodded.

"Going back upstream, we're next. Next to us was the old Traut place. Just past the Traut place is the Fischers'. They're friends of ours. The last upstream lot, right at the low-water bridge across the creek, belongs to a banker. The only way you can reach those five lots is by crossing the low-water bridge and driving down Waterfall Road. Anyway, the Traut place next to us is about ten acres. We heard it was sold last fall. The new owner replaced the fence with a big stone wall, all the way around, even along the creek! I'd estimate it's eight feet tall."

Julie jumped in. "According to the Coffee Creek appraisal records, the new owner's Richard R. Craft. We've never met him, never seen him. We call him the Hermit. According to the internet, he moved here from Houston and is at least seventy."

"Here's what worries us," Ham said. "The way Waterfall Road curves, from our gate, we can see the Hermit's gate. Some nights we'll see big SUVs rolling in and out a couple of times an evening. Black ones, tinted windows."

"More than one?" Alice asked.

"Oh, yeah. Usually two at once. But it's not for events at the Hermit's place because we don't hear music, and we don't see random cars coming in, like you would for parties. Just those two big SUVs going out usually in the afternoon and coming back late."

Julie added, "Plus we hear firing sometimes. Like target practice. It really bugs the Fischers. They say it sounds like automatic weapons."

"What's bugging me," Ham said, "you remember the guy with the dog? The one that scared our boy?"

Alice remembered.

"I think he lives there. I'm pretty sure I saw the same truck turning in at the Hermit's gate a couple of weeks ago. All matte black finish, no chrome, with a red and black decal I couldn't quite see. But he's not always driving that truck. I saw the dog in the front seat of a black SUV at the Y this week. The side windows were tinted but the SUV was parked right at the front door, and I saw that dog through the windshield. Can't forget that dog. I was on my way to the weight room, and when I walked in, that guy was walking out, covered with sweat. Gave me a look and kept on walking, straight out to the SUV." He paused. "Muscles everywhere. And some tats."

"You think Craft—the Hermit—is violating the covenants somehow?"

"Yes," Ham said. "I don't know exactly what's going on but it sure doesn't feel like residential use only. It feels commercial."

"But Craft's not the guy with the dog?" Alice asked.

"No," Julie said. "Craft's claiming the tax exemption for people over sixty-five, per the appraisal office records. The dog guy was maybe thirty-five. Right?" She looked at Ham.

"Right," he agreed.

"Could be family, though," Alice said.

"Maybe," Julie said. "But the target practice? It's pretty regular, like once a week. Doesn't last long, but it's intense and systematic."

"Have you seen anyone else besides the dog guy?"

Ham hesitated. "I've seen a woman going in and out during the day, sometimes driving one of those SUVs. But we don't watch all the time. We're trying to run our place." Ham and Julie stabled horses and kept some milk goats.

Alice wondered if the Hermit had a couple of live-in caretakers. A cook, or nurse. "Without more information on a specific violation I'm not sure I can help. The covenants prohibit target practice, which is common, but most people ignore that unless it really becomes a nuisance." On Sunday afternoons, several times a year, she heard pistol shooting for twenty minutes or so. She wasn't sure on which property, either. Her small ranch touched several others, and she'd never bothered to try to track down the pistol shooters. "You're sure the shooting's at the Hermit's place?"

"That's what the Fischers say." Julie handed Alice a stack of stapled papers. "I made you a copy of our deed and the covenants. I googled Craft, too. He shows up in connection with various businesses but not in Coffee Creek."

Alice scanned the restrictions. Typical of the eighties, nineties: no mobile homes, no commercial use, no target practice, no nuisances. Limits on residential structures, too; only a guest cottage could be built along with the main house. Maybe she could write a letter about target practice, but that didn't seem to be the real issue.

"I'll take another look," she said. "But if you want to claim he's conducting some business on his property, we really need more evidence."

"I know something's going on," Ham said, the bulldog jaw clenched. "I just don't know what. I know we shouldn't sit around if there's a violation, right?"

"Right," Alice said. "I think the statute of limitations is four years for suing to stop violations of covenants. Try to get the license plates on the truck and the SUVs so we know how many vehicles there are."

They nodded, thanked her. She walked them to the door, hoping that their neighbor wasn't running a meth lab. The sheriff had busted several small drug operations on isolated properties outside Coffee Creek in the past few years. Usually these involved a dilapidated house or a couple of mobile homes in the boonies, not pricey creek-side property. If someone did plant a meth lab on Waterfall Road, there'd be more traffic in and out than a couple of SUVs.

She googled Richard R. Craft and found one brief reference to a Houston-area LLC, apparently for restaurant consulting. When she typed in the name of the LLC nothing came up later than 2012. Scrolling down she spied a tempting headline: "Bank fraud charges…" with R.R. "Dickie" Craft's name in bold. She couldn't get the article to pull up.

No matter what he'd done in the past, maybe the invisible Hermit lay helpless in bed with a stroke, a hyperactive manservant and a cook watching over him.

She'd get Silla to dig a little more. Right now, Holly was foremost in her mind. She could feel, could almost see Holly's face, the glasses turned toward her. Time to "turn to," as her grandfather used to say. That meant get to work.

*****

By midmorning Silla had emailed Holly the draft will and trust documents to review.

Holly called her soon after. "Good news! Media Central emailed me the contract! They've finally signed it. I'm forwarding the email to you."

"Great," Alice said. "Did you see the drafts I sent?"

"All good. Can I still come by this afternoon to sign? Two o'clock?"

"Two o'clock."

New trust account and new will in three days? Maybe that's why Holly's such a successful writer, Alice concluded. Once she puts her mind to something, she's on a mission.

Well, I can match her. She opened Holly's email and scanned the executed Media Central contract. Yep, two million dollars to be deposited into the account as directed no later than the following Monday. That should take care of Marcy's bills.

*****

At two on Thursday, Holly walked down the street from her new office to Alice's. In the conference room, she executed the trust agreement, and her new will, with all bells, whistles, witnesses, and notarizations. Madrone Bank agreed to act as executor for the trust and finalized creation of the new trust account. Alice gave Holly copies of everything, including Alice's instructions to Media Central, sent by email and express mail, as to where and how to wire Holly's contract funds. Alice reminded Media Central the contract required deposit by the following Monday.

Holly stood up and whooped. "Yippee! What a relief!" She hugged Alice. "Now I'm celebrating. Oscar, our gardener, is taking me to Creek Nursery to buy flowers for Full House. I want old-fashioned roses, fragrant, with hundreds of petals."

Alice walked her out to Oscar's dusty sedan. With her eyes failing, of course Holly needed fragrance, needed all her senses to work overtime.

"What's that lovely smell?" Holly turned her face toward the shrubs along the office driveway.

"See that straggly bare bush? That's winter sweet, with tiny flowers the size of your fingernail. Just when you can't stand any more winter, you walk outside and there's that magic perfume."

"Maybe the nursery will have one for me," Holly said. "Will I see you Saturday at this crazy cowboy action event? Russ says he wants to try it out again."

Alice laughed. "Apparently he's not the only one! Yes, I'll see you there."

Holly made a wry face. "Writing about the Old West, I guess I should like it more, right? But that stray bullet that zoomed over our riding trail…I hope Russ will agree we don't renew the lease."

Oscar helped Holly into the passenger seat.

Spring. Tomorrow night Kinsear would join her. After Boyce's pot-luck, both Red and Kinsear had announced they were shooting on Saturday.

Alice couldn't wait to see the outfits.

Chapter Eight

Costumes Are Appreciated

Kinsear arrived Friday at sunset, bearing boiled shrimp, limes, and a jar of horseradish. He and Alice made red sauce.

"It needs a touch more horseradish," he said. "I like that burn to last several seconds."

"More lime juice too."

They peeled shrimp, dipped the pink curls greedily into the red sauce, licked their fingers.

Kinsear cleared the table. "You want to see what I'll be using tomorrow?" he asked.

"Of course," Alice said, even though she didn't.

They walked out to his Land Cruiser. He opened the rear.

"What the heck is that?" Alice pointed to a golf cart–like contraption lying on its side next to a black leather bag.

"That's my gun cart."

"Gun cart?" She was astounded.

"Yep. At the event you've got all your gear loaded in it. Right now, I'll just show you the guns."

He pulled out two long brown canvas cases and the leather bag and started back inside. "Also I want to be sure I'm ready for tomorrow."

"What made you sign up for this cowboy action deal?"

He smiled and shook his head. "A buddy took me out to watch when we first moved from New York to Fredericksburg. Wanted to try it myself. I shot for a while with the Fredericksburg group. There's a fun-loving spirit at the events, with the Old West costumes and camaraderie. And it's competitive. I liked the challenge." He unzipped the canvas cases and slid out a shotgun, then a lever-action rifle. He laid them gently on her coffee table.

"Cowboy action rules are strict. Safety's huge." He held up a leather pouch. "I've already loaded my cartridges."

"You loaded them yourself?"

"Yes. For competition, you light-load them, meaning you use less powder. Less recoil, slower velocity, safer. No one wants an accident, but if there is one you sure don't want it to be fatal."

"What caliber are they?"

"You can actually use the same caliber for your rifle as for your pistol. Most competitors will be using thirty-eights, as I am. You see how that would make sense, for cowboys?"

"So they wouldn't have to carry separate ammo for the rifle and pistol."

"Yep." He opened the black leather bag and removed a long-barreled revolver. "The rules require you to use vintage or reproduction guns of the type common on the frontier. That means single-action revolvers, like people used in the Old West. With single action, the shooter has to cock the hammer before each shot. For revolvers, even though they're six-shooters, you're limited to five bullets. Your revolver must be loaded with only five rounds and the hammer lowered and resting on the empty chamber. That way if you accidentally drop the pistol when you're walking around the venue, and it goes off, you don't shoot someone."

He spun the cylinder, showing the empty chambers. "I'll load just before I compete."

"Impressive," she said, eyeing the long blued barrel. "What's this one called?"

"The Colt M 1873 Peacemaker. It's pretty popular." He pulled a second matching pistol from the bag.

"Where'd you find these?" she asked.

"They cost me a pretty penny at that antique gun shop over in New Mexico." She remembered the shop: Kinsear hoped the owner would serve as an expert for his long-awaited book on South Texas ranch guns. "This model was originally developed in the 1870s. If I hadn't got these I'd have opted for the Ruger New Vaquero."

He put the pistols away. "Now here's my shotgun." He stroked its scarred but polished wood stock. "This gun barely made the cut, since it's early twentieth century, but I like it. It's not loaded either; you have to load your shotgun during the actual competition." He slipped it back into its case.

Then he pulled a rifle from the long brown bag. "This lever-action rifle was my grand-dad's. Fortunately, it qualifies under the rules."

"What about your outfit?"

"You won't see it until tomorrow morning. Listen, don't expect much skill from me tomorrow. I haven't shot cowboy action in years. It's not just accuracy, it's speed. If you watch, you'll see the serious folks get quiet before they shoot. They're concentrating on each movement in the sequence."

"I'm sticking to tennis as a blood sport," Alice commented.

"You're not gonna dress up tomorrow, like, say, Annie Oakley when she took her act to New York? Costumes are appreciated at these events."

"I am not." Alice knew her women forebears were gun users. As a child at her grandmother's house she'd held her great-aunt's small twenty-two, practically toy-sized, her initials carved into the stock. Guns were necessary household hardware on the frontier—for snakes, rustlers, and worse.

"People are still so fixated on that cowboy thing," Alice said. "But it only lasted about fifty years, right?"

"True," said Kinsear. He was sighting the rifle. "The classic cattle drives didn't really start until the railroads came and you could send your beeves to Dodge City and Chicago. Then came barbed wire, and the big drives ended."

"My great-grandfather rode on a cattle drive to Dodge City," Alice said. She'd looked at him in old black and white family photos; he stood straight and tall with white hair and a bushy mustache, and she wished she could hear him talk. He'd ridden home to his wife with a lovely gold brooch, starred with diamonds. Alice's mother had inherited that brooch, as had Alice, who kept it at the bank in her safety deposit box. She felt nervous and anachronistic on the rare occasions when she pinned on that brooch. But her mother had worn it to church most Sundays. A little piece of history.

"It was a colorful time," Kinsear said. "All those wild young men after the Civil War, jobless and wandering, looking for adventure. Trying to stay ahead of the law, out on the plains where you could see forever. You could also get bitten by rattlers. Swim your horse across the river. Try to stop a stampede. Sing to the moon."

"Eat nothing but beans and hard biscuit," Alice said. "Smell worse than we can imagine. Suffer from constant prickly heat. Did cowboys wash their clothes?"

"History does not record."

Alice wondered how it felt to wear the same pants and undergarments for months and shuddered. She bet her great-grandfather had stopped in Fort Worth at a newfangled hotel on the way home from his cattle drive so he could bathe and change before he rode the last sixty miles south to his waiting wife, the diamond brooch sewn in a silk bag and carefully tucked in his watch pocket.

She went on, "But these cowboy action events, they seem…"

"Silly?" Kinsear grinned at her. "Sure. But fun too. Shooting competitions—they're an old tradition out here. Shooting tin cans when you're little, glass bottles on a fence post, a silver quarter spinning in the air—who's the best shot? Yeah, just think, Alice, of all those old-time ranch barbecues. Old photographs show shooting was a frequent part of the event."

"Boys with toys," Alice said.

"Girls too."

She nodded, thinking again of her great-aunt. If Alice had lived then, maybe she'd have been a sharpshooter too, going after snakes and, once in her dreams, Comanches. Those dreams were why she always wanted her house on a bluff, under trees, where she could keep a lookout, see and not be seen. She liked to see what was coming.

"Have you picked your name yet?" she asked.

Red had said at Bryce's that under cowboy action rules, every competitor had to adopt a unique shooting alias.

"I'm the Rio Bravo Kid," he said. Rio Bravo was one of the names for the Rio Grande. "Which of course reminds me of our first night together, out in Big Bend." Kinsear put away the rifle and stood. "Come over here. Come comfort this lonesome cowboy. I mean, the Rio Bravo Kid."

Alice laughed, moved toward him, traced his cheekbone with her fingers.

Later she lay curled against Kinsear, enjoying his warmth, his skin. She moved closer, touching his feet with her toes.

"Mmm." He turned on his back, slipped an arm under her head, pulled her nearer.

Chapter Nine

How Many Coffins We Got?

"Big crowd!" Kinsear said as he edged the Land Cruiser into a parking place at the Coffee Creek Cowboys site on one corner of Full House Ranch. Shooting didn't start until ten a.m. Pickup trucks in a high state of polish cruised the lot, the drivers, deadpan, howdying by raising the traditional forefinger off the steering wheel. Kinsear parked between a giant Toyota Tundra and a larger Dodge Ram, Lone Star Edition, so tall Alice wondered how people could climb in and out.

"First things first," Kinsear said, reaching into the glove compartment. "You've got to wear your eye protection and ear protection." He handed her safety glasses and ear protectors. "These ear protectors are cool—you can adjust them so you still hear people talking, but when a shot goes off the sound is deadened. And keep the eye protection on at all times. Ever heard of shot-blasting metal?" She nodded. "You don't want little bits in your eyes."

Kinsear unloaded the gun cart and the rest of his gear. They walked to the entrance gate in the chain link fence. A Coffee Creek Cowboy volunteer, a red bandana tied around his left arm, stood at a table inside.

"Sir, you're shooting, right? Be sure to sign up for the posse you want," he told Kinsear, pointing to the posse sign-up sheet.

He made Alice and Kinsear sign releases, requiring name, age, phone, email, and a signature, which, Alice duly noted, released practically every potential cause of action against the Coffee Creek Cowboys. Alice wondered if Russ and Holly should insist that the form also release them as lessors. If they renewed the lease.

Once inside the fence, Alice and Kinsear surveyed the Coffee Creek Cowboys' domain. To the rear rose the cedar-covered hills of Full House Ranch. The Cowboys had cleared about eight acres, leaving a long berm of crushed caliche and limestone, at least ten feet high, behind the shooting area. "That's to catch lead bullets," Kinsear said.

Directly in front of them stood a semicircle of colorful false fronts, each about twenty feet from the next. They reminded Alice of stage sets from a Western movie, roughly constructed and repainted. A hand-painted sign hung on the roof of each porch. From left to right, they read, "Bad Day at Black Rock—Stage Four"; "Hideout Hell—Stage

Three"; "Rawhide Rodeo—Stage Two"; and "Saloon Shootout—Stage One." Each stage had a wooden porch where competitors stood to shoot through broad open "windows" at groups of metal targets in the cleared area beyond each stage set. Waist-high, faded red curtains on a wire separated the target areas behind the stage sets.

A battered three-tier grandstand (which wasn't very grand) sat about twenty feet in front of each stage.

Kinsear parked his gun cart by the battered set of bleachers, three rows high, in front of Stage Four. He inhaled deeply and straightened his shoulders.

Alice grinned at him, shaking her head in admiration. "Ride 'em, cowboy!" She patted the fringe on his buckskin jacket. Kinsear cut a rakish figure: scarf with an antique turquoise slide set in silver, leather vest, rancher twills, highly polished boots with…spurs! And his black hat. "You look quite convincing."

"Just wait." He opened the black leather bag and pulled out a black tooled gun belt with two holsters. He grunted a bit as he buckled it on. He reached into a compartment of the bag and slipped a revolver into each holster.

Alice's stomach gave the familiar lurch she felt at the sight of pistols. Long guns seemed safer, useful for hunting, for snake defense. Pistols? Only for shooting people. Although her Aunt Imogene routinely used her thirty-eight on the squirrels trespassing in her bird feeder. She did note that these cowboy-style revolvers reminded her more of Matt Dillon and Wyatt Earp than random shooters on today's streets.

Kinsear bent his eyes on her face. "I know that look," he said. "Do you think you'd feel better if I could teach you to manage a pistol?"

"Maybe. If it looks like those." Well, maybe she would, one of these days.

"I signed up for Posse One, with Red and Russ," Kinsear said. "Posses usually rotate through the stage sets, so maybe we'll start down there at Stage One. But first, I expect the trail boss will give the visitors an explanation of the rules, the sequence, and what to watch for."

He and Alice strolled over to inspect Stage Four. Kinsear pointed to the table on the left. "That's the loading table, where you load your rifle and revolvers before you shoot. When you're up, you place your shotgun and rifle on the designated shelves in front of the designated shooting window in the order required for the particular scenario. Then after you say your required quote and the timer sounds, you shoot. See those metal targets out there?"

Sheet metal targets of different shapes and sizes stood in three groups. "The closest are the five pistol targets, a little farther out the four shotgun targets, and then farthest out the five rifle targets."

He pointed to another table to the right of the shooting windows. "That's the unloading table where a volunteer checks your guns after you shoot to be sure they're empty."

About fifty yards off to the left of the stage sets stood a cedar log cabin with a sign reading "Men." A large mirror leaned against one end of its front porch. Several male competitors squinted into the mirror, adjusting hand-tooled gun belts, tilting their hats just so, loosening bandanas a touch, turning their bodies to check profiles.

"Heavens," Alice commented. They reminded her of her son, John, proudly wearing his Star Wars costume, practicing with his light saber in front of the mirror. Boys and their outfits.

"They're not just admiring themselves, Alice. Your gun belt has to be level, guns precisely placed," the Rio Bravo Kid said, fingering his own tooled holsters. He grinned at her. "I've got to check my holster level too. This is serious business! Okay, I'll meet you there, by my gun cart."

"Where's the ladies' restroom?" Alice asked. "And first, I want to find Red." Kinsear pointed to a second prefab restroom off to the right, past Stage One.

"Good luck." She kissed him. The Rio Bravo Kid tipped his hat and sauntered off toward the men's cabin, rearranging his gun belt as he walked. Alice noted the boot swagger. No question, the cowboy outfit was romantic. And more. She started humming ZZ Top's "Sharp Dressed Man."

"Alice!" Red appeared, lugging her gun cart, followed by admiring eyes. She twirled, showing off her vintage tan cowgirl boots with pink flowers and divided caramel suede riding skirt. A matching suede vest swished its fringe over her pink sequined shirt. "What do you think?"

Alice couldn't help beaming. "Good lord, Red! You're—a vision!

Not saying of what."

"Say hello to San Antonio Rose." Red adjusted the brim of her Stetson and posed, hands on the belt of her deeply tooled tan holster. "Like the hatband?"

Alice nodded. "I count six rattles on that hatband. The hatband counteracts the sequins. You shoot that snake yourself?"

"Yes, actually," Red said smugly. "It was menacing the horses in my stable. Listen, while I'm competing, you'll watch my stuff, right?"

"Of course." Alice accepted her role for the day: accessory wallah. "You nervous?"

"Not a bit. I can't wait. I'm all set."

Alice laughed. She'd never had a best friend like Red—so fearless, so ready for adventure. She could predict Red's usual response to even an outlandish suggestion: "Why not?" Red had convinced her to move to Coffee Creek; to Alice's amazement, despite her own native caution, her instinctive risk aversion, she'd never seriously second-guessed that decision.

"I'd better head to the restroom before this starts," Alice said.

"You don't want to miss a minute. Please hurry, then I can go preen. The ladies compete in the same posses as the men, you know."

Alice, enjoying her own boot swagger in her vintage Goodson Kells, strode briskly across the grass to the prefab portable women's restroom and up the steps past a large empty trash container onto the wooden porch. She felt pleasantly surprised by the clean facilities she found behind the door.

As she sat down in her cubicle she noticed someone was already in the stall next to her. She could see the red cowboy boots, pointing toward the back of the stall, heard the zipper being zipped, saw the boots turn and walk out the door, then heard the faucet running. When Alice opened the cubicle door, Red Boots, much taller than she, glamorous in a red satin jacket, with strawberry blond curls and Chanel sunglasses visible under a black Stetson, had pulled on red leather gloves and was applying scarlet lipstick. The little finger on her right glove bent at an angle. Ouch, Alice thought. Cowgirl must have had an accident.

Red Boots made a kissy face at the mirror then noticed Alice and smiled briefly. Alice was about to compliment the boots—tooled with a white fleur-de-lis pattern—but Red Boots pulled open the entry door and sauntered back outside with a sassy swinging walk.

Vintage boots and Chanel glasses. It was quite a look. Stunning. But no gun belt, and those sunglasses weren't required eye protection. She concluded Red Boots wasn't competing but maybe watching some cowboy.

Alice had just made it back to her bleacher seat, next to Red, when she caught sight of Holly walking toward them. She looked like something out of a Frans Hals painting: black jacket and pants, her face framed by a white collar like a Renaissance ruff around her neck, glasses glinting in the sun as she slowly turned her face, scanning the crowd. Alice winced, watching Holly's slightly erratic progress. She called out, "Holly! Come sit with us."

Holly turned her head toward Alice and found her way to the bench. "Take my seat," Red said. "I'm heading off for final lipstick."

"Good luck!" they chorused.

As she climbed onto the bench by Alice, Holly said, "I'm really glad you're here. Russ was so nervous this morning it's made me nervous too. I need someone to talk to while he's taking deep breaths to calm himself, trying to be Zen Cowboy. I've never seen him like this."

"It's hard to imagine Russ nervous," Alice said.

"Yeah, he always looks relaxed. But this cowboy action deal—I don't know why he's so wound up about it. He didn't even eat his breakfast. That's unusual for Russ. That man likes his breakfast."

"Can you see from up here, Holly?" They were on the second row—close, but elevated so they could see over most of the people in front.

"As well as I can see anywhere. Seems like my sight's worse every day, though I haven't lost all my peripheral vision. But"—Holly paused, choosing her words—"my head's so full of stories, so full of ideas, I know I can keep writing screenplays. I thought of another one last night. That's what I do when I wake up in the middle of the night; I plot. I know I can still take care of Marcy, even if the worst happens, even if I have to dictate instead of type. No question, I've felt bitter. You know, why me? But other people have worse problems than macular degeneration. I've got Russ, and the ranch—sunlight, moonlight, and my horse."

Alice stared off at Stage Four, thinking about what Holly had said. How would she feel in Holly's shoes? If she couldn't read or write, if she couldn't work as a lawyer…couldn't drive…couldn't travel alone. Would she be defeated? Could she, if push came to shove, find the courage to go on if she couldn't see, couldn't write, couldn't read?

"How's it going with Sandra?" she asked. "Is it helpful having a secretary?"

Holly laughed. "Drives me nuts. She's so solicitous. Always asking if she can get me a glass of water, make me tea. She's quick on the computer, prints the drafts out in great big type, adjusts the magnifying lamp. She's so helpful I can hardly stand it. But I'm not sure what I'd do without her. It's just—I've always written alone, handled everything myself. It's weird writing in a room with someone waiting to take charge of every page as soon as I finish it. Kind of cramps my style."

She turned her face to Alice. "You know what I do?"

"What?"

"I put on noise-canceling headphones to create artificial aloneness." She glanced at Alice. "Sounds weird? Like all those tech execs in the airport, who seem to be saying, 'I can't hear you so I'm really alone, and you can't bother me.' That sort of aloneness. It's a little bit rude, maybe, but it works. I can get more done now."

"What does Sandra do when you're in deep writing mode with headphones?"

"She works on other stuff. Travel plans, reservations. She returns phone calls, confirms doctor appointments." She sighed, tilting her face toward the sun. "Russ helps. He gives her lists of whatever we need from the hardware store, feed store, grocery store. That gives her something to do besides hover over me." Holly heaved another sigh. "You must think I'm ungrateful."

Alice shook her head. "I can't imagine the transition you're making."

"It's hard," Holly admitted. "But Russ is great. And Sandra seems like a sweet girl. She takes care of a brother somewhere, says he can't manage things like insurance and bills. She always asks about Marcy, too. I can't complain."

Her face, behind the thick lenses, turned slowly, watching the crowd of shooters and hangers-on beginning to congregate in front of Stage Four. Alice counted at least thirty hangers-on. Some of the shooters wore not just gun belts and holsters but leather vests, chaps, ornate belts for their shotgun shells, elaborately carved leather wrist guards. "Great costumes," Holly said.

"I like your outfit," Alice said. "Sleek. Clever."

Holly smiled. "Simplify, simplify. No purse, did you notice? I now rely on pockets. I'll only wear pants with pockets. One for my wallet, one for my lipstick, one for my phone. Bare essentials. That's it. If I trip I can catch myself."

The microphone blared static, then a laconic voice, total cowboy, said, "Okay, folks. Now I'm gonna try to explain what you're about to see."

Heads turned to Stage Four to watch a solid-looking man, slightly bowlegged in chaps and boots, leather vest, gun belt, and hat, scan the crowd. "My name's George Kimble, but out here I'm known as Caprock Kid. I'm serving as chief range operator, sort of the trail boss, for this bunch of rapscallion volunteers." Ragged cheers from the volunteers. "And I'm gonna walk you through the rules, which are very important in cowboy action, and then show you an example of what these competitors will be doing today. Of course, we hope some of you will be interested in shooting with us. If you have questions, ask one of us. We're all volunteers and today every volunteer's got a red bandana on one arm, like mine. Now, has everybody got eye and ear protection on? That's very important, for your own safety." He scanned the crowd. "Okay. Everybody ready?"

Spectators nodded. Kimble waved an authoritative arm, moving people back. "Folks, arrange yourselves so everyone can see. You ladies on the benches, can you see?"

Holly gently elbowed Alice. "Listen, I'm going to the bathroom now, so I'll be back in time to watch Russ. Will you take pictures of Russ for me till I get back? Of course I mean the Red River Rustler!" She groped in her pocket for her phone and handed it to Alice. "The code's 111111, easy for me to punch in," she said. "I'll be right back." Holly slid carefully off the bleachers and turned toward the women's restroom.

Alice watched the small figure, elegant in her black and white, marching with determination across the parking lot. Then she dutifully clicked on Holly's phone and focused on the Red River Rustler in his Doc Holliday get-up—black frock coat, white shirt, black string tie. She realized he and Holly matched, both in black and white. He and Kinsear chatted quietly as they watched the trail boss arrange his guns on the table at Stage Four.

The trail boss picked up the microphone, called the crowd to order, and walked them through the extensive cowboy action rules. Alice started counting the number of times he emphasized the strong focus on safety. She suspected counsel for the Coffee Creek Cowboys had approved this part.

She glanced over toward the women's restroom. No Holly yet. Over near the parking lot she saw Red Boots, peering into her handbag, then striding toward the entry gate. Sandra climbed onto the bleachers just in front of Alice, checking her phone.

The trail boss tapped the mike. "Okay, folks. It's almost competition time. This little talk is aimed at you visitors. We've got three posses, that's groups of shooters, competing today. As you'll see, each competitor is timed. For each stage, the competitor must hold his hands in the proper starting position, which we announce. Also for each stage, the order of use of arms will vary depending on the particular scenario. Each stage has multiple targets. Remember that the shotgun is not loaded and must be placed where the scenario requires. During competition, the shooter must run to the shotgun, load with two shells, fire, load with two more shells, and fire again. Like this." He placed his shotgun in the center shooting window and returned to the loading table.

The trail boss looked at the timer then bellowed, "Dyin' ain't much of a livin', boy!"

"Stand by!" yelled the timer. He held up the electronic starter and punched a button, which emitted a piercing signal.

The trail boss ran to the center window, grabbed his shotgun, loaded two shells, fired at the two right-hand shotgun targets, reloaded two more shells, and fired at the two left-hand shotgun targets.

"What'd I get, Frankie?" he called to the timer.

"Six seconds," Frankie answered.

A hushed murmur from the crowd.

The trail boss picked up the mike again. "Folks, at each stage the shooter must also use each pistol and the rifle. Unlike the shotgun, pistols and the rifle are loaded just before the stage begins. Before each stage, the shooters will learn the order in which the targets must be hit. For the pistol shooting we have five targets, and the shooter must fire five times with each pistol. The shooting order might require skipping one target and hitting another twice. If a competitor hits a target out of order, that results in a time penalty. Missing a target also means a time penalty.

"Each stage will be in use here, as each posse rotates through each stage. So, folks, be sure you know which posse your sweetie's in.

"Finally, you guests will want to be listening for your competitor to call out the required quote. Then the timer yells, 'Stand by,' and the timer beeps."

Alice turned and scanned the area between the bleachers and the women's restroom. Still no sign of Holly. A man in jeans and a black hat and T-shirt hoisted a compactor's trash bag onto other black trash bags and several hay bales that filled the back of a dusty black pickup parked by the women's restroom.

"All right, folks," the trail boss resumed, "You've got not quite ten minutes before we begin. Posse One, move on over to Stage One, and I don't need to tell Posse Two and Three where to go. Folks, you've got just enough time to grab some great brisket tacos from the food truck. Finally, the beer truck will be open"—cheers from the crowd—"but only after the competition ends. We want a safe event." He looked at his watch. "Whoops! Make that nine minutes."

Alice remembered what she'd promised Holly. She hopped off the bleachers and made Kinsear, Russ, and Red line up in front of Stage Four for pictures. They looked grim. "Come on, I need pictures of the Red River Rustler, the Rio Bravo Kid, and San Antonio Rose," she argued. "You look like Western movie stars. How about a smile?"

"Hey, I'm focused, Alice," Red said. No smile from her.

"We've got our game faces on," Kinsear added.

"Well, think of your favorite quote," Alice said. "What's it gonna be?"

"The San Antonio Rose would say, 'I'd say you're shy a few manners!'" Red announced.

Kinsear said, "I would favor, 'Get up, you scum-sucking pig!'"

"Both of you channeling Marlon Brando in *One-Eyed Jacks*?" Alice guessed.

Russ grimaced, holding his stomach, and said, "I've got to get some Pepto tablets out of the truck. Be right back." He hurried toward the parking lot.

"Don't tarry!" Kinsear called after Russ, watching the trail boss survey the waiting crowd, then pick up his mike.

"Okay, folks, it's time to roll," announced the trail boss over the loudspeaker. "We'll start at ten o'clock sharp. Posses, get on down to your stage. Time to show us whatcha got! Who's gonna win, and who's gonna lose? Who's gonna outshoot the others? Who's best dressed? Most important, let's have a clean match."

Chapter   Ten

A Trace of Gun Smoke

The Posse One crowd reconstituted itself on the bleachers at Stage One. Scrawled on a whiteboard by the Stage One porch were the names of the Posse One shooters. Russ was first.

Alice grabbed a seat at the end of the third row, high enough to see the entire stage. Through the left window she saw four shotgun targets—gray rectangles hand-painted to look like gravestones. Through the center window she saw five rifle targets shaped like cowboy hats with faces painted on. Finally, through the right-hand window she saw a wide wooden frame doorway with double swinging doors. The sign atop the doorway read, "Swingin' Doors Saloon." Above the swinging doors stood five round metal targets painted like faces, planted on metal stakes. A hay bale sat on the ground blocking the view under the swinging doors.

Sandra Sechrest slid onto the second tier of bleachers, in front of Alice, still clutching her phone. Head down, thumbs working, she didn't look up.

Alice kept glancing toward the women's restroom, just past Stage One. A young volunteer in elaborate cowboy duds, red bandana on his arm, carried a sawhorse with a warning sign to the far-right corner of Stage One. In big red letters the sign said, "STOP! NO PASSAGE!" The young volunteer adjusted his hat to a determined angle and strode past Stage One toward Stage Two. More safety first. Alice approved.

Where was Holly? Surely she'd be back any minute, before Russ stepped up to take his chances on Stage One. Sandra didn't seem worried about her boss...or her boss's husband. Where was Russ?

Kinsear, standing ready with his gun cart at the center front of Stage One, had his eyes on the parking lot. Alice turned around in her seat and saw Russ with Eddie's hot-tempered former partner, Brad Gorman. Brad was talking fast, holding onto Russ's jacket sleeve. Russ tugged his arm away, shook his head, and strode toward Stage One.

Off to the left gunfire erupted. Alice turned, saw puffs of smoke. Posse Two was already underway at Stage Four.

Alice inhaled, finding she rather enjoyed a trace of gun smoke. In fact, she was enjoying the whole cowboy action scene—costumes, competition, the required sayings. She was eager to see Kinsear and

Red strut their stuff.

Inside the gate to Stage One, the trail boss and his henchman, the timer, stood by the loading table, waiting for the first two competitors in the posse. Alice suddenly recognized the timer; he worked with her favorite vet. She'd seen him help give the burros their annual shots and worming. Not, however, while wearing a Billy the Kid getup.

The trail boss pointedly looked at his watch, just as Russ hustled past Alice, stopping only to drop an open pack of Pepto Bismol tablets on the empty seat next to Sandra. He and Kinsear carried their guns to the loading table and loaded pistols and rifles.

"All right, folks!" barked the trail boss. "Stage One's now ready to go. The arms order for this scenario at the Saloon Shootout is first, shotgun, then rifle, then pistol. For pistol, the sequence is 1-5-2-3-4. For rifles, the sequence is 1-1-4-4-2. Your quote is 'How many coffins we got?'" He held up a placard with the quote in all caps. "What's it from, folks?"

"*High Noon!*" someone called.

"You got it. Here are our competitors." He reeled off the names, starting with Red River Rustler and the Rio Bravo Kid, and ending with San Antonio Rose. "Red River Rustler, you're first."

Russ took a deep breath. He left his shotgun on the loading table and placed his rifle on the ledge in the center window.

Alice had her own phone out ready to take pictures of Kinsear. She stowed it in her pocket and aimed Holly's phone at Stage One. A flurry of dust blew across the stage set, and she shivered.

The trail boss pointed to the starting point. Russ walked to the window on the far left, by the loading table. Beyond the window the gray tombstones stood silent. Russ squared his shoulders, hands outside his holsters, in the prescribed position.

"Ready?" the trail boss said.

Alice took a still, then started her video.

Russ shouted, "How many coffins we got?"

"Stand by!" barked the trail boss. The timer hit the buzzer.

Russ grabbed his shotgun, loaded two shells and fired, loaded two more and fired again. All four gravestones clanged. He raced to the center window, picked up the rifle and fired at the five cowboy hats.

Ten clangs, no misses. Moving fast he replaced the rifle and hurried to the right-hand window. He fired his right pistol, then his left, at the five painted faces above the saloon's swinging doors. A rolling clang of shots hitting metal rang out. Alice counted nine, watching the metal targets shake. One miss? She'd expected more of a high-pitched ping. She inhaled. Plenty of gun smoke here.

Russ collected his guns and carried them to the unloading table.

The timer called, "Forty seconds." The crowd murmured. A sudden chilly gust blew dust in Alice's eyes and almost took off her Stetson. A scarf-size piece of black fabric blew off the rear of the saloon swinging doors and flapped across the target area. It caught on the wire holding the faded red curtain between Stage One and Stage Two.

Alice ended the video.

The trail boss threw up one hand, yelled, "Down range!" He walked around behind the stage set into the target area, joined by the timer. Alice couldn't hear what the trail boss said to the timer. But as the two men neared the back of the saloon doorframe, trail boss leading, she saw his mouth fall open, saw his lips say, "Oh my God!" The trail boss dropped to his knees, reaching behind the doorframe.

Alice stood, paralyzed. Kinsear, at the railing, turned to her, shaking his head and holding his hand up, signaling "stay put." Russ was running toward the trail boss. As Alice scrambled off the bleachers she heard Sandra say, "Who is it?"

Disregarding instructions, Alice pushed her way to Kinsear, by the first window. She saw what the trail boss might have seen: the hay bale did not quite fill the gap beneath the swinging doors. Some black, some white was visible above the bale. Russ, on his knees at the end of the doorframe, turned his face to the sky, howling, "Holly!"

The trail boss backed away, shaking his head, his face a study in sorrow and fear. Alice could imagine his fear: the Cowboy Action lease is up for renewal and now his landlady lies motionless on Stage One, in front of his landlord—her husband. Before a shocked crowd. After everything he told the crowd about his paramount concern—safety.

A whisper ran through the crowd: "The timer said…the timer told someone…" "Shot." "Shot dead."

The timer and trail boss were on their phones. Apparently in response to something he'd heard, the trail boss looked down at the ground, then back toward the rear of Stage One. He leaned over and gently tugged at Russ, who refused to move. The timer shrugged out of his coat. He put it over Holly, Alice realized. The trail boss, lips moving slightly, put away his cell phone. He walked heavily to the front of Stage One, picked up the microphone, then straightened his shoulders. "Folks, no one is to leave. The sheriff's on his way. Should be here in five minutes. I repeat, stay where you are. I'm an honorary deputy, folks, and that's an order."

The crowd fell silent, then burst into suppressed whispers.

Kinsear and Alice, at the railing, heard the timer saying, "We checked those guns! We've got all the shells!"

Kinsear whispered softly into Alice's ear. "I watched him load." Alice looked up at him. "Looked okay, as far as I could tell."

Sirens. The sheriff's SUV wheeled into the parking lot, spraying gravel, followed by the flashing lights of the ambulance. The sheriff himself hurried behind the doorframe, talking into his phone.

Two other uniformed deputies took charge of Russ, pulling him gently away from the body. "Sir, you must get back," Alice heard.

"But she's my wife!" Russ cried, agony on his face.

"We've got to preserve the scene, sir."

Russ looked at him, then let out a long breath and walked slowly back to the railing. One deputy led him through the gate and toward the now empty grandstand at Stage Two. Alice watched the deputy asking questions, taking notes.

* * * * *

Alice, Kinsear, Red, and Sandra, along with the trail boss and timer and groundskeeper, were there for three more hours. The sheriff's department commandeered the bleachers at Stage Two for interviews. The rest of the crowd provided contact information and eventually were allowed to head home.

Standing at the Stage Two railing, awaiting her turn, Alice watched from a distance as Sandra gave her statement to the deputies. Her answers seemed brief, businesslike. She apparently asked one question, but the deputies shook their heads.

Alice herself had some questions for Sandra. Why hadn't she gone to look for Holly? But then, she herself hadn't either. Maybe Sandra knew Holly didn't want her hovering. Who was Sandra texting or emailing while the trail boss talked? Maybe just ordering something online. Some lost detail nagged at Alice.

After her interview, Sandra left, walking slowly toward the parking lot, head down, staring at her phone. Alice and Kinsear were the last to be interviewed. Kinsear went first. She couldn't hear the questions posed to him. He still had that thousand-yard look of a man who has witnessed an incomprehensible death.

From Alice, the deputies wanted to know the timeline. When did Holly leave? What had she said to Alice? What about Russ and the trip to his pickup? Did she actually see him near his truck? No, but he did come back with a pack of those pink tablets. She pointed out that he'd seemed in need of the tablets and if he'd had them wouldn't he have taken them sooner? When the deputy asked about Russ and Holly's relationship, Alice said she thought they were still honeymooners, deeply in love. Yes, both of them.

"Will George Files be working on the case?" she asked. "I believe so," said the deputy. She was dismissed. She joined Kinsear.

"You didn't even get to shoot," Alice said.

"Thank God." He pulled through the Cowboy Action gate onto the highway. "Poor Russ. What a horror."

"Did the Trail Boss and Timer know something was wrong just from the sound of the pistol shots?" Alice asked.

"Well, Russ did miss one pistol shot. The rest hit the targets, spun one sideways. But when that gust of wind blew the black fabric away, the trail boss could see something more than a haybale back there. She—her body—must have been propped back there somehow. Covered up."

"Was she already dead? Or did he—" Alice couldn't finish the sentence.

"Obviously she was already *there*," Kinsear said. "I think she must have been killed by whoever put her there. He only missed one pistol target and even a miss shouldn't have killed someone if he used a light load. Unless it was a close-up shot to the heart, something like that."

"Who could have put her there, then?" Alice demanded.

Kinsear shook his head. "I sure don't think Russ had time. His teeth were pink."

Could've had those notoriously pink tablets in his pocket already, and not had to go to his truck, Alice thought but didn't say. Besides, Russ adored Holly. Didn't he?

Chapter Eleven

Hate to Add to the Bad News

Monday morning, after a ghastly weekend, Alice slumped in her office chair, staring blankly at her computer. She stood up, walked to the rear window, stared at the backyard pecan tree.

Holly was dead. Her client. Grief and a sense of failure settled on her shoulders like a dark gray cloud. Somehow Alice had felt her work for Holly—setting up a trust fund so Marcy could count on good care for decades to come—would confer a long and happy life on Holly. Irrational, she knew. After all, she'd also prepared Holly's will, talked with her about what happened if she died now, later, even later. Death was the necessary, the central topic. Still, she felt she hadn't protected Holly. Did Russ feel the same way?

She couldn't erase the image of Holly on Friday morning, making her way across the parking lot toward the bleachers, the black jacket and white collar setting off the smiling, vulnerable face, the thick glasses not quite aimed at Alice.

And now? A small body stored in a refrigerator drawer in the medical examiner's lab in Austin.

The office phone rang. Reluctantly Alice picked it up.

"It's Miranda, at Madrone Bank. I heard about Holly. What happened out there?"

"Someone shot her, but we don't know who. At least I don't know."

"Terrible." Miranda paused. "Well, I hate to add to the bad news. I've had a couple of unsettling calls this morning. The first was from River Road Group Home."

"Marcy's caretakers? Is Marcy okay?"

"Yes. But River Road is concerned because our trust department hasn't paid the bill they sent last week. Problem is, we can't."

"What do you mean? You're supposed to get the wire transfer for Holly's funds from the Media Central people today, right? We sent them instructions last Thursday that the money needed to be deposited no later than today."

"No. That's my second unsettling call this morning. I called Media Central and asked where their wire transfer was."

"And?" Alice felt her blood pressure rise.

"They said they'd already sent it, Friday morning."

"You should have it, then."

"They said they'd gotten new wiring instructions from Holly. They sent the funds to the new account." She stopped. "This woman I talked to, Kari Canaway, wouldn't disclose the new instructions. I think it'll take a call from Holly's lawyer to get those loose. I told her you'd call." She gave Alice the number.

Alice paced back and forth behind her desk, glaring at the speakerphone, as she always did for hard phone calls. She waited for Kari Canaway to answer.

Kari Canaway's voice was straight Southern California. Cheery, definite, and unwilling to help. "Sorry, Holly sent us new instructions."

"How do you know they were from Holly?"

"She emailed them to us. Let me look. Yes, from her phone."

"On Friday morning?" Wouldn't Holly have mentioned that on Saturday, at the cowboy action event?

Alice heard paper rattling.

"Yes, Friday morning."

"But you don't have a signature from Holly?"

"No, no signature. But we've done lots of emails with Holly. So I authorized the wire transfer."

"I need a copy of the wire transfer. I need you to scan it to me immediately. Along with those emailed instructions."

"But—"

"Look, I'm Holly's lawyer. And Holly died Saturday morning. Send me that wire transfer form so I can see where the hell her money's gone. That's the money she wanted used for her disabled sister."

That at least got an okay from Canaway. Alice waited, tapping her fingers, for Canaway's email. There it was. She opened the attached scans.

The wire transfer went to Palmetto Bank in Florida. The recipient? A limited liability company called Royalty LLC.

Was that Holly's? Why would she send her funds elsewhere than her trust?

She called Silla and asked her to try to find out where Royalty LLC was registered.

"Yikes!" Silla said. "I may have to search state by state. I'll start in

Texas and Florida."

"And look at the time on this email," Alice said. "Ten last Friday morning, presumably Central Time." She looked up at Silla. "I don't think Holly would've sent that email without telling us. I mean, she'd been here the day before, setting up the trust." She thought a moment. "Wait, I've still got her phone. I couldn't get Russ's attention Friday." She dug to the bottom of her purse, pulled out the phone, wondered for five seconds whether this was an unwarranted invasion of privacy. She looked at Silla, then gingerly tapped Holly's code into Holly's phone and searched "sent" email for the name of the media company. "I don't see this email."

Silla picked up the scanned email. "She must have sent it from a different account. She emails us on Holly1990@gmail.com. But this comes from Holly1991@gmail.com."

Alice checked Holly's phone again to be sure she was searching "all inboxes," not just the Holly1990 account. "That email is not in this phone."

"Alice, you realize you can set instructions for an email to be sent at a certain time?"

She had never done that, but, of course, Silla had.

"Plus, even if she doesn't have this account on her phone," Silla said, "it may be a business account she keeps on her laptop. I'll start looking for Royalty LLC." She looked again at the scanned instructions. "Can Miranda get us the contact info for this bank?"

Alice picked up the phone.

Miranda could. "Palmetto Bank. It looks pretty small. Never heard of it, but I wouldn't. Here's the contact info."

Alice scribbled it down.

Holly's laptop. It might be in Holly's office at Full House Ranch. Or…right down the street, on her desk, in Alice's rent house.

Could a landlord do that? For a murdered client?

Yes. Alice pressed her lips together and stood up. She checked to be sure she had the rent house keys in her purse. Silla was already glued to her computer, stalking Royalty LLC. Alice yanked open the front door and waved to her. "Be right back."

Chapter Twelve

Alarms in Her Ears

A lice marched down the sidewalk past the two lots between her office and the rent house. She climbed the porch steps and tried the front door. Locked, and no car in the driveway. She'd thought Sandra might be here, might want to tidy up affairs, be sure filing was up to date, whatever a private secretary did after her boss was murdered. Alice unlocked the front door and stepped inside. "Hello?"

Silence.

She walked over to Holly's desk, with its large glass magnifier on a swing-arm poised in front of the screen on Holly's open laptop.

Alice wanted badly to pick up the laptop. Years of litigation experience sounded alarms in her ears. She should not turn it on, much less search it. Should she unplug it or leave it in situ? Leave it, said the litigation alarm. Experts needed to mirror-image it before anyone messed with it.

Instead she took several pictures of the laptop with her phone. Then she called George Files. Voicemail. After the beep she said, "George, I'm the executor for Holly Dougal's estate. I'm worried someone's tried to clean out an account of hers. Can we secure her laptop? It's in her office, which is my rent house at 324 Live Oak. Can you call me?"

She turned to look at Sandra's desk. Spotless aside from a blank notepad. She saw no laptop.

Her mind whirled: how could she fund Marcy's future without Media Central's payment for the *Tales* deal? Holly had mentioned her new *Dark Song Trilogy*. What about those manuscripts? She'd seen Holly's printouts; surely Holly had digital files too.

Should she change the locks on the rent house? The lease had not expired…maybe not.

She called the ranch. Sandra answered. "Hi, Alice. No, Russ isn't here. He's gone to see Holly's parents up in Waxahachie. He'll be back tonight. Is there anything I should tell him?"

Alice asked for his cell phone number.

"Certainly, "Sandra responded. "But no message? I'll be glad to pass it along to him. I expect he'll be calling me to check in."

Check in? Why? "I'll just give him a call. Thanks."

Alice scribbled down the number, borrowing a sheet from Sandra's notepad. She left a message on Russ's cell asking him to give her a call. She checked the back door (locked), re-locked the front door, and started back to her office, thinking.

Holly could have sent new instructions. It was her money, after all. But the day after she'd created a new trust and a new trust account for Marcy? Why?

* * * * *

Walking back down Live Oak Alice noted the weight of her bag—slightly too heavy. Funny how she could detect when she'd forgotten her own phone, when her bag felt a few ounces too light. Ah! Holly's phone lay somewhere in the bottom. One more unpleasant topic for her call to Russ. Before she returned this intimate little device of his wife's to Russ, full of evidence of Holly's life, she needed to check with Files. He'd likely want it in evidence before anyone else touched it. Because it was evidence, wasn't it? She'd taken pictures with it, pictures that would help provide the time frame for Holly's whereabouts at the cowboy action site. At the same time Alice felt weird about violating Holly's privacy.

She called Russ's cell again. His "hello" was dull, flat. Alice explained that she still had Holly's phone and needed to give it to the sheriff. "Okay," he said. "I'll want it back, sometime. She took all our pictures…" his voice trailed away.

Alice asked about Holly's parents. "It's pretty hard," he said. "I called the night Holly died. You don't want to tell any parent their daughter's dead. You sure don't want to tell them someone…someone shot her. Her dad's about to go into hospice care. Her mom's got dementia. She doesn't understand what's happening to him, and she couldn't grasp what I said about Holly. She just kept looking at the door and asking where Holly was. Listen, I've got to go back in. Thanks, Alice."

Imagining how she would feel if anything happened to Ann, her precious daughter, Alice continued down Live Oak past her office over to the sheriff's annex next to the Coffee Creek Courthouse.

The annex waiting room smelled like burned coffee. She asked the desk officer for George Files and took a seat on a battered plastic chair with penal qualities—uncomfortable in any position.

"Alice." Tall, thin, rubbing tired brown eyes, Detective George Files gave her a mocking bow. "At least this time you didn't stumble over the body. Come on back."

They walked down the narrow hall with its institutional gray walls and fluorescent lights to Files's small office. Alice offered up her bag. "Holly's phone is in the bottom. Her code's 111111. She asked me to take pictures just before we all walked over to Stage One for the first competition. I also took a video of Russ shooting at Stage One."

That produced an interested expression on Files's tired face. With a baggie over his hand, he retrieved the phone. "I don't often get to rummage in a woman's purse." He turned on the phone. "Still has a charge," he said. "Let's look at those pictures. You think we'll only find your fingerprints and Holly's?"

"No idea who else has touched her phone, but I've had it since she handed it to me Saturday."

He and Alice bent their heads over the scarred wooden desk, looking at the shots of Kinsear, Russ, and Red. "That's at Stage Four, before the competition."

She showed him where to find the video of Russ, shooting. He watched it in silence.

"Okay, we'll take a look," he said. "What's this about her account getting cleaned out? And wanting us to grab her laptop?"

Alice explained about Holly's new trust account at Madrone Bank, the instructions to Media Central Alice had sent on Thursday, just four days ago, and Alice's unwelcome Monday morning call from Miranda saying that on Friday, Media Central had wired the funds for Holly's new deal to Palmetto Bank in Florida in response to new emailed instructions from a different email account than the one Holly used with Alice. She gave Files a copy of the new instructions Media Central had received.

"The media company didn't call you or her to check first?"

"Not me. We could check Holly's phone." She gave Files the phone number for Media Central. He peered at the list of incoming calls.

"I don't see a call from LA. Anyway, that's the feds' territory. We're just the Coffee Creek County Sheriff's Department. We'll need to call in the joint financial crimes team in Austin. Like, right away. They may need to try to freeze that Palmetto account before the money gets transferred to some offshore bank. They have more trouble sometimes with offshore institutions."

"But look," Alice said. "This may relate to Holly's murder. Media Company gets my instructions on Thursday. On Friday, Media Company gets new emailed instructions and sends Holly's money to the Florida bank. On Saturday, Holly gets shot."

Files was making notes. "Okay, back up. You drafted her will and these trust documents?"

"Yes. Not for Russ. He has a child by his first marriage, has a will, didn't want to change anything when he and Holly got married."

"He was divorced?"

"No, his wife died. Cancer."

"What about his kid?"

"He's older than Holly. He's thirty-four. Russ was only twenty-one when he was born."

"Draw me a financial picture," Files said. He leaned back in his chair, arms crossed behind his head, boots propped on the pulled-out bottom desk drawer.

"Okay." Alice paused, remembering. "Holly just got a deal for an initial two million plus residuals for a new streaming series based on her historical novels about early trails in Texas, including the first cattle drives. That's a trilogy called *Tales of the Road*."

Files whistled. "Wish I could write."

"No kidding. What with streaming these days, a promising series can get a writer some money. Anyway, two million was to be wired to the trust account Holly set up at Madrone Bank to help pay ongoing care for her little sister, Marcy. Marcy suffered brain trauma from a car wreck. Lifetime assistance needed.

"Holly also took out an insurance policy for five hundred thousand. Her sister's the beneficiary." Alice sighed. "The insurance was supposed to be a backstop, not the main event."

"Getting that insurance paid any time soon could be an issue," Files said. "What other resources does Holly have?"

"A couple of IRAs, a brokerage account. Plus she and Russ jointly bought the Full House ranch."

Files lifted an eyebrow. "I went turkey-shooting out there once, ten years ago. Man, I wanted to own that place. Those big cypresses along the creek." The tired eyes gazed out the window. "Oh well. So the ranch is his now."

"Yes. But one thing nobody's getting."

"What's that?"

"Holly's brain. She had more projects on tap, screenplays for streaming media. She talked to me about them."

"I hear she was practically blind. Was she more valuable dead than alive?"

"Alive, of course!" Alice said, bristling. Then she leaned her head back, gazing at the ceiling. "Maybe she was more valuable to some parties than others. Media Central stands to lose out, two ways. First, this upcoming series based on Holly's novels could be more valuable if viewers look forward to follow-ons. Second, as part of the two million the company paid for that series, the company also got a right of first refusal on any future screenplays."

"Is the two million contingent on future screenplays?"

"Nope. Holly got that free and clear whether she produced more or not."

"What about Russ's will?"

"As I recall, he leaves the bulk of his to his son. He's got about the same amount of resources she does, minus her two million. They both wanted to take care of his son and her sister and then each other."

"Where's the son?"

"Colorado Springs, I think. Teaching at the Air Force Academy."

He sat up. "What about the secretary? Did you ask her whether she sent the instructions?"

"Not yet. I wanted to talk to you first." She tried to explain her discomfort. "Sandra wasn't in on discussions of the will and trust documents. I mean, I doubt Holly shared them with her. Sandra hadn't worked for Holly long enough, you know. They weren't…intimate. More boss and employee. However, she might know more about the Media Central contract. I didn't handle that."

"Give her a call right now. Put it on speaker."

Alice dialed Sandra. The competent voice said, "Alice. Good to talk to you. Isn't this dreadful? I don't know what to think. How can I help you?"

Alice said, "You recall that Holly made a new will after she and Russ married?"

"Mm-hmm."

"And you know Holly takes financial care of her sister, because of her accident?"

"Yes." Sandra's voice softened. "Holly was a very generous person."

"Holly established a trust for her sister, which was to receive a wire transfer from Media Central. This would help pay for her sister's care. We sent instructions last Thursday about the wire. This morning Media Central told us that they'd gotten new instructions and had already wired the money to a Florida bank, Palmetto Bank, for an account owned by a company called Royalty LLC. Do you know anything about that company?"

"Never heard of it."

"Well, did you send any wire instructions for Holly to Media Central?"

"No, Alice. Listen, why are you calling me about this? I mean, I'm feeling somewhat insulted by this call."

"Why? I'm just trying to find out what happened to Holly's money. Don't you want to help?"

"Has it occurred to you that perhaps Holly was dissatisfied with the arrangements you made for her? That she took her fate into her own hands? I mean, Holly was no idiot."

"Of course not. But she gave me instructions she wanted carried out, and I'm obligated to look into what happened."

"Then either you screwed up or she changed her mind. As she had every right to do. I think there's been, if I may say so, some arrogance on your part. I've mentioned my opinion to Russ, in fact."

Alice felt her gorge rising, felt the wave of fury that meant she might yell at Sandra, felt Files's watchful brown eyes on her and took a deep breath. "Do you have access to Holly's email accounts?"

"I respected her privacy, *Miss* lawyer. She never complained in any way about my services. Nor has Russ! Both have said how grateful they are!"

"I'm only asking whether you have access to Holly's email accounts. Can you tell me that?"

"She has occasionally asked me to send an email for her. I have always done just as she asked. This is ridiculous. I feel obligated to report to Russ how unprofessional and unkind you have been."

The line went dead.

Alice turned to Files. She was shaking with anger.

"Nice young woman," Files said. "So pleasant to see your professional accomplishments recognized, Alice. She got a thing for Russ?"

"Maybe," Alice said through clenched teeth.

"Let's get that laptop right now. You've got keys to her office?"

"Yes. The lease is in Holly's name and therefore part of her estate."

"You're executor for Holly's estate?"

"Yes. At least until someone fires me." She wondered who could.

"And lawyer for the trust she set up for her sister?"

"The bank's executor for the trust, so they'll choose the counsel. Normally they'd choose me."

"I think I'm covered. Let's go. I'll drive."

Files's footsteps echoed behind Alice as they climbed the porch stairs to the rent house. She unlocked the door, and Files followed her in. Silence inside, and the faint scent of Holly's perfume. Alice had asked Holly what it was, and she'd said, "*Eau Moheli.* Russ picked it out when we went to Paris."

Sandra, she remembered, wore only *Coco.*

"This it?" Files gestured at Holly's desk. Wearing gloves, he carefully unplugged the laptop, with its charger, and slipped them both into an evidence bag. He added Holly's magnifying equipment. "Anything else we should take right now? Besides"—he pulled out the lap drawer and added pens, pencils, a daybook, and the large print calendar that Holly used as a desk blotter—"these? Anything someone else might have touched." He looked around at the wall shelves behind Holly's desk. "See anything we should sequester? All these books, I expect they can stay, for now."

Alice pulled out the file drawer under Holly's desk. "These folders," she said. "Media Central." Files bagged them.

Files and Alice stared at Sandra's spotless desk, with its blank notepad. He pulled open the lap drawer. Completely empty save a pencil and two gel pens. He opened the file drawer. Also empty.

He looked at Alice, who shrugged. "Maybe she's keeping everything digitally," she said.

"I'd personally like to take a look at *her* laptop," he said. "And *her* phone."

"I don't usually let people talk to me like she did, you know," she said.

"That's my impression." He permitted himself a lopsided grin.

"If we hadn't been trying to get her to answer about the wiring instructions I would have had a conniption."

"I know. Thanks for reining it in."

They pulled the front door to. Alice relocked it.

Outside the air was cool, damp. Soon it would be time for bluebonnets and South by Southwest, the annual invasion of Austin, with music everywhere, even out west in Coffee Creek. Alice's heart wasn't ready for South by. Holly's death made that annual celebration irrelevant. Even though her children were coming home for spring break, even though she knew she'd want to celebrate with brisket at their favorite barbecue joints, with some wild new beer and pizza at Jester King, with music coming at them from every direction, right now all she could focus on was the small body dead behind the doorway of the Swingin' Doors Saloon.

She had to learn who killed Holly. And she needed to turn around that wire transfer.

Files dropped her off at her office. Before she climbed out of the Coffee County Sheriff's Department SUV she made him promise to call back to tell her what he learned from the financial crimes unit.

Waiting for his call, she dived into the federal banking regulations. Within minutes she felt like she was trying to swim the Sargasso Sea.

Chapter Thirteen

Another Round of Bad News?

When he called back, Files confirmed the time pressure they faced. "Listen," he said. "I'm assigned to Holly Dougal's murder—at least it looks like murder. In that connection I've pulled in our financial crimes officer, Burt Hooks. He coordinates with the Central Texas Financial Crimes Task Force."

"What's that?"

"The federal Secret Service has financial crimes jurisdiction around Austin, including Coffee County. They deputize some local officers like Burt as federal marshals so they can operate with both state and federal jurisdiction. I sent him the fake email. He's in contact with Palmetto Bank about the Royalty LLC account. With this much money at stake, Burt's only got a short time to try to freeze that account before the money could go somewhere else."

"What if it gets sent to another account?"

"I mean, if Holly's money gets sent offshore to a country that doesn't cooperate with the U.S. financial crime police, it could be impossible to undo a fraudulent transfer. He's maybe got a fighting chance, if we move fast. I gave him the basics, on Royalty LLC and Palmetto Bank. He's in Austin. He'll get in touch with you to jumpstart the process."

Alice hung up, feeling nauseous. Marcy's shaky future, given her brain trauma, depended on that money—for therapy, for support, for food, for the roof over her head. Marcy's parents couldn't help—her mother suffering from dementia, her father dying. Russ? Even if he wanted to help his dead wife's sister, Russ's assets weren't that big. Alice gritted her teeth, thinking of Holly's money, hard-earned after years of work, disappearing down a rabbit hole.

The feds had to identify precisely who owned the Palmetto account, who or what was Royalty LLC. She heard Silla's fingers tapping on her computer across the hall, trying to beat the feds to the answer.

Alice called Russ's cell again. At the beep she left a message to call her as soon as possible. She explained as briefly as she could: someone using what looked like Holly's email had sent different wiring instructions for Holly's two million dollars. Alice needed to identify who'd sent the instructions, and who held the account. If the instructions weren't authorized there might still be time for financial crimes officers to freeze the account.

Could Holly herself, after spending all those hours in Alice's office on Marcy's trust fund, have decided the hell with it? Could she have opted to send her two million to Florida, then on to another bank somewhere and, with or without Russ, spend her life in tropical pleasure?

Alice envisioned Holly, face pink with excitement as she dreamed up stories to hold readers rapt. That was the true Holly—she *assumed*. Then she tried to picture Holly in a bikini, lolling in a hammock, sipping iced rum beneath swaying palms by blue-green waves. Even when she added Russ to the picture, imagining him tanned and smiling, striding up the beach like a middle-aged James Bond, she didn't believe this story. In the hours she'd spent at Alice's office, Holly had convinced Alice that she intended Marcy to thrive, not merely survive.

Alice had sat through a state bar continuing legal education class on the current epidemic of financial crimes. What if someone had used Holly's information to create that email, just one digit off, so the media company wouldn't catch it? Reportedly that happened all the time. Fraudsters hacked a title company to learn what buyers might be using it, forged a title company email to a prospective buyer, and directed the unaware buyer's down payment to a wrong account. The down payment merrily disappeared into hands unknown. Here, instead, the fake instructions went to the media company.

Another possibility: What if the media company's computer system had been tampered with? What if the miscreant was someone at the media company who knew a big wire transfer was going out? An inside job?

Or what if the sender was closer than an anonymous fraudster? Would Russ stoop to this? Lord knew he probably had the requisite knowledge. He knew Holly was signing a new will, knew Alice was creating a trust account, surely he could access Holly's email. Alice shook her head, hoping that scenario was wrong.

Her phone buzzed. She grabbed it. Russ's slow rumble.

"You needed to talk to me?" Not a friendly tone. His usual warmth was absent.

She explained the situation. "Do you know Holly's email addresses?

Specifically, all the gmail addresses she used?"

"Holly1990@gmail.com."

"Nothing else?"

"Well, she had a gmail for her website. Readers could contact her at TalesfromHolly@gmail.com."

"No other email with 'Holly' in it?"

"Not that I know of."

Of course, he could have *created* one, but that question should come preferably from Burt not Alice. "We'll need to tell the financial crimes unit who could have had that kind of information, that kind of access. And I'm assuming you didn't send the new instructions last Friday, right?"

Silence on the phone, just the sound of tires on the highway. "Of course not. I can't think of a solitary soul who'd do this to Holly." He paused. "And don't go blaming Sandra for it, Alice. That woman loved Holly. You hurt her feelings, cross-examining her the way you did."

Clearly Sandra had run to Russ and said Alice treated her roughly.

"I didn't cross-examine her. I'm sorry if it seemed that way to her. I'm trying to figure out what happened, who sent those new instructions, so I can make sure Holly's wishes for Marcy are carried out."

"Well, weren't you the one who sent the first instructions to the media company?" His voice rose.

"Yes."

"So I suppose you're putting yourself on the list? I mean, you or someone in your office could have sent the new instructions for all I know."

Alice took a deep breath. "Of course we didn't. I expect the police will confirm that. They'll turn over every rock. But we don't have much time."

Silence.

"Russ, Holly's my client. It's my duty to her to get done what she wanted."

"Yeah. Okay." He hung up before she could tell him he'd be hearing from Burt Hooks, that she'd given Holly's phone to Files, that Files had Holly's laptop. And now she'd have to tell Files—or Hooks—to check *her* accounts and Silla's. Russ's accusation hurt deeply.

Or maybe Files had already put her—and Silla—on the list.

She walked into Silla's workspace and reported what Russ had said. "Aw, hell," Silla said. "What an ungrateful…well, I'll start assembling whatever the feds want. Our info and Holly's too." She dived back into computerland.

Frustrated, restless, mind whirling with her to-do list, Alice was about to call Burt Hooks herself when he called her.

Hooks said Palmetto Bank acknowledged that it had indeed received instructions directing it to forward the Media Central payment to a Caymans account. He'd told Palmetto the money had reportedly been sent based on false instructions and that the federal financial crimes unit was taking steps to freeze the account. Identifying who'd sent the false instructions, as well as the party who'd sent further instructions to Palmetto, was a top priority. He sounded calm. Too calm.

"Holly Dougal needed that money in a trust account for her sister!" Alice burst out in frustration.

"We understand. We're working as fast as we can." He hung up.

The phone rang. She reached out, heart still pounding, arm halfway to the receiver. Pick up or not? Another round of bad news?

Chapter Fourteen

Pick Up the Pieces

Alice picked up the phone.

"Ms. Greer?" Young woman, nervous.

"Yes. Who's calling?"

"My name's Mia Varez. I'm—I was a friend of Elena Ramos. Is it okay for you to talk right now?"

"Yes. Definitely."

"Her brother Tonio told me about you. At her parents' house." Silence. "He said you helped him find her."

Alice closed her eyes against the memory of Elena's bare legs, the drying blood, the rising vultures. Tonio's agonized face. She could kick herself for not calling Tonio in the last few days, just to see how he was doing.

"What can I do for you?"

"Can I come by? If now is okay, I can be there in two minutes."

She must already be in Coffee Creek. Silla had left for lunch. Alice sat at her desk, willing herself to let silence wash through her head. Breathe, she admonished herself. She turned her head and saw, outside, a battered gray RAV4 pull up at the curb. A young Hispanic woman bundled in a pink down jacket hurried up the sidewalk, stopped at the door, and raised her hand. She paused, as if unsure she wanted to knock. Alice answered the door before the young woman had made up her mind.

"Mia?"

"Yes."

Alice ushered her into her office. "Let's sit over here." She waved at the wing chairs by the tea table at the window. Less threatening, more collaborative.

"So, how did you know Elena?"

Mia looked up. She was young, like Elena, with smooth skin and big brown eyes. "High school. We both graduated from Bowie last year and then started at ACC. We carpooled when we could."

If they were at Austin Community College, they were likely part of the vast number of local high school students not rich enough to afford full-time undergraduate college. Like their peers, they worked, raced to class, raced to work. "We were both working at Hecho en Mexico part-time. You know that restaurant?"

"Yes." Down in southwest Austin by the infamous "Y" intersection of Highways 71 and 290.

"We both wait tables, nights. Anyway, Elena was in this journalism class—"

"Journalism?"

"Yes, she was passionate about investigative reporting. She said those reporters turn over rocks, shine a light at what's under the rocks, try to do some good." Mia paused, eyes flickering behind the lashes, looking at her hands. "Me, I'm getting the prerequisites for nursing school."

Alice nodded, waited.

"Anyway, Elena had this idea. One night after we cleaned the tables, stacked the chairs, all that, she told me she was going undercover."

Alice stiffened. "What did she mean?"

"She'd heard about some scam near Coffee Creek, some manager type using undocumented workers like slaves. She said she was going to join up and get some dirt for her term paper, maybe even tell the police what was going down."

"Did she say where exactly these people were working?"

"No, not really. She said she'd heard maybe they worked events, you know, served, cleaned up." Mia rubbed her hands, palms down, on her thighs. "She was planning to get picked up close to the highway just west of Coffee Creek. There's an old shopping center, mostly vacant. She said you just waited for someone in a black SUV to stop and offer work."

Alice thought she knew the shopping center.

"Did she go?"

Mia nodded. "She called me while she was waiting. She was excited, nervous, said she had to hang up the minute she saw that black SUV. Word was that they didn't let you use phones."

"When was this?"

Mia chewed her upper lip, staring into space. "Our last shift together was a Tuesday night. She called me two days later."

Alice and Tonio had found Elena's body on Monday morning after that phone call.

Alice frowned. "Have you told the police?"

Mia flushed, looked down, looked back up into Alice's eyes. "I don't have legal papers. I've got my Dreamer application in, you know, DACA, but it's all up in the air. I'm afraid to go to the police. I told Tonio. He said I should talk to you."

"Maybe the police don't already have Elena's phone number, her email, but they'll need it. You can give me that, right?"

Mia nodded.

"Can you give me your phone number too?" Alice asked. "And your address?"

Silence. Then, "If I can qualify for nursing school, then get in, graduate, then get a job, I can help my family," Mia said.

Alice knew this meant, Don't out me. "But okay," Mia said, finally. "For my friend Elena. Who wanted to make things better for people like me."

"Elena was a U.S. citizen, though, right?"

Mia nodded. "Born here." She smiled at the arbitrary nature of the world, her lack of papers, Elena's lucky break. Now useless. Mia's face hardened. "I want her killer found. Call if you need me." She'd make a good nurse.

Alice called George Files, who confirmed the department had made no progress on Elena's death. They'd found no bullet or casing. They already had Elena's email and phone number, and they were looking into her account.

Alice passed along what Mia had told her. "Any chance this will help?"

"Talk about slim and none," Files replied. "You know how many black SUVs there are in this state? Or running around all the event centers and wedding venues we've got popping up out here? Coffee County, Hays County, Blanco County?"

"But have you heard any rumors about undocumented workers being used?"

She heard a long sigh. "I'll ask around," he said.

"What about that shopping center?"

"I'm already thinking about that. If it's the one I'm thinking of, it's notorious for some off-the-books activities. Big-city activities moving out here from Austin, up from San Antonio. The gig economy, y'know? Side hustles, but on the dark side. But, yeah, I'll take a look. And tell that young woman that if we need to talk to her, we'll try to keep ICE out of it."

Then he asked Alice, "How're you doing, after finding Elena?"

She shook her head at the phone, then realized he couldn't see her. "I'd like to erase the picture in my head, but more than that I'd like her back alive."

"Oh, yeah."

"I feel…empty." She couldn't believe she'd revealed that. She did feel empty, vacant. But what about Files? He had to deal with the slaughter of the innocent—and guilty—every day. "How do you manage? What keeps you going?"

He waited a few seconds before speaking. "Well, first, I want closure for the family."

"But is that enough? Just knowing who killed your loved one and maybe, maybe getting the murderer off the street?"

"It's at least something, Alice. It's horrible when you can't even tell a family what happened, who killed their family member. Families hope for justice. There's never enough justice, of course. But families are grateful for some closure." He stopped, perhaps waiting for a response, then went on. "I have bad days. But somebody's got to pick up the pieces. Besides, violent death is not just at the hands of humans. People drown, get hit by a bus, get struck by lightning. They overdose, have heart attacks, die of cancer. The word is we're all mortal."

"Yes, but to have another person snatch your allotted years away?" Alice wanted control, wanted to keep her loved ones safe, but Files was right. Some people died in bed, some died when a tree fell on them, but the word was, all would die. Even her children. Even her. Without a choice, necessarily, as to when or how.

Alice strongly objected to not having a choice. What about the Romans? What about Brutus who chose his own time, his own death, falling on his own sword, after clasping the hands of his friends? He found that preferable to capture.

On the other hand, she never wanted to fall on any sword. Forget that.

Pick up the pieces? What if there weren't any pieces to pick up?

Silla opened the front door, walked into Alice's office, peeling off her jacket. "Got some good gossip at lunch from one of Jane Ann's clerks."

Jane Ann ran the title company Alice used for real estate transactions.

"Oh?"

"Someone's making offers on multiple wedding venues around here. She's got at least three deals in the works. They haven't closed though."

"Did you tell that clerk to tell Jane Ann to tell the parties they should hire us to paper some of those deals?"

"Of course. But she says this buyer's got Phoenix money. Using Phoenix counsel."

Bells rang. Phoenix. Brad Gorman. Eddie's former partner.

Alice reached Eddie on his cell phone. "If you lose me it's because I'm out in the vineyard putting in more vines," he said, the wind all but blowing his words away. "Some petit verdot grapes. What'd you just say?"

"Someone's making a move on wedding venues in Coffee County. I wanted to see if you've heard any more from our friend Gorman."

"Nope. Radio silence." He paused. "However, there's a place next to me, right across the road, I've been thinking about making an offer on. Meant to call you about it, but we've been busy planting. What would you think if I got another hundred acres or so?"

"For vines? For a bigger venue?" Eddie's tall glass-walled tasting room looked out over the vines, carefully trained on their wires, and now just old enough to produce real vintages. Below he'd planted olives that flowed down the slopes, the gray-green leaves softening the rocky limestone ledges.

"That land sits on the next hillside over. It looks out toward my property. Has some southeast exposure. I could plant vines and maybe more olives."

Alice mentally lifted an eyebrow. "You know what I always say when someone asks whether to buy a particular piece of dirt? How will you feel if someone else buys it and you had the chance and didn't?"

"Exactly." The wind roared again through his phone. "Listen, I'll call you in an hour. I'll look up the owner on the tax records and come up with an offer."

"Sounds good," Alice said. "I don't want Brad Gorman hovering over me in any way whatsoever."

An hour later Eddie called back. "It's owned by some Houston folks named Graves. Elderly, they don't come up here any longer. Appraised market value on the tax rolls is a million five for most of the acreage, but the part down on the creek is fifty thousand an acre. The whole parcel, except a little ranch house, a cabin really, is already in ag use, for wild-life management. Assuming I can keep it there, that means big tax savings. Definitely worth it if I can swing it." He paused. "I'll need to borrow some money if we're looking at about a million six offer. And not a cent from Gorman, either. So, I'll work on the money, and you get a draft contract going, okay? Get in touch with the Graves people?"

"Will do." She hung up and called Silla, whose magic fingers extracted phone numbers from the World Wide Web. Yes, the Graves family would entertain an offer; they'd already received one offer, so please get in touch with Houston lawyer Joel Grassley.

She remembered Joel Grassley from a joint summer clerkship after her first year at UT Law. Where was he now? She found his contact info on the Texas State Bar website.

"Joel? I don't know if you'll remember me, but this is Alice MacDonald—"

"Alice!"

She sent a competing offer that afternoon to Joel Grassley.

Chapter Fifteen

My Way

The next morning when Alice pulled into the office driveway she heard raised voices as soon as she opened the car door. She pushed open the office door to find Brad Gorman in her entry hall, arguing with a white-faced Silla.

"What the hell are you doing?" he demanded, swinging around to face Alice.

"What the hell are *you* doing?" she asked, furious that he'd scared Silla.

"I'm taking you to the fucking State Bar!" he yelled. "You're violating my client rights!"

"You are not my client," snapped Alice. "I represent the limited partnership that you're no longer part of."

"You've got the grossest conflict of interest I've ever seen!"

"Mr. Gorman, either leave or go into the conference room and calm down. If you can be civil I'll join you. Go!" She pointed. He inflated like a bullfrog, then turned and stalked down the hall.

She pushed Silla ahead of her into the kitchen where, thank God, the coffeemaker was dripping elixir into a pot. "What happened?"

"He was waiting on the street. When I unlocked the door, he barged in right behind me and wouldn't leave. He's having a fit about that offer to the Graves family."

"Eddie's offer?" Maybe Brad had already made an offer. Maybe he was the "Phoenix money."

Alice took her coffee back to the conference room. Gorman, arms across his chest, glared at her from the other side of the conference table. He uncrossed his arms and slapped his hands on the table, leaning toward her, chin jutting at her, cheeks turning purplish. "Listen, missy," he hissed. "I'm buying that Graves property. No way you're getting it."

"So far as I know," Alice said, "it's still a free country. The limited partnership's entitled to go after that property."

"What'd you offer?"

"Oh, come on!" scoffed Alice. She managed a one-sided smile. "Tell me what you offered."

"You don't understand. I've *got* to get that parcel. Tell Eddie to buy something else. I'm—let's just say I need that hundred acres way more than he does."

Alice narrowed her eyes, trying to read him. "You don't live here. You don't need that land for an existing business. There's plenty of acreage for sale around here. That parcel's right next to Eddie's vineyards, and he's got plans for it. Those acres are directly related to his business, not yours. So what's your beef?"

He snorted, averting his eyes. The room was silent. He looked back across the table at Alice. "Y'know, I'm in a different market from you. I got to satisfy my boss. I got to get that parcel. That's my job."

She studied him. "Who's your boss?" He looked at her, his dark eyes unreadable. "Maybe you need a different job. If the Graves family likes our offer better than yours, that's how it's going to unfold."

"Okay, missy. I've tried to make this crystal clear. You playing dumb, that'll get you in serious trouble."

"Is that a threat, Mr. Gorman?"

"Oh no. It's the facts of life."

He stomped past, almost hitting her with his shoulder as he barged out of the conference room.

Silla emerged from the kitchen. They watched him pull open the front door, not bothering to close it, and stomp down the walk to the black Jeep.

Too late Alice realized he hadn't told her the name of his boss. Maybe he wasn't driving his own car. "You remember that MYWAY license plate, Silla?" Alice said.

"Sure. Arizona vanity plate. The Jeep looked like last year's model." Silla's apparently effortless eidetic memory amazed Alice.

"We may need to ask Tyler to run the number." Alice's criminal law buddy, Tyler Junkin, had extensive resources Alice didn't usually need in her sedate trusts and property practice.

"Sure."

She called Eddie. He must be working outside again; she could still hear the wind blowing when he answered. "I hope I didn't whistle up a storm bigger than both of us," she said.

"What's up?"

"Gorman's already made an offer on that property. He stopped by the office to tell us to back off. You know, his manners are deplorable."

She didn't tell Eddie that his ex-partner had managed to upset the unflappable Silla.

"Lord God," Eddie said. "That's all I need." Wind rattled the phone reception. "How mad is he?"

"Mad," Alice said. "Do you have security out there?"

"I've put up some video cameras, night cameras. I've hired a couple of security guys. Doesn't feel like the Hill Country, this kind of crap."

Alice concurred. She hung up, called Silla in, told her to call their own security people, beef up the office alarm system. Motion detectors, lights, video. "Got us a six-month contract," Silla reported.

Alice hoped Gorman would have left town by then.

*****

Alice stared at the stack of drafts on her desk. A couple of wills. One land trust. One power line easement. She made a field trip to the kitchen for another cup of coffee, plopped back down at the desk, stared at the fine print. It didn't speak to her.

Usually Alice felt a magnetic pull from contracts, wills, documents. She had only to pick up a number 2 pencil, very sharp, and start through a document before the structure started erecting itself in her head, and she could see where the window was leaking, the foundation uneven, the floor plan wrong. This part of the deal needed more specifics, that part needed some contractual warranties. Her pencil started constructing just what was called for.

But today? The drafts waiting patiently on her desk could have been written in Basque, in Icelandic for all she could grasp. Her mind whirled with visions of Elena's bloody legs, Gorman's purple cheeks and enraged eyes, Holly's little body slumping sideways below the saloon's swinging doors.

She stood up, dialed Kinsear, waited for his voice, waited for that warm masculine baritone saying, "Alice!"

Well, where was he? She left a message. "Date night?"

Silla came in with a short stack of the month's client bills and their transmittal letters, ready for Alice's signature. She glanced at the untouched drafts on Alice's desk. "Thought you wanted at least to get the will drafts out today?" she said, with a raised eyebrow and one-sided smile. Silla the taskmaster.

Alice nodded, unable to muster a responsive grin, and grimly signed the transmittal letters. As she handed them back, Silla said, "Go home. Go for a run, brush the burros. I'll wait for the security people. They're showing up before five. Those wills will wait." She twirled around and headed for the hall, her red ponytail swinging, and added, "As soon as those security boys get done, I've got a hot date at the Beer Barn. Gonna do a little show-off dancin' tonight. It's the Lufkin Low-down."

Now that sounded like a life improvement plan. The Beer Barn... music, some good cooking, some better beer. Unclear yet how good the band was. She'd never heard of them. Alice picked up her phone, tried Kinsear again. No answer. She tried him at his bookstore in Fredericksburg. "The Real Story, may I help you?" said a prim female voice. Must be his new clerk. "I'm so sorry, Mr. Kinsear is out. No, he has a dinner engagement. You know, that new place on Main Street?" What new place on Main Street? What dinner engagement?

Alice hung up, lips pressed together. Well, Kinsear was an adult male, unencumbered except by his daughters. He could go out without letting her know. Without inviting her. To that new place on Main Street.

So, what are friends for? She called Miranda. "Beer Barn?"

Chapter Sixteen

Extensive Downside Risk

The portable lighted sign at the Beer Barn read, "'What care I how time advances? I am drinking ale today.'—Edgar Allan Poe." The entertainment was listed below: "Tonight! Lufkin Lowdown! How low can you go?"

Alice was still in the parking lot when Miranda's Jag slid around the entrance, spraying gravel. Miranda grinned an impudent non-banker smile as she parked and climbed out. "I'm ready!" She looked at Alice's grim face and said, "Hmm. We'll need to talk, won't we?"

As she and Miranda pulled open the double doors to the beer hall, Alice realized how she loved the smell—years of beer, its millions of bubbles popping quietly and lending their effervescence to the air. History, a twenty-something male grad student making tuition by bartending, stood smiling behind the antique curved bar near the entrance. She and Miranda installed themselves on barstools.

"Dos Equis," Miranda said. History nodded.

"Who's cooking tonight?" Miranda asked.

"Jaime," History said. "I highly recommend the fajitas."

"Done," Miranda said. "Corn tortillas, please, not flour."

"Same," Alice said. "And a Modelo Especial."

History nodded and vanished. Miranda turned to Alice. "You look a little down in the mouth. Where's Kinsear, may I ask?"

"At a dinner engagement at the new place on Main Street in Fredericksburg."

Miranda raised a delicate eyebrow. "With?"

Alice shrugged.

"You don't know? Could be work, could be his daughters, could be some author?"

"I know. I'm being ridiculous."

"Your order's on the way," History announced. He placed two beers, beaded with moisture, on their coasters, and popped them open.

Miranda held up a manicured hand. "Alice. A moment of reverence. Or mindfulness, whatever. First sip." They each picked up the beers, eyed the faint vapor emanating from the tops, felt the wet labels under their fingers, sniffed the bouquet just slightly, and took a slug.

"Ahh." Miranda took another sip. "Never mind about that new place on Main Street. It's really Holly who's got you down, right?"

Alice nodded. "Also Elena."

"And this mess about Holly's money?" Miranda asked.

"Russ pointed out Silla or I could've changed the instructions. Scolded me for hurting Sandra's feelings by asking her if she'd sent different instructions."

"Well, come on, Alice. The man's just lost his wife. But, of course, I haven't met Sandra. On the make? Ready to bring her best casserole to Holly's funeral?"

"Maybe." Alice remembered Sandra, stroking the pastel nursery samples. "Could be her biological clock is ticking."

"Any more info on who sent those new instructions to the media company?"

"No," Alice said. "The techie wizards have to look into the internet service provider of the person who sent the faux email. They'll also look at Holly's emails to see if they can match up the fake-instructions email with other people who emailed Holly. And make sure she didn't do it herself, of course. Which, no way." She finished her beer. "I'm worried. They've only got a few days before it'll be too late to freeze that bank account. The thought of Holly's money disappearing…makes me sick."

Miranda grimaced. "As a banker, I too feel sick. Disappearing money…which could be sitting safe as houses in my bank." She looked down at her empty beer and then up at History, just as he arrived with a big tray holding two oval platters of fajitas, salsa verde, salsa roja, a dish of guacamole, and a bowl of sour cream.

In unison Miranda and Alice said, "Ahh!"

"Another beer?"

Both nodded, too busy arranging their condiments to look up. "I ran three miles this morning," Alice said.

"I went to barre class," Miranda said. "So, we can demolish this entire dish. In between bites, you can tell me whether George Files has found out anything more about who killed Elena."

"Nope." She didn't mention Elena's class project. Another dead end? Would Elena get justice?

The male components of the Lufkin Lowdown lumbered onstage and began their soundcheck. Beer Barn patrons began moving with intention toward the dance floor. Across the room Alice spotted Silla, who never lacked for dance partners. One of the three owners, Jorgé

Benavides, jumped up onstage to introduce the band. "Here tonight from down in the piney woods at Lufkin—you heard 'em at South by Southwest, you heard 'em at Kerrville, and now you're hearing the Lufkin Lowdown here at the Beer Barn!" Cheers from the crowd. The lead guitar rolled into a slow bluesy lick, the drums picked up and a young woman sporting blue hair brushed up like a Hokusai wave surprised the crowd with Carolyn Wonderland's "Texas Girl."

Alice perked up. Another successful night for her favorite client, the Beer Barn. Sweaty dancers swarmed the bar for more longnecks and rushed back to the dancefloor to sweat some more. Maybe life wasn't so terrible. Her feet were tapping, and…

Someone was kissing the back of her neck. Someone who smelled good. She whirled around to see Kinsear, a quizzical expression on his face, pointing to his phone. "Turned off your sound again, Alice?"

Miranda laughed, stood up, got her hug from Kinsear. "I'm heading home. Have a good night, you two."

Alice pulled her phone out, thumbed to messages, looked at the string from Kinsear.

"Let's dance," he said. "I like that girl's voice." He grabbed her hand, tugged her down toward the dance floor. Alice liked to dance with someone who knew what he was doing. Kinsear's strong sense of rhythm, the fun he had choreographing her into a twirl, and the confidence he brought to the enterprise always made her smile. But tonight, with the Lufkin Lowdown, the seductive R&B vibe, and the self-mocking smile Kinsear put into his, yes, frankly low-down moves, Alice found him ridiculously, outrageously sexy for a grown man, a rangy late forty-something in a blue chambray button-down shirt. In fact, Miss Hokusai Wave was gazing straight at him while she sang.

Alice's response must have shown in her eyes, because Kinsear waggled his black eyebrows, now flecked with gray, twirled her, pulled her close, and said into her ear, "Take me home now, Alice!"

And so to bed.

*****

At six the next morning, after biting her tongue several times, Alice plunged ahead and asked Kinsear how sophomore year was going for his daughter Isabel. She had no intention of offering any advice, ever, on his childrearing. But he'd been upset, so she felt the need.

He took a sip of coffee. "Life-giving," he said, and took a second sip. "I've been thinking. She needs another role model. She's got a pretty limited view of the world."

"What do you mean?"

"Her problems are all first-world problems. She spent summers at the fancy camp in New Mexico, got into the fancy boarding school, grew up with a house in town and a ranch where she could ride horses all day long. She wants the latest jeans? She gets them. Never has she had to wait for clothes to go on sale or choose her baby-sitting job over going out with her friends." He frowned. "Sometimes I disapprove of my parenting. But like Heraclitus maybe said, you can't step in the same river twice. No do-overs. We change, the river changes."

Too early for philosophy. "Any volunteer work?" Alice asked.

"Oh, sure. Last year she volunteered at a day camp for low-income kids. She's done some volunteer work at an equestrian program for kids with disabilities. But she doesn't see it, Alice. She doesn't see the big picture."

Alice thought he might be selling his daughter short. She probably kept her secrets, kept her thoughts from her dad.

"Anyway," he went on, "what I thought would be really helpful, would be for her to meet you. Have lunch with you."

"Me?" Alice's worst nightmare.

"Yes, you. She's talked some about going to law school. My war stories about New York law practice in hedge fund land aren't juicy enough, don't convey enough about real people with real problems that a lawyer could help solve, the way you do. Anyway, it's time you two met, spent some time together."

"Doesn't she already hate the idea of me?" Alice asked.

"Probably. But she could learn from you. She doesn't have to like you. And you don't have to like her either. How about next week?"

Alice managed a smile. "Can't wait." She doubted this nineteen-year-old would have any interest whatsoever in her small-town law practice. Though, to be sure, Alice had lived through some interesting times. Still, she could see extensive downside risk from this lunch.

Chapter Seventeen

The Bully Posture

Kinsear left before seven for a breakfast meeting in Fredericksburg. Alice sat by the kitchen counter, with an empty coffee cup, in her empty house. Once again anger and grief snuck up on her. After a couple of minutes, she sat up straight and called Detective George Files at the Coffee Creek Sheriff's Department. Early, but she bet he'd answer.

"Good morning. Anything new on Holly or Elena?"

"Not yet," he said. "By the way, I'm not on Elena's case anymore. It's assigned to Detective Eads. He's new. I've got my hands full with your writer friend."

Alice's heart sank. "I thought you'd work both these cases."

"We've got some new assignment protocols. Have to spread the work, you know." He paused. "I'll look over his shoulder now and then."

Alice heard herself say, "I hope he knows what he's doing. I hope a newbie's not being assigned to Elena just because she's a Mexican-American kid."

"And I hope you don't really think that," Files said stiffly. "But try not to get on the wrong foot with Eads. He's a little oh, let's say he can be a bit oversensitive."

"I just want him to find out who killed Elena."

Silence on the phone. Files said, "I know."

"Thanks." She hung up.

Thoroughly disgruntled, Alice emerged from her house dreading a day in the office. Two women lay dead; the normally insouciant Eddie now patrolled his property, fearing attacks on the vines; Russ mistrusted her.

At least her three donkeys stood waiting for her at the wrought-iron gate, ears twitching, brown eyes fixed on her in hopeful anticipation. Alice pushed against the gate until the donkeys finally got out of the way. They followed her out to the workshop. She grabbed three donkey treats from the bag on the shelf. Three muzzles sniffed, three donkeys lifted their upper lips and gently mouthed the treats.

Alice stroked the ears of Princess, the youngest, then gave donkey hugs to the two older donkeys, Big Boy (the smallest) and Queenie (the most regal). Donkey hugs meant leaning into their sides, firmly stroking their necks. The donkeys instantly settled, leaning back against her. The weird thing was how the donkeys settled her. She felt her own breathing slow. The donkeys weren't like dogs, loyal and needy, or cats, neutral as Switzerland and non-needy. Donkeys were ancient residents of the planet, tough, independent, curious herd animals with their own inner life. They bemused Alice's visitors who loved to feed them carrots. Alice would say, "They keep the grass down." But she felt the donkeys, with their watchful eyes, somehow kept her honest.

Honesty required her to evaluate the pen around the donkeys' shelter and to check the barn for hay.

Pen: the mineral block, a thin sliver. Barn: no hay. An eye to the north showed a hard blue-gray wall of advancing clouds, a classic Texas norther moving south. She hoped it was the last before spring. She ached to see wildflowers.

Grumbling to herself, she climbed into the familiar seat of her old Toyota truck and headed out the creek road to town. At Miller's Feed Store she acquired a new mineral block and six bales of hay—enough to spread a bed in the shed that shielded the donkeys from heavy rain and north wind.

She sped home, climbed into the truck bed, and rolled the mineral block off the tailgate into the pen. She pushed and kicked the bales off the truck toward the open side of the shed. She clipped wire and broke open the bales, kicking the golden-green grass into a comfortable layer. The donkeys watched, unblinking, behind her. As soon as she quit kicking they began eating their bed. She just hoped they wouldn't finish it before the norther arrived.

Kicking the bales out of the truck made her feel better.

As she drove the truck back across the pasture to the driveway her pocket vibrated. She pulled out her phone and looked at the screen. "Coffee County Sheriff." She punched "accept."

"Detective Eads here. Is that Alice Greer?"

"Yes."

"I need to talk to you about Elena"—he paused—"Elena, um, Elena's death. Are you available right now?"

"Yes."

"I'm at your gate. What's your gate code?"

Damn. Not a lot of warning. What was the deal?

She watched the sheriff's department SUV move down her drive. Files would have called, would have asked what time was convenient. She could see Eads's head swing left, swing right. Files wouldn't be driving down the drive at three miles per hour, checking out her place. Alice stood by her truck, waiting. She felt movement behind her. The donkeys were slowly coalescing into a small retinue. She was feeling pretty stiff-necked by the time Eads pulled up. He wasn't going to get any offers from her, coffee or otherwise.

Eads dismounted from the SUV, hat pulled low over his forehead. Files never wore a hat. Tall in his tan chinos and leather bomber jacket, Eads assumed the bully posture, belly and chest sticking out, head slightly tilted, eyes narrowed. She'd never seen Files do that.

Alice let her eyes wander from Eads's hat, to the badge, to his hands, to his boots, and back to his face, not saying a word.

"Ms. Greer?"

She nodded once.

"I've got some questions for you about"—he looked down at a steno pad—"Elena something. Umm."

Still can't get the name right, can he? Bad sign. She waited, curious. He glanced once at her house, then back at her. She ignored her mother's semi-automatic hospitality training. No, she did not plan to ask him in.

"How long had you known her?" he asked.

"I never met her. Until the morning we found her." She waited.

"Where were you the night before you found her?"

"Here."

"Anyone with you?"

She shook her head no. "I assume you've seen the statement I gave the sheriff's department." Why was he here?

"Did you move her body?"

"You mean from under the fence where we found her? No." She added, "We did disturb the vultures, however."

He looked at the steno pad. "Why was this Elena stuck under your fence?"

"I don't know," Alice said. "Did you find where the shot or shots were fired from?"

He looked up. "What do you mean?"

"Based on where she was found, didn't you search upstream? Past the blood tracks in the grass?"

His face reddened. "If you disturbed the crime scene you're in big trouble," he growled.

"We could see blood in the grass from where we were standing, on my property," Alice said. "As I said in my statement."

He looked down at the steno pad. "This Tonio guy, how long have you known him?"

"At least five years."

"He works for you?"

"Yes, most weekends. All the ranch work."

"You think he's reliable?"

"Completely."

"Is he legal?"

"I believe so." What did this have to do with Elena's murder?

He shifted, put his weight on the other leg. "What firearms do you own?"

"I've never bought any."

"Well, what do you have?"

"My husband's shotgun and pistol."

"No rifle?"

"No rifle."

He shifted back to the other foot, tilted his head the other way. "I need to see your guns."

She stared back. "Detective, you have no warrant, do you?"

He reddened. "No."

"I will show you my dead husband's guns. As a courtesy."

She turned and headed for the house. "I'll be right back."

First, find the guns. The last time she'd hidden them, before a Christmas party with children, she'd put them upstairs…maybe in the closet behind all her son John's Star Wars figures and his vast collection of Legos. There they lay: a 45 pistol in a canvas holster and a beautiful Scottish shotgun, both dusty. Alice grabbed a washcloth and hand towel from the bathroom and tenderly picked up each. She carried them outside.

"Here they are." She laid them on the tailgate of her truck.

Eads reached a hand toward them. She shook her head, lifted a warning finger. "These have not been fired since well before my husband died."

"You're sure there's no rifle?"

"I'm sure there's no rifle. Jordie was a bird guy."

Eads stared at the two weapons. Then his eye traveled to the holes in the steel truck bed. After a moment he said, "Are those bullet holes?"

Alice nodded. Instantly in her mind it was a year ago, and she was frantically evading the helicopter shooter who'd tried to kill her and her elderly client, out on a lonely road rich with spring wildflowers, her truck hurtling toward an overpass, bullets banging. She added, "You can ask George Files. He knows all about it."

He stared at her, then back at the bullet holes, then back at her. She refused to drop her eyes, staring him down.

"I think that's all," he said. "For the moment." He stared back.

Grr. Okay, what had he investigated, given that he didn't even know Elena's surname? "Are you guys any further on finding who killed Elena? Did you find the people who were supposed to pick her up at that shopping center on Highway 290?"

"We have a team on this," he said.

"What about the info I passed on about her class project? From her friend Mia? Anything come of that?"

"We'll be in touch if we need anything further," he said shortly and turned and headed for the SUV.

It was only eight-thirty a.m.

Poorly handled, Alice told herself. How can you get information if you horse off the investigating detective? She sighed. Files had warned her. But she objected to being bullied in her own driveway. Bad morning. A sudden blast of chill arrived; the windmill in the yard squeaked and began to spin. Alice looked up at the lowering blue-gray cloudbank. The norther had hit. The donkeys flicked their tails and moved off toward their shelter.

Alice shivered in her fleece. She climbed into the Discovery and headed to town. Maybe work would take her mind off Eads. Maybe at least Hooks would have called and cleared her email and Silla's and the office's from any charge of sending fake instructions. Maybe her office would feel warmer. Also safer. In the meantime, she turned up the volume on Art Tatum, "Aunt Hagar's Blues," followed by Count Basie, "How Long Blues." Cause that's how she felt.

Chapter Eighteen

Dead End, in Every Way

Ham and Julie beat her to the office that morning. Silla met her at the front door to alert Alice: "They're in the conference room, with coffee."

Alice dropped her bag in her office. When she opened the conference room door two tense faces looked up at her.

"We just dropped off the kids at school," Ham said. "We took a chance you'd be here. We really need you to send our next-door neighbor a cease and desist letter, or whatever you call it. Now he's hauled a trailer onsite. He's definitely violating our covenants!"

"See?" Julie said, pushing her tattered copy of the covenants across the table. "Down here under Prohibited Acts. No trailers!"

"Is it possible he's making a commercial use of the trailer?" Alice hoped to develop a stronger case before showing up in court with a fight between neighbors.

Julie glanced at Ham, then said, "We're not sure. It's gotta be something, though."

"Tell me more about the trailer."

"You can see it from the front gate," Julie said. "It's parked just past the big house, on the part of his land that's level before it slopes down to the creek."

"Well," Alice said. "I can at least draft a letter attaching the covenants and stating that we want the trailer off the property in two weeks. When did you or your neighbors last try to enforce the covenants? Also, what are you really afraid of?"

"That dog guy," Julie muttered. It wasn't enough. Not yet, anyway.

"We and a couple of neighbors did enforce the trailer covenant about five years ago," Ham said. "That time, it just took a letter. What we're afraid of—the commercial use issue—is critical. We're worried about Waterfall Road getting taken over by wedding venues. They're popping up like measles all over Hays County and Coffee County. Meanwhile, we've invested all our resources buying our creek land for the quiet life and stars at night. We're not interested in shrieking bachelorettes and bands past midnight and drunk drivers careening around."

Alice knew all too well what he meant. Denny Springs Road on the far side of Coffee Creek had become a welter of venues, one after another. She tried to avoid it during prime wedding weekends—

April through June, October through November—and felt sorry for long-time residents who found their once-peaceful country road now abuzz with streams of cars, buses, and limos all weekend long. Silla's gossip with Jane Ann's title company employee confirmed what Ham feared: investors were prowling Coffee County, trying to corner venue property.

Ham went on, "Some people run a nice venue, but we don't want that on our road. We bought where we did because it offered both the creek and the school district. Our area's supposed to be residential only, except for animals and crops. We're determined to enforce these covenants."

Alice walked her friends to the front door. "I'll draft a letter today," she said. "We'll ask for the trailer to be removed and remind them that no commercial use is allowed. Find out if any of your neighbors want to sign on. If you learn more about what's going on with those SUVs, let me know."

Julie nodded.

"Maybe get the license plates," Alice suggested. "See if they're registered to Craft or someone else."

*****

Silla's voice from the workroom, "Call George Files back on his cell! I left the message on your desk."

Alice grabbed her phone and dialed. Files had his own button now in her phone's favorites. Files answered.

"It's Alice. You have news?" She heard papers rustling.

"The financial crimes people are still working on that phony email with the wire instructions."

"Meanwhile the account's still frozen?"

"Yes."

"Are you any closer on who shot Holly?"

"No. But I've got the ballistics report here. The day she died we documented all the guns brought onsite by the competitors and the cowboy action volunteers. The bullet that killed her looks like it's from a Ruger New Vaquero. Several competitors had pistols like that."

"What about Russ? He was the only one who shot a revolver at Stage One that day." And missed once, she remembered.

"He does use Ruger New Vaquero revolvers, so we've sent his guns to ballistics for testing. You said you heard him fire each revolver five times and miss once—you heard the shot, but no ping on the metal target, right? The volunteer timers say the same, and the volunteers who checked the guns before the competition swore his revolvers had an empty chamber, per safety rules. You remember watching them check the guns?"

"Yes."

"And afterwards they tell me they picked up all ten shells on the porch, like they always do," Files said. "No extras. Finally, whoever shot her got her right in the heart with a bullet that we don't think was cowboy action compliant, wasn't light loaded. The medical examiner thinks Holly was shot from just a foot or so away. Lots of residue on her clothes. Not on her hands, though."

"Holly wouldn't have shot herself!"

"And I'm trying to tell you it looks like she didn't. It's also hard to see when Russ could've shot her. We'll have ballistics back from his guns in a few days."

Alice remembered Holly asking her to take pictures and then leaving for the women's restroom. She remembered Russ standing with Red and Kinsear while she begged them to smile for their picture, and Russ leaving, wanting stomach tablets from his truck. Holly had said he was too nervous to eat breakfast. Later she saw him returning from the parking lot and brushing off Brad Gorman. She too couldn't see how he'd have shot Holly.

Files interrupted her thought. "But here's what I called about. No one can identify the guy you saw picking up the trash bag at the women's restroom. You remember anything else about him?"

"No more than I've already told you. Black outfit. Black truck. Black trash bags. Wasn't he a Cowboy Action volunteer?"

"The trail boss and the timer can't identify him and no one else can either."

"What about the black trash bags?"

"There's not a trace of the bags or the truck. Of course, whoever it was could've just dumped her body behind the saloon doors at Stage One and driven right on out of the venue while you and all the spectators were still up at Stage Four. But no one we've talked to saw any such thing."

"And no one saw Holly in the restroom?"

"No one we've been able to track down," he said.

Dead end, in every way. Alice closed her eyes against the memory of Holly's small body.

She sighed. "Well, can I ask you a question? What about Elena Ramos?" she asked. "What's Eads found out?"

"You know that's not my case. By the way, what'd you do to Eads?"

"Nothing," Alice said.

Momentary silence. "After he got back from your place he asked me about your truck, you know, the perforated one."

"That man came out to my place with no warning and no warrant and wanted to search my house," Alice said stiffly. "We conducted our business in my driveway." She paused. "I got a little tight-jawed that he hadn't bothered to learn the victim's last name."

"We've got a lot going on," Files admitted. But Alice thought she detected a faint tone of disapproval.

"Did he learn anything from that shopping center where Elena was supposed to meet the SUVs?"

"I don't know. It's not my case. I'll ask him to give you a call. Gotta go."

*****

Meanwhile, Alice had a plan. It would soon be March; the days were perceptibly longer. The weather service predicted a storm in the Gulf of California might bring rain by the weekend. She emailed her draft letter to Ham and Julie and headed home by three.

She didn't want her plan rained on.

Chapter Nineteen

Worse than Unneighborly

Down the empty drive to her empty house she drove, arousing a greeting from Big Boy, who hee-hawed as usual when she drove through the gate. Once inside, she trotted upstairs to the storage closet and dragged out the plastic storage bin of fly-fishing gear. She hadn't opened it since Jordie's death. His flies, his waders, his vest, his net—all on top. She dug underneath and pulled out her own waders and stream boots. She added her vest, with its dangling clippers, and her fly box. She chose a stream-sized rod and went back downstairs to don her outfit.

The sight of herself in the hall mirror momentarily convulsed her in laughter. She left a message for her next-door neighbor Hal, a semi-retired financial fraud consultant who traveled extensively and only spent weekends at his place in Coffee Creek, that she might trespass.

Alice climbed down her stone stairway to the creek wearing her waders, vest, and stream boots. She intended to confirm with her own eyes the presence of a trailer before she sent a demand letter to Ham and Julie's neighbor, the Hermit. Clients sometimes exaggerated; she needed certainty. She picked up the rod like she meant business and waded into the creek. She could feel the chilly current through her waterproof waders. "Whoo!" she said aloud. Then she started her slow walk upstream toward Ham and Julie's, trying to avoid the deeper holes in the gravel bottom.

Alice's house sat on the steep bluff along the north side of the creek, as did her neighbor Hal's. But unlike Hal, she also owned acreage on the other side, the low side, where spring and fall floods tore up the fences and deposited chunks of rock and logs every year. Her fence on the far side abutted a vacant lot belonging to the owners of the Calico Ranch, a big spread that lay south of the creek. Elena had been found underneath the fence between Alice's land and the vacant lot.

Calico Ranch's owners had carved out five large creek lots on the low side of the creek, reachable only by Waterfall Road, which crossed the low-water bridge across the creek and ended at the Calico Creek vacant lot. The ranch owners had kept the vacant lot abutting Alice's property but sold off the other four. Next to the vacant lot came Ham and Julie's property, then the Craft domain, then the Fischers' property. A banker owned the last lot, at the low-water bridge.

Alice was glad Ham and Julie and their kids had been in Oklahoma City showing their quarter horse the weekend she and Tonio found Elena's body.

Hal's creek frontage stretched all the way to the low-water bridge, giving him a view of Ham and Julie's, the Hermit's, the Fischers', and the banker's property. His part of the bluff was higher than Alice's, and so steep he'd had to build a wooden staircase that zigzagged down to the creek. She planned to use his stairs as her vantage point.

Alice stepped slowly along beneath the limestone bluff, still green with graceful clouds of maidenhair fern. Winter rains had soaked the porous karst layers under the thin soil of the plateau. Water dripped off the limestone ledges, plopping into the quiet creek. She could feel cold water pushing against her legs.

Just ahead on her left she saw the fence line between her land and the vacant lot, where she and Tonio had found Elena dead, face down under the lowest wire. Again, she wondered how exactly Elena had traveled to that point. The sheriff's officers hadn't reported finding any sign other than the short bloody trail near the fence. Had she perhaps tried to travel down the creek itself, where any trace might be washed away?

It was hard to pick up pieces when there were none.

Now, past her own fence line, she waded past Ham and Julie's place on the low side, and Hal's, on the bluff above the water.

Her legs were chilly but still dry. In the clear blue-green water a few fish darted like small torpedoes through the bigger pools. Watching the fish, she nearly fell right into a hole.

Time to amp up her disguise. Alice stopped in the shallows across from Ham and Julie's place and tied on a fly, a woolly booger. With a fly on her line, she'd start casting gently, quietly, at the shaded pool just ahead. Down in that cool water lurked a big 'un, she felt sure, but she planned not to catch it.

Protective coloration for both of them—a shady patch for the bass, a convincing fly on the line of this anonymous fisherwoman, systematically casting her way upstream. She tried another cast, loving the curve of line in the air, the way the fly settled on the water. But she should keep moving. She reeled in her line, prepared for another cast farther upstream.

On her left, still as statues, Ham and Julie's horses watched from behind barbed wire. They were fenced out of the creek. "If they get in the water I'll never get 'em out," Julie had told her. "I always tell the kids, 'You leave that gate open, you're totally in charge of rounding up those horses.'" Beyond a locked gate in the fence, a path led uphill to Ham and Julie's house, with its comfortable porch and creek view.

Just past Ham and Julie's she reached the Hermit's place. He'd erected an eight-foot-tall limestone wall between his land and Ham and Julie's. The wall stopped only fifteen feet short of the creek bank. Alice shook her head. Who in the world would buy creek-front property and then spend that much money on an eight-foot limestone wall, all the way down the property line? Most river houses, as on the Blanco River in Wimberley, left their side property lines open so each house could see the entire stretch of the blue-green river. Even though they knew precisely where their property line lay, neighbors usually wanted their view to include as much river as possible.

The Hermit was not neighborly. He'd effectively blocked Ham and Julie's upstream view.

Moreover, Alice could now see he'd continued the stone wall along the creek itself, even a worse offense. The limestone barrier along the creek was interrupted by a business-like gate of iron bars as tall as the wall. She squinted. Razor wire on top of the gate? Crazy. He's wrecked his own creek view. He's left only a few feet of rocky shore outside his wall. And what happens to his new wall in the next flood? That'll be a mess.

She stopped, lifted her rod, gazing upstream, and cast. As she retrieved her line, she glanced across the creek through the iron gate. Aha! Beyond the stone wall, maybe fifty feet from the creek on a level patch, sat a white trailer. Beyond and atop a rise, she spied a second white trailer. That must be the one Ham and Julie could see from the road. Both were single-wides resting on cinderblocks. On the nearer trailer, curtains covered the single window she could see and—she squinted to be sure—yes, there were bars on the window. No window in the door.

The yard sat undisturbed in the late sun. Not a soul moved anywhere. Through the gate Alice could see thick-trunked pecan trees, perhaps from an old orchard, shading the lawn near the creek. Past those, close to the trailer nearest the creek, next to the wall adjoining Ham and Julie's land, she spotted a big stump, the raw wood still yellow. Someone had cut down one of those old pecans.

She peered past the trailers, looking for the main house. Beyond the second trailer she saw a gate and parking area. With the stone wall running to and along the creek, the other side of the strip of land holding the trailers was closed in by a tall game fence, she guessed eight feet tall. Someone had covered the entire game fence with green shade cloth. She couldn't see through it, but she saw a tall roof beyond it. She'd checked out the Hermit's property on Google using the Coffee County appraisal site, but it was out of date and didn't show any structures.

She wanted to see the Hermit's house. The limestone wall ran farther up the creek, past this fenced-in trailer section.

Alice sauntered on upstream, rod pointed forward, slowly scanning the water for fish. On her right, on the bluff side, she dodged a deeper pool in mid-creek and reached Hal's rickety wooden staircase. Midway up, on a landing, Hal had chained a couple of kayaks. At the gravel bar by the stairs she clambered up the bank onto the staircase and began climbing. At the kayak landing she turned to look. Hal's stairs provided a generous view of the Hermit's domain.

The Hermit's limestone wall continued about five hundred feet before it turned and ran back uphill toward Waterfall Road. Directly across the creek from Hal's stairs, a wide ornate wrought-iron gate, waist-high, interrupted the wall. The main house stood on a rise maybe three hundred feet from the water. Three stories, dressed limestone, mullioned windows. Faux Tudor in the Hill Country. A broad two-story wing extended from the house toward the parking area, maybe a multicar garage? Apartment upstairs for the help? Beyond that wing two black SUVs were parked in the driveway.

A terrace stretched across the lawn below the house. Three oversized umbrellas shaded three empty chaises and a wheeled tea cart. Formal jardinières held evergreens pruned into topiary pyramids. No casual Hill Country plantings here, no salvia and sage, no pink yucca or agave. Instead, immaculate green lawns sloped down toward the creek, requiring watering and mowing. No low-maintenance buffalo grass for the Hermit.

What did the place say about the owner? Alice guessed he wasn't from the Hill Country. He ignored Hill Country penury about water usage, ignored neighborly norms, and obviously did not welcome drop-in company.

She climbed almost to the top and sat down, huffing, behind the stair railing. From this vantage point she felt somewhat concealed. She could see beyond the Hermit's house to the road he shared with his neighbors, Waterfall Road. Nothing moved. No one spoke. She pulled her phone from the chest pocket of her waders and took pictures of the trailers on one side of the property and the Hermit's house and terrace on the other.

Suddenly she heard the squeal of brakes: a black pickup, matte finish, roared up to the Hermit's gate. Alice replaced the phone in her chest pocket and grabbed her folding binoculars. The gate swung slowly open. The driver had short tawny hair and wore aviator glasses. Could it be the man who alarmed Julie so? The truck accelerated toward the one-story wing, then disappeared. Alice decided to watch for five more minutes.

She was about to pick up her rod and start back down the rickety staircase when she saw movement in the fenced-in trailer yard. The tawny-haired man stood outside the door of one of the trailers, wearing a bright red one-piece spandex outfit, like a wrestler's. He talked to someone at the trailer door, then pulled the door to and locked it from the outside. He stalked over to the game fence, unlocked a gate Alice had missed, and reappeared on the other side of the fence, walking lightly back down the immaculate green lawn toward the elegant gate by the creek. She noted his graceful walk, his long muscles: a dancer, maybe?

He disappeared momentarily behind the stone wall along the creek, then reappeared by the wrought-iron gate, now holding a set of free weights in one hand and a full-length mirror—a lightweight back-of-the-closet-door type mirror—in the other. He leaned the mirror against a pecan tree. She watched him as he watched himself lift weights. After a couple of minutes, still facing the mirror, he plunged to the ground in plank position, held plank for a long count, and began pushups, the advanced sort, heaving himself into the air and clapping his hands before returning to the ground. Alice watched, fascinated.

The man stood, dusting his hands, then reached for the weights again, and worked his biceps and triceps. Then he hit the ground again for plank on one arm, lifting a weight with the other. In the early spring sun, slanting down the creek from the southwest, she saw sweat began to impart a gloss to his sinuous, well-defined muscles. At last he stood, breathing heavily. Then he retreated behind the wall and emerged with a yellow line with two rings on one end. He threw the line over a pecan branch close to the mirror, grabbed the rings and began working his abs and obliques, turning his body slightly so he could see himself in the mirror. The air was so quiet she heard him panting.

She wanted to remember his face clearly so she could describe it to Ham and Julie. She lifted her folding binoculars.

He straightened up, looked over his shoulder at himself in the mirror for a few seconds, turned back to face the mirror, brushed his hair back with one hand and posed: first, legs apart, arms folded across his chest; then profile, both sides, with biceps flexed; finally an Elvis slouch, head cocked, ending with a fond smile at the mirror. What a dog. The Hermit had Narcissus as a guest. She focused her binoculars on the face reflected in the mirror. Pale eyes.

But she bumped against her fishing rod, which clattered down two steps, and when she leaned to retrieve it, her hat fell off. Narcissus turned, looked up sharply, stared intently. Don't show alarm, she said to herself. She tucked the binoculars inside her shirt, adjusted her hat, picked up her fly rod, and started slowly up the last few stairs, trying to look like a woman who'd just taken a little afternoon casting practice. At the top she leaned over the gate, unhitched the latch at the top of the staircase, and walked across the top of the bluff toward the back of her neighbor's house, still trying not to hurry. She hoped Narcissus had gotten the message she intended: "You don't know me. I've just been fishing."

He couldn't see her now. She changed direction, diverted her steps toward the fence between her neighbor's pasture and hers. But she wanted one more look. A cedar thicket that crowned the bluff offered opportunity. She stashed her fly rod beneath one thickly branched cedar, then pushed aside branches and moved toward the edge of the bluff. Hoping she was well hidden, she peered over. Across the creek she saw Tawny Man vault lightly over the wrought-iron gate and walk straight into the creek, slowing as the blue-green water swirled around his crotch. Did he intend to add cold-water exercise to the workout?

No. Not flinching at the water, he moved across the creek toward her neighbor's property. He reached the staircase. He stood silent, head tilted back, scanning the bluff. Behind the prickly cedar branches Alice tried not to move and held her breath.

He stared up the steps, eyes narrowed. Finally, he turned back to the creek, splashing fast through the water. He vaulted back over the gate and disappeared behind the wall.

Alice shoved her way back through the cedar thicket, found her fly rod and hustled toward the ranch gate between her property and her neighbor's, trying to memorize the face she'd seen in the mirror. Bushy pale brows, stubby nose, thin reddish lips. That unusual hair. What she remembered most was the eyes. Pale eyes.

Her phone beeped with a message from the neighbor: "Fine. I'm not home today. Can you manage our gate?" She could. It was padlocked, but she climbed over. Safely back on her property, she climbed up rocky ledges toward the live oaks that sheltered her house and walked back into her empty home.

Had she picked up any pieces? She'd spotted two trailers. She could certainly send the Hermit a severe letter requiring him to comply with the no-trailers covenants. But also, someone was inside one of those trailers. Someone Narcissus had locked in. She felt a chill, thinking of those pale eyes, the locked trailer, the barbed wire on the gate, the silence. The Hermit's place was worse than unneighborly.

Chapter   Twenty

My Best
Viognier

"You heard back from Joel Grassley," Silla called, as Alice walked into the office the next morning. "He only had a couple of comments on Eddie's offer for the Graves property next to his winery."

Alice scanned Joel's response to her draft sales contract. Good—only minor issues. She called Eddie. "Can you close a week later than we offered? The owners want to come up here for one more weekend this year."

"Sure. Gives me more time to scare up the money."

"Also, they want you to buy the equipment in the barn. It's that orange Kubota tractor and a riding mower." She added, "Sounds like they just don't want to have to deal with it."

"If they throw in the lawn furniture and the two kayaks you can add a little money to the contract."

They talked details. She called Joel back, finalized the deal, sent Joel and Eddie the revised draft, and called Eddie again.

"Joel's taking the contract to the owners to sign. When can you come in?"

"Can't. I'm here all day, working on getting my concrete tank installed."

Concrete tank? Septic system? What did he mean?

"It's my new concrete wine tank, the one that sent Brad into conniptions," Eddie explained. "We're not the first in the Hill Country, but we're pretty early. Unlike the usual steel tank, concrete lets the wine breathe a little. Micro-oxygenation, it's called. On a wine with a tight structure, like petit verdot, a concrete tank can help the wine get properly drinkable sooner, which is great for a small winery like ours, both on cash flow and storage."

"Brad was not in favor?"

"'What a dumb idea,' he said. That was Brad's favorite response to any of my ideas requiring us to spend capital. So now he's gone."

But not forgotten. Alice recalled Gorman's angry invasion of her office. "So, you can't come sign today? Can't Conroy help?"

"Nope, he's got to go see his therapist in Austin." Alice knew Eddie, former pro center, had hired his old teammate Conroy Robinson, who'd played pulling guard next to Eddie, to help at the vineyard. Eddie had explained briefly that Conroy still had some post-concussion syndrome. "He likes this quiet life, working the vines," Eddie had said.

"But as soon as the tank installers leave, I've got to start rinsing it out, getting ready to move my petit verdot in there."

Alice could hear the excitement in Eddie's generally low-key voice. He added, "I expect I could come by your office tomorrow."

She agreed and hung up. Then she looked at her to-do list. Only two tasks left for the day: a phone call with a new client wanting a will and finalizing Ham and Julie's demand letter to the Hermit, telling him to move those trailers.

She'd get those done, then maybe this afternoon she'd run out to Eddie's place.

*****

"Ready to go." Silla handed Alice two original letters addressed to Mr. Richard Craft. Ham and Julie had reported the Fischers, two of their neighbors, wanted to join in the letter; Alice had double-checked with the Fischers to confirm.

Alice signed both originals. "One by regular mail, and one certified, return receipt requested." How would the Hermit respond? Comply and move two trailers within two weeks? Pepper Alice with protestations and letters from opposing counsel? Or go on the attack and accuse his neighbors of their own violations of the sacred covenants? Her mind wandered to the tawny-haired man and his dog. She brushed that away.

Time for a little road trip.

*****

McElrath Road inevitably reminded Alice of her evasive driving lessons with Eddie LaFarge. Approaching the S-curve on the poorly banked two-lane blacktop, she estimated the apex of the first curve, slid into it, enjoying the feeling, and was just about to accelerate into the next curve when a Coffee County Sheriff's SUV appeared in the oncoming lane. At an unimpeachably sedate speed, she gave the traditional forefinger wave from her steering wheel and continued on toward Raptor Cellars.

No other cars or trucks, no cyclists, no one but the sheriff was out on this lonesome stretch of road. Eddie had found a piece of paradise: rugged limestone hills sloping down to a creek, with plenty of southeast exposure for grape vines. If French wine grapes could think, and Alice expected they could, what opinions did they hold about this new terroir, this hot-in-the-summer and occasionally viciously cold landscape, where Cretaceous limestone, old seabed, offered crevices for long roots? Did the seabed present a New World challenge?

Eddie had excavated straight into a limestone hill to build his winery, creating his own underground wine cave. Upstairs, the tasting room's tall glass walls framed views to the southeast and southwest, over green waves of vineyards and a streak of grey-green olive trees. Downstairs, the homemade wine cave stayed a reliable sixty degrees or less, allowing Eddie the consistent cool temperatures he needed to age his wines in the stacked rows of oak casks. The back wall and one side of the cave were unfinished solid limestone, chalky white with golden streaks, sometimes weeping a little moisture. Alice had seen fossilized seashells protruding from one section of stone. Eddie did most of his work down in the cave.

She turned into the winery at the big rock bank jutting up by Eddie's gate, which stood wide open. The parking lot was empty.

Maybe the delivery truck delivering Eddie's new tank had finished and left.

She didn't see Eddie's truck either. Maybe he'd parked behind the winery; a dirt road led off the parking lot downhill to a large overhead door on the lower level at the rear of the building, where Eddie took deliveries.

She climbed out, clutching the manila folder with the sales contract in one hand and her phone in the other. She rang Eddie's cell. No answer. Reception could be sketchy out here. He might be involved with a customer or a winery chore.

Slowly, still scanning the hillside below in case Eddie was out working in the vineyard, she walked toward the tall winery door.

*****

"Eddie?"

No answer. She saw no one on the main floor, one long high-ceilinged room with tables at one end where customers could taste wine while admiring the view of Eddie's vineyards. She walked to the far end and looked down at the dirt parking area behind the building. There sat Eddie's old red Ford 150, by the delivery entrance that led into the wine cave.

She retraced her steps to the iron spiral staircase that led downstairs to the wine cave, where a long wooden tasting table stood amidst the oak casks and steel tanks. At that table Alice had watched Eddie work his magic on clients, pulling wine from casks and offering previews of upcoming vintages.

Alice disliked spiral staircases; she usually felt like the steps went the wrong direction. Her steps clanged and echoed as she clutched the handrail and tried not to drop her phone or the manila folder. She descended into the lower level's heady chill, redolent with resting wine. And a new smell. Like construction. The concrete tank?

She spotted a cell phone on the tasting table. Eddie's? Next to it lay a thick publication titled "Tank Specifications."

Where was the man?

"Eddie?" Her voice echoed against the stone walls.

She laid down her folder and set out for the rear door and Eddie's truck. One glance showed her his truck was empty. The next glance revealed a welter of dusty footprints by the door. She followed them past the stainless steel tanks lined up on the back wall to the new concrete tank looming in the corner. A pressure washer leaned against the tank, extension cord trailing over the floor.

Three of the heavy iron chairs from the tasting table seemed to float against the tank. She moved closer. No, not floating: the tank entry hatch was a small rectangle, two feet above the ground, with a vertical steel door handle. On the tank next to the hatch was a vertical steel handlebar. Someone had wedged one iron leg from each of two chairs, crisscrossed, through both vertical handles. For good measure, the leg of a third chair was jammed behind one of the crisscrossed legs.

No one inside could push open the hatch.

"Eddie? Eddie!" Alice yelled, pulling and shoving at the wedged chairs. They didn't budge. She dragged over another tasting table chair and tried prying the wedged chairs loose, using one iron leg as a lever. Useless. Sweat dripped into her eyes. Finally, she pushed the chair she'd dragged over under the wedged handles, climbed onto that chair, with her back to the handles, put her hands under the seat of the third chair, and shoved upward with all her might. She dodged that chair and it tumbled loose, clanging on the concrete floor. Next she succeeded in dislodging one, then the other of the crisscrossed iron legs. She grabbed the vertical door handle and pulled it to the horizontal position. The hatch door opened.

A rush of fetid air. With foreboding she peered inside. The big footballer's body lay sprawled on his back on the floor. In the dimness his face looked blue.

Alice crawled through the hatch and reached his bloody hand. Still warm. "Eddie!" She leaned over and blew in his face. "Eddie!"

An eyelid flickered. "Eddie! Wake up! We've got to get out!" He blinked, then the eyes closed again. She tried to lift his shoulders, get him to sit up. It was like trying to lift a queen-sized futon mattress. She saw blood on her forearm and realized it was from the back of his head.

Desperate to get both of them more air, Alice reached under his back and grabbed him at the armpits, with his head lying against her chest. She began backing toward the hatch, trying to cradle his head. Panting, she reached the hatch, and, one leg at a time, backed her lower body out, then sank to her knees. Still holding Eddie, she ducked her own head out of the hatch and took a deep grateful breath of fresh air. She tugged at Eddie's armpits again, trying to work his head through the hatch so he could breathe. No way to get him out, not without some help, she thought.

Now she was stuck, holding his head outside the hatch.

"Eddie!" Were the grizzled blue cheeks a little pinker? He took a deeper breath.

Her shirt was a mess of drying blood. She needed help. She wriggled sideways, holding his head out the hatch, and pulled the phone from her pocket. She dialed 911. Please let there be reception down here, she prayed.

Breathless, she told EMS how to find them. She looked down to see Eddie staring at her.

"Alice?"

"Yup. Can you move? Like, a hand, or a foot?"

He blinked, without moving his head. His eyes moved. He flapped his right hand, then his left. Then he slowly moved one leg.

"Alice," he mumbled. "Guess I took a hit. Never saw it coming. Musta been a safety blitz."

"Eddie. Can you get out of this hatch?"

He took another deep breath, blew it out. "I think someone—"

He slowly pulled his head back inside the tank, got to his knees, and began to maneuver his big body through the hatch—head, one arm, then the other, then his long back and legs.

"Like being born again," he gasped, and sat heavily on the floor, eyes closed. Alice examined the matted hair and blood on the back of his head.

"Did you fall, in there?"

He shook his head. "No. I was cleaning the tank." He thought a minute. "Someone called me. Outside. I stuck my head out to see who." He laid a delicate finger on the back of his head. "Bastard hit me."

Alice suddenly recognized the smell. "Hit you with a wine bottle?"

She looked past the rounded corners of the concrete tank. On the floor in the far corner she saw a wine bottle, broken. The shoulder of Eddie's white T-shirt was stained pale gold.

Eddie lifted his head and sniffed. "The bastard hit me with a bottle of my best viognier."

"Who was it?" Whoever it was had meant Eddie to die, to asphyxiate slowly in the tank.

"Don't know," Eddie said. He paused. "Gorman came out earlier, said he wanted to see the tank. Still pissed at me. I think he'd left, though."

"But Eddie! How long have you been in there?"

"What time is it?"

"Five."

He slowly shook his head. "I guess Gorman came by about noon.

He left after, oh, fifteen minutes. Then I went back to finish wiping down the tank."

"You were turning blue, Eddie." Alice felt rage surge into her temples.

He was still a proud football center.

"But then I couldn't open the hatch." He looked at his hands. Dried blood on the fingers. "Guess I passed out again."

"You didn't have your phone?"

"Nope," he said, staring down the long cave at the carefully stacked casks. "And there wasn't enough air."

"Micro-oxygenation," Alice said.

"Not enough for this guy," Eddie said. His voice sounded more like the Eddie she knew, low-key, ironic, deeply confident, able to laugh at himself.

He'd almost died. "Would Gorman have the guts to bash you?" Alice asked. "And why would he?"

Eddie snorted. "Gorman and guts? He's mean, but basically he's nothing but a big mouth. Turned out the real reason he was here wasn't to see the tank. He told me to lay off buying the land across the road. He said his buyers were going to sign the contract first thing tomorrow morning. I told him, no dice." He squinted and gingerly felt the back of his head with one hand.

"What about your head? Should I be checking to see if you've got a concussion?" She got in front of him, stared at the tired blue eyes.

"I've got one. I can tell." A little grin. "Yeah, in my former line of work I learned to know when I'm concussed."

"Are you saying it's bad, but not so bad that you don't know you're hurt, and you keep telling the coach to send you back in?"

"Right." He still hadn't tried to stand up.

"Stay here." Alice ran upstairs and got a glass of water from the tasting room sink.

He drank it all and held the glass out for more. She ran back upstairs and saw an ambulance roll into the winery parking lot. She pointed the EMTs around to the driveway leading to the downstairs rear of the building, and then went for more water.

As she turned on the faucet she belatedly realized that she'd sent them into a crime scene.

"Wait!" she called, clanging her way down the wretched spiral staircase. "I've got to call the sheriff too! He was attacked!" They nodded but continued attending to Eddie.

She dialed the sheriff's department. "George Files, please." No way would she ask for Eads. The operator put her on hold. Files picked up. Alice blurted a hurried summary of the attack. "Brad Gorman came out earlier today to try to talk Eddie out of buying the land next door because Brad's buyers want it. Eddie and Brad already split the blanket over their earlier deal, so they're crossways. But Eddie's not sure who hit him."

"Can he give us Gorman's contact info? Phone?"

"Silla can. The EMTs are trying to load Eddie. I'll call back."

Eddie began arguing with the two EMTs, both young, one wiry and red-haired, one broad-shouldered and dark-haired. "No, I'm fine. I just need an ice bag."

"We need to see if your skull's fractured," the broad-shouldered EMT said. They were looking from his bulk to their gurney, measuring the lift. Eddie threw off their arms, crawled to his feet, grabbed the gurney, and sank onto it.

"It's not fractured," he said. "But maybe you can give me some hits of oxygen on the way. Always did like oxygen."

The wiry EMT exited to back the ambulance closer to the open door.

Alice said, "Eddie. I'll follow you to the hospital. Listen, do you still want to buy the land?"

He nodded. "Damn straight."

She held out the contract and a pen. He scribbled his name and initialed where she pointed.

Alice watched his gurney bounce across the gravel outside, then closed the downstairs doors and ran upstairs. She called Files back. "I'm leaving the winery front door unlocked. Look downstairs at the concrete tank and the wine bottle. And Eddie's phone. At least I think it's Eddie's. Okay, they're taking him to the hospital now."

She headed for the Coffee Creek hospital but made a quick detour to the office. Leaving the car running, she ran up the steps and handed

Silla the signed contract.

"What in the world happened to you?" Silla gasped.

Alice had forgotten her blood-stained shirt. "Not mine. Not my blood, I mean. Listen, Eddie's in the hospital. But he'll be okay. Can you email that contract to Joel Grassley over my signature? Tell him it's fully executed: the sellers have signed and Eddie has too."

"Hey, at least change your shirt! You'll terrify everyone at the hospital."

Alice reluctantly agreed.

"Yoga bag," Silla said.

Alice yanked off the bloody shirt and wriggled into a cleanish tee from the yoga bag in her office closet. Her pants were bloodstained where she'd wiped her hands. Oh well.

Hightailing it to the hospital, Alice wondered if she'd been hasty. Was Eddie really okay? Okay enough to sign that contract? Okay enough to take on more land, more debt, more vineyards?

Chapter Twenty-One

Blood, Sweat, Wine

"Where's my damn phone, Alice?" Eddie asked, when the ER nurse finally permitted Alice to come check on her client. She tried not to let shock show on her face. Eddie looked pale and drawn. His eyes lacked their smart-ass twinkle. He looked older, maybe due to the helplessness that came from having his shirt cut off and his head bandaged and a backless hospital gown tied around his neck.

"I left your phone at the winery, for the police to see," she said. "It's part of the crime scene."

"Don't do that to me!" he said. "I've got business to take care of!" He lay back on the pillow. "For one thing I've got to call Conroy. He'll worry when he can't find me. And I've got to have some clothes."

Alice asked Eddie for Conroy's phone number. He squeezed his eyes shut, gave an annoyed grunt, took a breath, and reeled off the number. She dialed and handed him her phone, thinking that for Eddie to remember Conroy's number was a good sign.

"You on your way back from Austin?" Eddie asked Conroy. She listened to Eddie giving his friend a stripped-down version of the tank attack. "I took a pretty good lick on the head. But I'll be okay. You going to stop in on your way home? Okay, good. Listen, if you need to call me before then, you'll have to use this number. Here's Alice."

Alice introduced herself and repeated her phone number. Then she phoned George Files.

"I'm at the winery with the crime scene team, about to come talk to Mr. LaFarge," Files said.

She passed along Eddie's request to get his phone back. "No problem," he said. "I'll bring it with me. Sounds like he's able to talk to me, right?"

"Yes."

Time to face her worry over the contract issue. She turned to her client. "Eddie, I sent the sales contract back to Joel Grassley with your signature. You're sure about buying that land?"

"I'm sure. Already got the vine varieties laid out in my mind." He grabbed her hand and squeezed it. "Don't worry, Alice. I've got a hard skull. However." He looked away, then back at her. "I'd be dead if you hadn't shown up."

"Just give me a bottle of that viognier," she said.

"Viognier for life. How about that?"

Footsteps in the ER hall. The flimsy privacy curtain jangled. Detective George Files stepped in, followed by a dark-haired young uniformed guy Alice thought she'd seen before at the sheriff's department. He was toting an equipment case.

"Mr. LaFarge. I'm George Files, Coffee County Sheriff's Department. Honored to meet you. This is Deputy Romero from our crime scene team. I understand someone beaned you?"

"I guess I've lost a step," Eddie said. "Yeah, someone beaned me and shut me up in the wine tank. Hadn't been for Alice here, you might have a murder case."

Files took Eddie through the timeline, asking when Conroy left, when Gorman arrived. He handed Eddie's phone to him and asked him to identify the recent phone calls. Eddie pointed. "This last one at 12:30 today? That was right after Gorman left. I called the tank manufacturer, the concrete tank guy. I wanted to double-check the cleaning protocol for my spray washer before I finished prepping the new tank."

"You gave Gorman a bottle of"—he checked his notebook—"Vee-on-yay, that how you say it? Before he left?"

"Yeah. Viognier. Waste of good wine, right?"

"Where were you when you gave him the bottle?"

"Upstairs. He was on his way out. Then I went back down to the tank."

Files beckoned Romero. "We're going to take your fingerprints, so we can establish who all touched that bottle."

While Romero worked on Eddie's big hands, Alice stepped over to Files. "Was the bottle wiped?"

Files nodded. "To some extent. We found some of Gorman's prints on the bottle. Got a preliminary match from some old prints of his on file in Phoenix. But most of the prints were smudged, like by someone wearing gloves." Then he said, "The chairs, though—the ones jammed in the hatch—were wiped." He looked at Alice. "Except for some which are probably yours, I believe."

"Did you find Gorman?" Alice asked.

"Yes. We talked to Silla and put out an APB on that license plate, found Gorman at that new Distillery Bar outside Coffee Creek. He's been sitting in a hard chair at the department, talking to my new assistant detective, Alan Joske." Alice lifted an eyebrow. Maybe Files had fired Eads.

Romero finished with Eddie and departed.

The curtain jangled again. A young woman in black glasses and white coat and stethoscope strode in and grinned at Eddie. "I'm Dr. Roscoe, from radiology. Your skull's not fractured, I'm glad to say, though your chart suggests you're concussed. Are you really Eddie La-Farge, like, the best center ever? I've gotta ask, why weren't you wearing your helmet?"

Eddie grinned back. "I'd like your autograph," he said.

"You know about post-concussion syndrome, right?"

"Lots," he said.

"So you know that during recovery you might notice bouts of anxiety or depression."

Eddie nodded. "I've seen it happen, but not to me. Yet."

"I understand you did lose consciousness today. But you didn't experience a seizure, right? Still no headache? No nausea?"

He shook his head no.

The doctor scanned his face, maybe looking at his pupils. "Just to be sure, given all the circumstances, we're going to keep you overnight." She glanced at Alice, then back at Eddie. "After you're discharged, if there are signs of mental confusion or nausea or headache, you need to come straight back to the ER."

"Yeah, yeah. But I need to get back to the winery. I've got to move some wine."

"Well, I'm advising against that. Don't worry, we'll reevaluate first thing in the morning. But your room's ready and"—she pulled the curtain and looked into the hall—"here's my favorite orderly, ready to roll you up there." She grinned again. "Once you're settled I'll come get that autograph."

"I'm gonna tell Conroy to bring me some clothes by seven tomorrow morning," Eddie said to Alice. He turned his face to Dr. Roscoe. "Got that?" he said. "I'll be walking out of here by seven! Right?"

Alice said not a word. She felt relief that Eddie would be kept here overnight, not back at the winery fending off another attack by—Gorman?

Files turned to leave just as the curtain rattled again and a huge African-American man peered in, face serious, eyes anxious.

"Hey, Conroy," Eddie said. "Meet my lawyer Alice and Detective George Files. This is Conroy Robinson." Alice and Files both shook hands with Conroy—his hands were like catchers' mitts—but Conroy only had eyes for Eddie. He moved past the waiting orderly to the side of the bed.

"Can't even leave you for a minute," he said. "Who did this to you?"

"We're not sure yet. Gorman came out there but I thought he'd left," Eddie said.

"Is your head all right, man?" Conroy squinted uneasily at the bandage around Eddie's skull.

"Yeah. I'm just pissed, is all. Hey"—this to the orderly—"what's my room number?"

The orderly repeated the number for Conroy, who nodded. "I'll be back with your clothes tonight."

"Then we'll talk about re-cleaning the floor of that concrete tank," Eddie said. "I had it spotless. But now—"

"Left a little of yourself on the floor, did you?" Conroy said. "Like blood?"

The orderly pulled back the curtain and rolled Eddie out and down the hall.

"Mr. Robinson, can I ask a couple of questions?" Files said. "We're trying to get the timeline straight, like when you had to leave for your appointment."

Files got contact information for the Austin therapist. He asked when Conroy left for Austin and when he started back to Coffee Creek.

"I had to leave the winery today right after the tank was installed, to make it to PCS therapy," he said. "We have two sessions, first individual and then group. Usually lasts over three hours."

"PCS?"

"Post-concussion syndrome." He frowned and shook his head. "Eddie's been lucky so far. I sure don't want him getting PCS."

"No fun?" Files asked.

"No fun at all." Not a smile, not a twinkle. Just sadness. "But"—he said, nodding slightly—"I'm getting better."

Files exited and disappeared down the hall before Alice could quiz him.

She looked up to see Conroy waiting politely for her, holding back the curtain.

"It's peaceful out at Raptor Cellars, right?" Alice said.

"Yes. Thank God for that peace. I'm gonna go get the man some clothes. I guess his were a mess, after…what happened?" He nodded at the blood stains on Alice's pants.

"Yes," Alice said. Blood, sweat, wine.

*****

Alice unlocked her car in the hospital parking lot and headed for the ranch, mulling over the day. Had Gorman really whacked Eddie with a wine bottle and left him to suffocate? No question Gorman had a temper, she'd seen that in her own conference room. But was he just a yeller, or would he actually try to murder Eddie? Maybe he'd counted on someone—Conroy, for instance—showing up to open the hatch before Eddie died. Gorman had hinted he was being pressured to buy the property next to Eddie's; maybe he just wanted to keep Eddie locked up long enough to get his own deal done. She couldn't make up her mind whether Gorman really would have left Eddie to die or not.

She called Files. "What did Gorman tell your new deputy? I'm worried that whoever whacked Eddie will come back to finish the job."

"Joske's charged him with assault. He posted bail, so he's out loose. According to Joske, Gorman swears he didn't whack Eddie. He says he just left the winery and drove straight to Flores Tacos for lunch. You know, the place on the highway."

At Flores the customers ordered at one window and picked up their order at another. Most folks got their orders to go; the only seats Flores provided consisted of two picnic tables in the yard.

"Does anyone remember him?"

"Not really. You know what those lunch lines are like. He paid cash, but so do lots of customers. Even if someone actually remembered him they wouldn't know what time it was. That's important, given Eddie's phone call to the tank manufacturer."

"Which tacos did he get? Does that help him?" Flores had a famous blackboard menu. Alice herself often chose the Acapulco Wave, fish tacos, but the taco menu held many temptations.

"He says he got the daily special, which he thinks was chorizo and potato. Flores confirms that was the special, and says they sold a lot today. Gorman could've easily seen that on the menu board outside, just driving by. One thing, though; Gorman does claim he saw a motorcycle on the road when he pulled out of the winery."

"Did anyone see the motorcycle? Or Gorman?"

"The neighbors saw nothing, but they weren't watching particularly."

"Thanks." She hung up. As she hit the creek road, her phone beeped. Message. She glanced around to confirm no officers were lurking. Coffee Creek's ordinances forbade cell use while driving inside the city. Then she checked the message. Silla: "Grassley called to say owners accepted Eddie's offer."

Ha! Alice felt a rush of triumph, sat straight up in the car seat, grinned at herself in the rearview mirror. Take that, Brad Gorman.

She looked again in the rearview mirror. Headlights, approaching fast. Alice detested tailgaters. Of course, sometimes she herself …

The driver flashed high beams. She slowed down, furious. No, she wouldn't speed up for this joker. Another flash. She turned down the dirt road that led to her own gate. The headlights behind turned too. She was just picking up her phone to call the sheriff when she recognized that particular automobile: Kinsear's Land Cruiser.

She was still mad when they reached her house.

"Why didn't you call?"

"Couldn't you tell it was me?"

"I could not!"

In response, Kinsear unfolded his rancher coat and wrapped it around her, then turned her chin up for a kiss.

It had been a long time since she'd enjoyed a kiss quite so deliciously warm, such a comforting contrast with the chilly spring air on her porch. Alice decided encouragement was warranted. She kissed back. Kinsear rearranged her against the porch wall, by the front door, and kissed her from her ear, to her neck, then farther down. She squeezed her eyes shut and let his hands and the following sensations take their course.

Finally, she fumbled with her hand behind her back, opening the front door. Kinsear followed her inside. They dropped their coats on the living room floor, kicked off their shoes in the hall, and found themselves in the bedroom. Alice closed her eyes, reveling in being alive, with Kinsear, as alive as she could be. Then she forgot about being alive and concentrated on matters at hand. Sometimes he whispered comical thoughts in her ear; sometimes not.

At three a.m. the moon had circled partway up the sky and was lighting the entire valley below her house. She could never sleep when the moon silvered the world this way. She found a robe and crept out onto the deck behind the house, astounded at the bright silence. Somewhere down the hill an owl called. She pulled her robe tight, listening, looking out across the valley. A deer snorted, then careened away in the underbrush. A rabbit squealed; the sound abruptly ended. Someone… something…was hunting, somewhere down below the deck. Nature, red in tooth and…poor rabbit. She realized she hadn't told Kinsear about the attack on Eddie. He'd want to know.

The owl called again and she hooted softly back. The owl waited, perhaps puzzled, or intrigued, or challenged, then called again.

Alice returned to the bedroom and slipped under the comforter, trying to keep her icy toes from poking Kinsear. Nevertheless, he reached over and buried his face in the back of her neck, then the front of her neck. "It's too bright to sleep," he muttered. "Let's do something else."

*****

After such a night Alice was caught totally off guard when Kinsear, after only one cup of coffee, leaned across the kitchen table toward her and said, "Could I beg you again to have lunch with Isabel? Or even just coffee?"

At first Alice couldn't respond, since she herself had only had two sips of coffee. Finally, she said, "What's happened?"

"Midterms loom," he said. He shook his head, looked straight at Alice. "I don't think she understands about studying."

"Surely that hotshot boarding school taught her how to study!"

Kinsear frowned, pushing back the hair from his forehead (more gray in that black, Alice noticed). "I misspoke. I don't think she understands that she's by God got to study! Because everyone else at UT Austin knows that's what's needed!" He sat up and heaved a long sigh. "Honestly, I don't have a clue what to do. I thought if she went to lunch with you, saw how you operate, how you focus, how hard you work for your clients, she might get an inkling of what it means to have a career. That she might think there's some point to getting grades good enough to allow you even to apply to a professional school someday. Because I know she thinks she's smart. That's part of the problem. She's sure she's too smart to have to work at night…or early in the morning…or all weekend."

"What if she hates me at first sight?" Alice asked. "And then I'm mad at you, and you get mad at me for being mad at her?"

"Or at her for being mad at you?" Kinsear added. "I know I'm asking a lot. But I'm desperate."

Alice's thoughts went to her children, John and Ann, one a senior, one a junior in college, children she loved more than life itself. Children who had been considerate enough, in college, to hide from her anything too frightening they were doing and to present her with decent enough grades that she didn't obsess about their futures…most of the time. Maybe her children hid their private disasters from her; if so, she was grateful. She wished Kinsear had the same comfort. For her to get involved felt risky. But he was asking.

She nodded. "Sure, I'll have lunch with her. When?"

No hesitation. "Monday?"

She nodded. "Can she meet me at the office at, say, eleven? Then I can introduce her to Silla." Alice thought Silla would be pretty bracing.

"What a relief," Kinsear said. "I'll get that scheduled right away." He took out his phone, then walked out on her deck.

She watched Kinsear forcefully talking, pumping one hand. Then waiting. Then rolling his eyes and looking heavenward. Then raised eyebrows. She lip-read his "Okay? Okay." Then a relieved face as he opened the deck door. "Okay." Then his hands on her shoulders, with a kiss and a hug. "I owe you. Big time."

"I always tell you I expect to reach senility before I reach maturity," Alice warned, "so don't expect perfect behavior from me."

He laughed.

"I mean it."

C h a p t e r   T w e n t y - T w o

Can't Back Down

On Monday morning Alice stood by the office coffee pot, thinking of all the things that could go wrong at her lunch with Isabel. Instant antipathy on Isabel's part. Or on hers. If she detested Kinscar's child, what effect would that have on their relationship? She shook her head and stared at the floor.

"What's going on?" Silla peered around the corner. "You've been standing there for five minutes."

"Dread," Alice said. She explained. Silla looked at the wall clock.

"It's only eight. You've got time to marshal your ideas, right?"

Alice looked hopefully at Silla. "You want to go? I thought if she met you she might recognize a work ethic when she saw one."

"Fat chance," Silla said. "This is *your* party."

"I could cancel. Get sick. Throw up."

"No way." Silla whirled back to the morning mail.

*****

Five minutes later Silla slapped a letter on Alice's desk. "You poked a stick in a wasp's nest, Alice. Whooee!"

Alice looked at the letterhead: big Houston firm, with an Austin office. First sentence: "We represent Richard Craft, who owns certain Property at Waterfall Road, which is the subject of the intemperate letter received from you on behalf of certain neighbors." Intemperate? "We reject entirely your unfounded demand for removal of any property, including trailers, from the Property. Based on our review, the covenants are inapplicable." Why inapplicable? "Further, we reject your strained reading of these archaic and irrelevant covenants. In addition, your clients are estopped by their own actions including their own violations of the covenants."

Blah, blah, statute of limitations, blah, blah, estoppel, blah, blah, unclean hands. Wrong. The Hermit couldn't claim the covenants didn't forbid trailers, because they did. Instead, his lawyers were throwing in everything but the kitchen sink and attacking the neighbors. The letter ended: "If you do not withdraw your demand within five days from the date of this letter, we will have no choice but to institute an action against your clients for injunctive relief to preclude further harassment and interference with our client's property rights."

It was ridiculous, but dangerous.

"Email a copy to Ham and Julie and the Fischers, the neighbors who signed on," Alice told Silla. "Tell them I'll call in thirty minutes."

But before Alice could call them Ham and Julie had already called her. She put them on speakerphone.

"Alice, you've got to do something! We can't have Waterfall Road turn into wedding venue central."

"Remember we don't have proof yet of a specific commercial use, just the trailers," Alice warned. "And remember, there's always the chance a court may say you're wrong. The court might say the covenants unreasonably restrict property rights. We'll need to draft affidavits and be solid on our facts. This could get expensive."

"But we did get the trailer provision enforced before," Ham argued. "That was going to be heard by Judge Sandoval, even though we settled before he had to rule. Can't we get in front of him again?"

"We can't back down," Julie chimed in. "If they're threatening to sue us if we don't back down, don't we want to file first?"

"Filing first has some advantages," Alice said. "It means you get first choice of jurisdiction, of where to file. On the other hand, if you warn the defendant one more time by letter, and then the defendant is the first to file, maybe he looks more trigger-happy."

"We're fighting for our property," Ham said. "I think we should go ahead and file. If these covenants mean nothing, if they aren't worth the paper they're printed on, we need to know."

Ham had a point. As property values rose in the Hill Country, he and Julie wanted to know whether the covenants were enforceable, and whether their land could remain their quiet country utopia. If not, they would have to decide whether to stay, watching the steady advent of lights, noise, and traffic, or go, maybe selling their place for significant dollars.

Alice sighed. Her warning letter was one thing; filing suit, another. She'd spent enough early years handling litigation that she hated the risk and expense exposure for clients. Especially in neighbors' land disputes, she urged clients to avoid letting disagreements morph into litigation. She told them they wouldn't enjoy feeling their blood pressure go up every time they drove past the neighbor's house. But what if the neighbor was a bully? Ignoring bullies—and a statute of limitation—carried other risks.

"Check with the Fischers and let me know right away if they're still on board to be plaintiffs," Alice said. "I'll send a draft petition for everyone to look at. If you're sure you want to go this route, we'll file first and ask for a hearing." She hung up and went to talk to Silla.

"Whoa! If you want to file first, we need to get busy," Silla said.

"Right. Let's start with facts for the affidavit," Alice said. "I don't want to be blindsided. We need to check the tax appraiser's records for any commercial personal property that's being assessed to Ham and Julie or the Fischers." Silla nodded. "But we'll need a windshield survey too, of houses on both sides of the road, to be sure no one out there's running a business or has a trailer onsite." Her mind raced, thinking of the petition, the exhibits.

"Here's an idea," Silla said. "What about getting Isabel to help? Sort of a short-term internship? If you make your mind up before lunch, when Isabel gets here I could sigh and moan a little about how I need some help."

"Work here?" Alice shook her head. "I haven't even met her. That's a bridge too far."

"I'll get you a reservation for noon in Wimberley, and you can let me entertain her for a few minutes before you leave."

Alice always marveled at Silla's ability to maneuver past Alice's stubborn introversion. Silla correctly evaluated herself as generally ir-resistible. Maybe this time a few minutes with Silla would do the trick with Isabel.

Alice headed for her desk, head down, clutching her copy of the Hermit's lawyers' response, mind already drafting the petition, orga-nizing the exhibits. She turned to her computer and typed in the first paragraphs, reciting the parties and their addresses, then the claim for violation of the covenants. What about affidavit proof that trailers were on the property? She had certainly seen them but shouldn't be a wit-ness; the affidavit should come from her clients. She called Julie.

"Can you just walk down to the creek and peer through the first gate to confirm that both trailers are still there?" Remembering Narcissus, she said, "Be sure you're out in the middle of the creek when you do this. Not on the Hermit's land. Take a picture."

"Got it," Julie said.

"Email it to me."

Chapter Twenty-Three

You've Got to Understand Motives

Alice heard voices in the hallway, then Silla's laugh, then more conversation. Go, Silla! In a few minutes Silla opened Alice's office door. "Isabel Kinsear is here," she said.

Alice jumped up and came around the desk and stuck out her hand.

"Alice Greer," she said.

"Isabel Kinsear."

Isabel had her dad's height and black eyebrows, with dark hair pulled back in a ponytail. She wore a houndstooth wool miniskirt and black tights. No jeans. She'd dressed up for this. No smile yet, though, just a long look from those hazel eyes.

"It's good to meet you," Alice said. "I see you've met the resident barrel racer."

That got a one-sided smile from Isabel, who turned to look at Silla. "I'm seriously impressed with barrel racing," Isabel said. "I never got the hang of it, couldn't seem to send my horse the right signals on those curves. I like straightaways, though."

"Racing?"

"When I was eight I wanted to be a jockey. But I kept growing."

"Well, let's head for lunch," Alice said. "I'll drive. Silla suggested a place on the river in Wimberley."

Alice wanted to drive because she knew driving would let her feel in control, give her something to do with her face and hands while she got to know this young woman.

"Your dad said you've shown some interest in law school," she tried. "I wondered if you'd like to hear about small town versus big city practice."

"He told me you've done both," Isabel answered. "What keeps you busy in Coffee Creek? It's not even as big as Fredericksburg!"

"Right," Alice said. "Well, I've got a mixed practice, real estate and trusts and estates. People need wills, need to settle estates, need to buy and sell land, need to create entities to accomplish some of that. Sometimes litigation's involved. I get plenty of substantive issues and much more people contact every day being in Coffee Creek. That's different from my work downtown. Of course, big downtown firms can offer economic security and big clients with big litigation, which has its exciting moments." She glanced at Isabel's profile. Isabel was staring straight ahead down Ranch Road 12.

"So, Isabel, which environment would appeal to you? Or something different entirely? Attorney general's office? Public defense? Immigration? In-house counsel? Private equity deals? Any of that sound interesting at all?"

Isabel gave Alice a short glance from the corner of those hazel eyes. "Really? If I had to tell you, I'd be a private detective. Climbing up gutters, catching jewel thieves abroad, peeking in windows, solving crimes."

Alice laughed. "Wow!" She looked at Isabel. "Cat suit and all? I love it."

Just ahead in Wimberley lay the driveway to the Leaning Pear. Alice enjoyed the view downhill from the restaurant, green lawns running down to the fast-moving stream below. She asked the hostess for the booth in the corner. Always protect your back, sit where you know what's coming, that was part of her creed.

"Iced tea," Alice answered the waitress. She'd have preferred wine, some false courage for this lunch. But it called for iced tea.

"Iced tea," Isabel said.

They ordered salads.

"What are your choices for majors?" Alice asked. "I know it's early days, but what sounds interesting?"

Isabel looked toward the window, then at her plate, and said, "Clinical psychology."

Alice digested that. "Fits with your private detective thought, right? If you understand motive, you understand actions?"

Isabel nodded. "Yeah. You know that mystery series where the detective says, 'If you know how you know who?'"

"Sure," Alice said. "You don't agree, do you?"

"I say, if you know *why* you know who. You've got to understand motives."

Their salads arrived. Alice picked up her fork, but then sat thinking of the murders she'd had to help solve. In every case, learning *why* had been critical. Sometimes the why lay far in the past. Not always, though.

Isabel went on. "When I say clinical psychology, I'm not just talking about abnormal psych. I want to learn more about this new research into how people make ethical choices. Have you read about the experiment where people are to imagine themselves standing on a bridge where they can see an oncoming train that, depending on the choice they make, could kill either one person or a group of people? They have to choose. That's just one example. But it's exactly what interests me."

Alice nodded. "Me too. Are the prerequisites tough? Is it hard to get into this major?"

"I don't know yet," Isabel said, looking faintly surprised. "How do I find that out?"

"Your adviser should tell you. Sounds like a fascinating major, but if you don't want to waste time, get your adviser to help you lay out your strategy, so you get all the prerequisites you need in time to get the courses you want."

Isabel looked blank. "My adviser…is that the kind of thing he should be telling me?"

"Yes, of course he should," Alice said. "He can't do it if he doesn't know what you're thinking about, though. Do you have time to meet with him before this term ends?"

Isabel slowly turned pink. "I don't know. I haven't met with him since the first week of September…until this past week, and we didn't talk majors."

Alice said nothing, just expelled her breath. "Maybe go tape a note to his door, ask for an appointment? If you really care about this line of research, and obviously you do, you owe it to yourself."

Isabel's eyes filled with tears. "I already made a D on one midterm."

"Too late to drop the course?"

Isabel nodded.

"Go talk to the prof. Go talk to your adviser. I'll bet you can improve the situation. Maybe ask to write an extra credit paper?"

Isabel blinked angrily and stared out the window.

"Isabel, I got a C- in philosophy my first semester. Philosophy sounded cool, but it turned out I had no clue what the hell philosophy was about." Alice paused. "Still don't, really. It never occurred to me to go talk to an adviser. If I even had one. My kids dug themselves into some holes their first year too."

Isabel perked up. "Really? From what Dad says, they're paragons."

"Not freshman year. Thank God, Ann's adviser told her she needed to straighten up and buckle down. Mixed metaphors, but Ann said later she realized that she was actually going to have to work in a different way."

"I can work," Isabel said defiantly.

"Without doubt you can. So, after you meet with your adviser, do you think you'd have time to help me and Silla for a few hours this week?"

Isabel looked back, nonplussed.

Then Alice added, "This may sound crazy. Silla and I could use some help."

Isabel gave her a longer look, eyebrows up.

Alice explained Ham and Julie's concerns, the Hermit's refusal to comply and threat to file suit, and the work crunch she and Silla faced. "We'll need someone to take a look at the houses on their road, just a windshield survey, but also a look at property taxes, to help put together an affidavit. Accuracy is key, because our request to the court has to be sworn."

"Sworn?" Isabel asked.

"You can't ask a judge to issue an injunction, to compel someone to do something or stop doing something, without sworn testimony in the record. So, we'll file our petition with an affidavit attached and ask for a hearing." She watched Isabel's face. "We'll pay you, of course." Alice paused. "You could call it a paid internship if you want. On your resumé. But we'd need a solid six hours this weekend so we can get this petition done, and you'd need to drive your car. And it absolutely can't interfere with your studies."

"Done," Isabel said.

"Wait. I mean this coming Saturday," Alice said.

"This *Saturday?*" Disbelief on Isabel's face.

"Dessert?" chirped the waitress.

*****

On the way back to the office Alice explained to Isabel the urgency of her assignment. "We want to file our petition by next Monday demanding that the Hermit move any trailers off his property. We need to attach an affidavit from our clients, the plaintiffs, including pictures. We need to be able to tell the court there are no other trailers, no mobile homes, on any property along Waterfall Road, from the low-water bridge all the way to Ham and Julie's. I'll give you the appraisal district map showing who owns what." She added, "And be sure you see no signs for businesses at any of these residences either. You know, people advertising that they provide accounting, upholstery, law practice, whatever, in their homes."

She glanced at Isabel, who appeared to be paying attention. "Here's why. On the stand, I want our clients to tell the judge that no one on their road is violating either the no trailers or the no commercial use covenant. And I don't want them to be wrong."

Isabel's face cleared. "I see." Then she frowned. "But what is their neighbor, the Hermit guy, doing? Why does he need two black SUVs? Those tinted windows are a dead giveaway."

"To what?"

"Transporting people that don't want to be seen! You know, fancy business types and young girls. Like that guy in Florida." Isabel shivered. "Tinted windows—ugh. They creep me out."

People who don't want to be seen? Or people that the Hermit doesn't want seen?

"Okay," Isabel said. "Saturday morning. I'll even show up with gas in my car."

At the office she hopped out of Alice's car, gave a saucy wave, and got into her own battered blue Passat.

Gas in the car. Alice smiled to herself. Kinsear had complained that Isabel never changed the oil, never checked her tires, and that at least three times she'd run out of gas between Austin and Fredericksburg. "I just keep a five-gallon can in the trunk," he'd said, rolling his eyes. "What doesn't she get about cars?"

Alice decided she'd actually try to get Isabel to check her gas gauge before she cruised out Waterfall Road. And check whether her cell phone was charged.

C h a p t e r   T w e n t y - F o u r

Fireworks Could Start

L ate Saturday afternoon Isabel burst into the office with the report on her windshield survey of Waterfall Road. "No trailers visible from the low-water bridge all the way to Ham and Julie's," she declared, scrolling through the pictures on her phone, showing them to Alice. "No signs for home businesses either."

Alice sighed in relief. "Good job."

Isabel allowed herself a smile, looked away, then added, "But wait! There's more!"

Alice froze. Was something stirring at the Hermit's? "Well?"

"At about two this afternoon I was turning around in Ham and Julie's driveway when…" she paused.

"Come on!" Alice pressed.

"The Hermit's gate opened. Two big black SUVs pulled out ahead of me. I stopped for a second in the road, fiddled with my phone, waited for them to get a bigger lead. Then…I started after them."

"What?" Alice felt blood drain from her face. Kinsear would never forgive her if anything happened to Isabel.

"Don't worry. I just trailed along behind. At the end of Waterfall Road they turned onto Camp Drive and then Denny Drive, you know, where all the wedding venues are. Then they turned into Bluff Wines and Weddings."

"Did they spot you?" Alice demanded.

"I don't think so. I boogied on down Denny Road back onto the highway."

"They might have been going to a wine tasting," Silla commented.

"At two on Saturday?" Alice queried.

"Not a wine tasting," Isabel declared. "The Bluff Wines gate was covered with white ribbons and bows and a big sign saying 'Angie and Tim.' I'm definitely guessing wedding."

"Maybe the Hermit was ferrying the bride's family or the groom's family to the wedding venue. Could be he's running a posh B&B?" Alice wondered.

"I've been to a wedding at Bluff Wines," Silla said. "The wedding party stays in casitas overlooking the creek. It's a big operation."

Alice caught Isabel's eye. "Are you certain no one saw you? Could they recognize your car?"

"Well, when I first pulled up behind them, the guy in the second SUV, he adjusted his rearview mirror. I slowed way down. Got way back."

Oh Lord! How memorable is a used blue Passat with a dent on the—Alice peered out the window at Isabel's car—right fender? And a sorority parking tag dangling from the rearview mirror? And Isabel's memorably pretty face?

And if the Hermit was not running a B&B, delivering wedding guests to Bluff Wines, who sat behind the tinted windows in the two SUVs?

*****

Seven thirty, Monday morning, Silla called from the workroom, "The petition's ready. The affidavit's ready too. Also the discovery requests to Craft and deposition notices for him and his employees, which he won't like." Silla peered out at the street. "Julie's here to sign."

Silla and Alice had spent Sunday afternoon finalizing the petition. It asked the court to require the Hermit to comply with the covenant against trailers, attached the covenants, attached Julie's photos of the trailers, and would also attach her affidavit swearing to the facts in the petition.

Julie bustled through the front door. "Where's my pen?" She looked over the affidavit and signed it; Silla notarized her signature.

"Will the judge rule for us?"

"I believe so." Alice paused. Sure, the covenant violation was clear and obvious. But she suspected Judge Sandoval might take his time, might not feel any urgency. He might point out that Julie couldn't even see the trailers unless she climbed up and looked over the wall or waded out into the creek. Alice suspected he'd move faster if the trailers housed a business that also violated the covenants. As yet, Alice had no such evidence. If she found it, she'd amend.

Silla left for the courthouse. She'd file the petition and get copies of the petition and discovery requests served on the Hermit. Then the fireworks could start.

*****

Alice's phone rang.

"Alice? George Files here. Listen, we're trying to find Brad Gorman."

"About bashing Eddie on the head?"

"Also about another matter. Do you know where he works? Where he lives?"

"No." She remembered the LLC agreement. "Let me check with Silla; I think we only had a post office address for him. Hang on."

She asked Silla to bring the file and hit the speakerphone number.

"We've got a cell number for him. Here's Silla."

Silla read Files the number.

"He's apparently not using that phone now."

"Gorman's car?" Silla said. "Black Jeep with an Arizona vanity plate, MYWAY. Last year's model." The office phone rang, and Silla went to answer it.

"Yeah, we got that when we booked him. We can't find it now. Thanks anyway." He hung up before Alice could ask his second reason for chasing Gorman.

Silla leaned around Alice's door again. "Miranda's on the phone."

Uh-oh. Alice picked up. "Miranda?"

"Sorry to call you again about Holly's trust account. We got another bill from Marcy's group home. I still have nothing to pay it with."

"I'll do something. There's a small account in her separate property that's supposed to go in there." But Alice needed the Media Central funds. She hung up and called George Files back.

"Have you released Holly's money yet?" she asked. "We're getting bills for her sister's care."

"The financial crimes people are working on it."

"I don't want Holly's baby sister to lose her spot in that group home."

Files paused a moment. "Okay. Listen. Gorman's disappeared. But get this: the fed unit's tech wizards now say—still tentative—the email directing Holly's money to Palmetto?"

"Yes?"

182

"Came from Gorman's email account."

"Gorman's?" Alice's mind raced. Gorman sent the fake email instructions? What possible connection did Gorman have to Holly Dougal? Holly hadn't mentioned Gorman. But Alice had seen Gorman talking to Holly's husband, Russ, in the cowboy action parking lot, watched Russ shake his head no.

"And no one has claimed that account?"

"Nope. Hey, Hooks has cleared a bunch of folks of any involvement with the fake email. You should call him. I know you've got questions."

Yes, I've got questions. Have the feds cleared me and Silla and our office account, for instance? She hoped to God they hadn't been hacked. What about Holly, Russ, and Sandra? Plus, how long could the feds freeze the account?

"Wait!" Alice said. "How could Gorman know how to get into Holly's email, how to forge those instructions?"

"Maybe he hacked her account," Files said.

"But why? How would he know about the media company money?"

Files sighed. "We don't know yet."

"But…" Alice pondered a moment. "Is the Palmetto account his?"

"That's the odd part. Gorman swears it's not, swears he didn't send the fake email either. I almost believe him. He seemed, I don't know, shocked, in fact, when we questioned him. He said he'd have no idea how to hack anything." Files paused. "I'm not sure he's got the bandwidth, mentally."

"But then who set up the account?"

She heard papers rustling at Files's end. "There's a registered agent for the Royalty LLC account but the name and address are no good. The law requires you to keep that information current. We're still chasing it down."

"So the funds stay frozen?"

"Yes, at this point."

"How much time do we have before we can't retrieve that money?"

"That depends on how close the financial crimes unit is to figuring out the ultimate owner."

"George, I've got to get that money. Holly meant it for Marcy!"

"Yeah, yeah. And I know you're about to ask; no, we don't know who shot Holly either. But this will interest you. We got back the ballistics on Russ's revolvers. They don't match the bullet that killed her."

Alice leaned back in her chair, momentarily relieved, then assailed by dread. Russ and Gorman…could Russ have gone after Holly's money? Could Russ have had Holly killed? She shook her head, remembering how Russ kissed Holly as she slid down off her horse. But did Russ have enough of his own money to run Full House? The ranch cost a lot to run…his wife was going blind…her money would mostly be going to her sister…how did Russ plan to live?

Not for the first time Alice noted that her legal training left her with dark thoughts about people who seemed so very…good.

She left a message for Hooks.

Chapter Twenty - Five

Something Lay Underneath

Early Tuesday morning Alice had just passed her gate, heading to the office, when she met Tonio's Ford coming toward her. She stopped and rolled down her window; he did the same. He said he had a couple of hours before work and could start cutting cedar for her. Tonio looked ten years older, his face permanently etched with sadness. Alice felt her heart contract.

"Have you had any news, on Elena?"

"*Niente*," he said. "They tell us nothing."

Alice shook her head. "I'll call," she said.

"*Gracias.*" He lifted his hand in a half-hearted wave and drove on toward her gate.

Driving down the creek road, Alice couldn't get her mind off Elena's family, grief-stricken and in limbo. She'd worked herself into a dark mood by the time she got to her office, where she already faced one unpleasant phone call.

*****

Alice smelled the fresh brew and gratefully diverted her feet to the kitchen. First, coffee, then phone call. "Bless you, Silla," she said.

Silla patted her hair. "What do you think?"

Alice gazed at Silla's new hairdo: red curls upswept into a fetchingly untidy clip. "Italian chic?"

"I'm not sure it'll work for barrel racing."

"Probably not."

Alice recalled Silla's fierce competition at last summer's Coffee County Fair, with her red ponytail streaming out behind. "How do you keep your cowgirl hat on when you're racing?"

"Professional secret." Silla narrowed her eyes at Alice. "Listen, don't you need to get started on your executor's filing for Holly? The probate court clerk said the judge is about to approve your request to act as executor. Then the clock starts ticking on what you've got to file for the estate."

Alice heaved a sigh. "I know. That means calling Russ. He's already pissed at me."

Once authorized, Alice had to gather Holly's assets, notify creditors, and pay Holly's debts and taxes. Only then could Alice distribute assets to the beneficiaries.

She also dreaded the possibility that she might have to sell assets if she couldn't find sufficient cash somewhere in Holly's accounts to pay Marcy's group home bill. And what if the media royalty money was permanently—gone? Disappeared?

Slowly Alice carried her coffee back to her desk, sank into her chair, and flipped through Holly's will file to find her draft list of financial assets. What else? Horses? Cars? Insurance policy? Jewelry? Book inventory? Social media and website accounts? Agent and publisher contracts?

Nothing for it but to pick up the phone. She dialed Russ's cell. He answered, voice noncommittal, uninflected. Alice explained what she needed. She waited, fearing he'd refuse to help.

"Alice. I find I... might have been a little hasty with you. You want to come on out? What you need, we probably should just dig through Holly's office."

Alice sat back, surprised. She'd expected open hostility. A quick look at her desk calendar: no conflicts. "I can be there in half an hour."

"Um, Sandra is here, but she's out in my new office."

"She's still working for you?" Alice wondered what her tasks might be. Surely not working on Holly's papers, Holly's belongings? She hoped not.

"Yeah, I've got her double-checking the contractor's bills for the renovation. She, um, needs the money. She told me her brother's having some issues, needs some counseling. She wants to help out."

"I see." She wondered where the brother was. "Does he live around here?"

"My understanding is he's been trying to break into acting in Hollywood."

California, then. "That's a tough gig. Okay, I'll see you shortly."

*****

On the way she called Hooks again. No answer. She left another message.

*****

The bay and the palomino stood snorting by the fence when Alice parked. She reached down into her briefcase for the apples she'd grabbed at the last minute from the office refrigerator. "Miss Fancy," she crooned, as the bay delicately took the apple from Alice's palm. Did the horse miss Holly? she wondered. "You're gorgeous, sweetie," she told the palomino, offering another apple.

She heard a door close across the courtyard and turned to see Russ striding over in his boots and down vest.

Again surprising her, Russ offered a sideways hug. "I haven't had the heart to ride much lately," he said. "These horses miss their morning exercise."

Four brown equine eyes were fixed on Russ's hands, hoping for more apples. "Maybe tomorrow," he told them.

Russ turned to her. "I know you're just doing your job, Alice, trying to take care of Marcy and do what Holly wanted. Any chance the feds are going to get her money back?"

"The feds aren't saying. They're showing Palmetto Bank the email was fraudulent."

"But who sent it?"

Alice realized she hadn't told Russ about Gorman. "The federal crimes unit has apparently cleared some email accounts: yours, Holly's, mine and my office's, Sandra's. They're saying it looks like the scam email came from Gorman's account."

Russ stopped in his tracks. "Brad Gorman? That grifter from Phoenix?" He snorted. "He was after me to rent the cowboy action place to him. He wanted to use it for a wedding venue!"

"What'd you tell him?" Alice asked.

"No way, José. Can you imagine? Ol' Brad said, 'Russ, just think; the bride and groom could ride in on a buckboard wagon and get hitched right out there in the target area! The guests could sit in the grandstands!'" He shook his head, staring at the house. "After what happened to Holly…" He turned back to Alice. "Was the detective serious? He thinks *Gorman* sent the email?" He stopped, visibly running through the idea. "Come on, he'd have to know her email. And know about her royalties contract. How in the hell would he know?" He turned to Alice. "They never even met, did they? If they did, I sure don't know about it."

"I'm just telling you what the financial crimes people said."

They reached the front door of Full House. Russ stopped in the foyer, lifted his eyes, sniffed. "I always hope for a little whiff of Holly." His smile was strained. He walked across the living room to the hall and the door to Holly's study. To Alice's surprise, instead of opening the door Russ stood in the hall, pulling a key out of his pocket. "Sorry," he said. "I just thought, with all her books and records—"

"No, it's great!" Alice exclaimed. "I mean, to...to keep everything intact, keep it the way Holly left it." He lived there by himself, except for servants he trusted. Sandra was out in his office. Perhaps it was unusual for him to lock the door to his wife's office, but she was relieved he did.

"Well, you know," he said, looking down at the key, "it's part emotion. I want whatever last waves—brain waves, fragrance, invisible Holly—I want that to stay in here. In fact," he confessed, "I sneak in here and sit in her chair at night, hoping to feel her hand touch my forehead, ruffle my hair."

"I know," Alice said.

"You do?"

"My husband's helicopter went down in the North Sea. We never found him. At night I'd stare at his favorite chair, waiting for a sign."

Russ watched her face. "You think the dead come back? To visit?"

"Yes," Alice said. "Then they kind of...lose interest. Fade away. Decide you're doing okay and begin to disappear, become transparent. I did see Jordie—my husband—in a sort of dream." Never mind, she told herself. You are not telling this man that you saw your dead husband appear as a bear. But she continued. "When I check on the stars in the morning sometimes I get the feeling my parents—they're dead—occasionally hover over the house, above me, just checking. Just touching base. And then they're gone." She added, "Don't rat me out on that, okay? I haven't told my children. They'd worry."

He laughed. "I like that. 'Just touching base.' I woke up the other night and I swear Holly was by my bed, touching my forehead. But…I wanted her to talk, and she didn't say anything."

Alice nodded. Neither had Jordie. Ever again. Why was Jordie on her mind? And then she remembered. This was the day before the five-year anniversary of that phone call from the Scottish platform off Aberdeen, out in the North Sea.

Russ turned the key in the door, and they were in Holly's office.

Alice pulled out the asset form Silla had handed her. "My cheat sheet," she explained. "I need to find a recent statement from her bank or savings or brokerage accounts and ask you all kinds of rude questions about who owns the cars and trucks and horses, see the deed to the ranch, things like that."

Russ nodded. "Understood. Some of that's in her desk." He sat in Holly's desk chair and began pulling out vertical files. "Bank stuff, she kept it all in this folder." He plopped it in front of Alice. "Holly owns Miss Fancy, of course. Miss Fancy's folder is this one, with her papers." He put the folder on the desk. "Deed to the ranch is in the safe in my new office. I'll go get it."

"Another thing," Alice said. "I've also got to find papers for the assets Holly wanted in Marcy's trust. That's not just the royalty money from the LA people. Holly told me she'd written screenplays for a new trilogy, *Dark Song*. She showed me the hard copies, in an envelope in her desk. I need to check her desk."

Russ said, "*Dark Song?* She mentioned something about that."

"Even if we can't get the Media Central money back," Alice said, "those screenplays might be able to fund a chunk of Marcy's care."

He nodded. "Look around in here, Alice. I'll go check in my office for the ranch deed." He looked slightly embarrassed. "And I want to double-check how Sandra's doing."

She watched him leave the room and shut the door. She couldn't quite read his views about Sandra. Was he helping her straighten out his office accounts? Or…leaning over her chair? And why had he been reasonably welcoming today, after the harsh judgment he'd imposed on her in his Waxahachie phone call? Had he changed his mind? What was going on?

Now she was alone. Time to get to work.

She opened the drawer where Holly had stashed the sealed screenplay envelope. Not there. She looked again without luck. She pulled open the other drawers. No screenplay envelope. Nor did she see any screenplays minus the envelope. Where would Holly have put them?

She hastily tried Sandra's desk, listening for footsteps. Empty, except for one pen and one pencil.

She stood back and surveyed Holly's bookshelves. Here and there between groups of books she'd put her artifacts. Alice had seen them on her first trip to the ranch and been tickled by this glimpse of Holly's writing companions: a deer skull, Cretaceous fossils, a trilobite, a collection of arrowheads from the Hill Country. The shelves held much-used books, some tattered, including the *Chicago Manual of Style*, sticky notes stuck hither and there. One shelf, a row of three-ring binders, all labeled. She flipped through them, checking for screenplays. One binder held press clippings, another held blog entries, another contained book talks Holly had given, but no screenplays. Research material took up three shelves: histories, historical fiction, Texas geology, handbooks of local flora and fauna. Handbooks of springs and rivers. Folklore collections. Manuals on ranch management.

No screenplays.

Alice sat back down at Holly's desk, looked around the room, drummed her fingers on the desktop. Something struck her as slightly different. She stared at the top bookshelf behind Sandra's desk. There Holly had placed an old mahogany mantel clock, still ticking. "My grandmother's," she'd told Alice. On each side of the clock sat a small bronze sculpture of Greek masks, one of comedy, one of tragedy. Such was life. But she noticed that the masks and clocks sat not on the shelf, but on a fringed embroidered Mexican stole. Was that new? She didn't remember seeing it on her first visit. Maybe she'd missed it.

Alice climbed up on Sandra's office chair, holding tight to the bookshelf in case the chair swiveled. She looked at the embroidered stole, tapped it. Something lay underneath.

She pushed the clock and sculptures aside and lifted the cloth. Three typescripts lay flat beneath it. She slid them out, carefully balancing in Sandra's chair. She replaced the clock and Comedy and Tragedy, whose empty eyes watched Alice clamber down from Sandra's chair and hurry to her briefcase.

Heavy footsteps in the hall. She zipped the screenplays into her briefcase, then made a show of busily stacking up the papers on Holly's desk as Russ opened the door. She debated whether to tell him or not. Had Holly hidden the screenplays? If so, from whom? She wanted them secure—scanned and encrypted and then locked in her office safe. Anyone who got hold of them and recognized their value might decide to rathole them for a few years and then pass them off as their own. But why not tell Russ? Surely he'd want those screenplays to benefit Marcy? What was holding her back?

Russ carried a manila folder in one hand, a carved wooden jewelry box in the other.

He looked back down the hall, then closed the study door. "You finding what you need in here?" he asked.

She smiled and pointed at the stacked papers on Holly's desk. "This is a start. I'll get copies made. Did you have any luck with the deed to the ranch?"

"It must be in the safety deposit box," he said. "It's not in my office safe. But the jewelry box was. This is where she keeps—kept—the nice stuff."

He set the box on the desk and opened it. In blue velvet compartments lay a silver and turquoise squash blossom necklace, a single strand of pearls, a large opal ring, and two antique-looking silver bracelets, likely Navajo.

Russ picked up the opal ring. "I gave her this. She said it reminded her of sunrises at Big Bend. Also, Holly loved the old New Mexican stuff." He touched the squash blossom necklace. "We got this in Santa Fe. And the Navajo bracelets. Holly always said she liked something with a story, something other people had worn."

"That sounds like her," Alice said.

"The pearls were her grandmother's. I loved to see her wearing those pearls. They had a history too," Russ said. "She told me pearls benefit from being worn. Is that true?"

"I don't know. Nice to think so, though."

"This is all she kept in the jewelry box. I thought, if you need to sell something to pay Marcy's bills…well, do what you need to do. Holly had a bunch of earrings and stuff, what do you call it, costume jewelry, upstairs in her dresser. I'll get it if you want."

"Not right now." Alice took pictures of the jewelry. "If you have an idea of value for these, that would help."

"I'll look." Russ handed her the manila folder. "Here are the car titles. Truck's in my name, my Toyota Highlander's in my name, Holly's old Volvo's in her name. She hasn't driven it in over a year. Battery's probably low."

Alice used her phone to take pictures of the car titles.

"Thanks."

He colored a bit. "If you're done I'll walk you out," he said, after a moment. "But I need to lock this in my office safe. Be right back." Carrying the jewelry box, he exited the office. Alice put the remaining papers into her briefcase and stood by the door. He came back, pulling the key from his trouser pocket and relocked the office door.

From the car Alice called Silla. "I've changed my mind. Call the locksmith and get the locks changed on the rent house. Doors and windows." She should've done it in the first place. Russ was protecting assets; so was she.

Back at her office she finally reached Burt Hooks. "Files told you it looks like the fake email came from Brad Gorman's account, right?" he said.

"He did."

"At this point, yeah, you're clear," he said. "You, your secretary, your website email, you're okay."

Alice closed her eyes in relief. "And the victim herself?"

"Yeah. She's clear."

"Russ Vay?"

"The victim's husband? Yeah."

"What about the secretary, Sandra?" Alice asked, holding her breath.

She heard paper rustle. "Her Gmail account, yes," Hooks answered. "And look, all I'm saying is, the fake instructions email didn't come from any of those accounts. So right now, we're still trying to determine the actual owner of the Royalty LLC account, but the bank account stays frozen. If that's all—"

"Thanks," Alice said. She hung up. Hallelujah! Time to turn up the heat.

Chapter Twenty-Six

Take the Bull by the Tail

S tanding at her desk she called Media Central and asked to be connected with the company's general counsel. She was transferred four times and had to identify herself four times. "Yes, it's an urgent matter."

Finally, a cool emotionless voice. "Kathy Castle."

"Alice Greer, from Coffee Creek, Texas. I represent a writer you've contracted with, Holly Dougal. Your company agreed to pay her two million dollars for her *Tales of the Road* trilogy. On her behalf I sent instructions that the money was to be deposited in the trust account Holly created for her injured sister."

"So, what's the problem?"

"Your company got fake email instructions, not on Holly's own email, but from a hacker. You sent Holly's money not to the trust account but to an unrelated account at a bank in Florida designated in a fake email. Right now, the Central Texas Federal Financial Crimes unit has frozen that account, but the Florida bank has already received instructions to send the money to an account in the Caymans."

"How do I know an agent for Holly didn't send that email? How do I know she's not running a scam on us?"

"You can check what I'm telling you with the Central Texas Federal Crimes Unit," Alice said sharply. "Call Burt Hooks. Here's his number." She repeated it slowly for Castle. "Listen, your company did not call me or Holly to confirm the validity of that fake email before acting on it, despite the fact that most well-run companies these days are on the alert against financial hacking. Bear in mind that if the feds have to unfreeze the Florida account and your two million vanishes somewhere in the Caymans, your company will still have to pay Holly's trust account two million dollars."

"What? You can't ask us to pay twice!"

"Nope. I'm demanding that you pay us once, though. So far you haven't paid Holly at all. I'm demanding that you immediately put your liability carrier on notice of your company's recklessness and negligence. I'm demanding that you promptly put two million into the trust account as my letter instructed. You'll receive a letter to that effect today."

"Hold on, I'm looking up the file. I see this Dougal contract."

Pause. "I see your letter."

"Look at the cockamamie email changing the payment instructions. It's not even Holly's email."

She could hear Castle's intake of breath.

"I'll expect that payment within three days, into the trust account at Madrone Bank, as my letter instructs."

Castle argued for a couple of minutes, wanting Alice to postpone the payment obligation. Exasperated, Alice said, "Look. I want you to put your carrier on notice immediately. You pay big premiums for liability coverage, right? In exchange you're entitled to service. Your carrier will want that money found at least as badly as you do, so the carrier will hire an expert to help the federal crimes unit unravel Royalty LLC and the shell LLCs behind it. The carrier will not appreciate one minute of delay on your part."

"That makes some sense," Castle acknowledged.

"Sometimes you have to take the bull by the tail and face the situation squarely," Alice said. They hung up.

Alice drafted the demand letter and gave it to Silla to email and mail.

"Whooee!" Silla said. "Hope this doesn't catch fire in the mailbag."

*****

Loose ends for clients? Nothing to do in Ham and Julie's case; Craft's answer and discovery responses weren't due yet.

Eddie's new vineyard? Jane Ann was handling closing.

*****

Not her job, but heavy on her heart: follow up on Elena.

She called the sheriff's department and, reluctantly, asked for Eads.

"Ms…ah…Greer, is it? Something you need to know?" Eads drawled.

"Yes. Have you made progress on finding Elena's killer? The family says you've told them nothing. It's been three weeks since we found her body!"

"We'll let them know if and when there's something to report."

"Let me try this again. Did the neighbors on Waterfall Road see anything, hear anything? Did you talk to Elena's friend Mia? I gave you her contact information."

"Ms. Greer, we're busy here. I don't disclose my investigations to nonrelatives."

"That's not department policy, so far as I know," she retorted. "Have you or have you not spoken to Mia?"

"I'm not disclosing details to you."

"Or following up on any of the leads I've given you?"

He hung up. Furious, she called Files. "I asked if he'd followed up on Mia, Elena's friend, or any other information I gave him. As far as I can tell, Eads hasn't done a damn thing! Can't someone else take the case?"

"I'm sure he's working it," Files said.

"Sure?"

"But I'll touch base."

"One question—when Elena was found, did she have her phone with her?" Alice asked.

Files paused. "Not that I remember."

Alice thanked him as best she could, tamping down her fury at Eads, fumed awhile at her desk, then stalked into the kitchen for coffee. She rooted in her purse and found Mia's number scribbled in the notebook she carried everywhere. As she dialed the number she saw Isabel walking up the office steps. Didn't she have classes? Alice beckoned to Isabel and waved her to the chair in front of the desk. Alice pushed a legal pad at her. Isabel grabbed a pen.

"Mia? Alice Greer here." She put the phone on speaker.

"Hi." Mia sounded deflated. "Tonio told me the police still don't know who killed Elena. He says they aren't really looking."

"I've asked another detective to find out the status," Alice said. "But listen. I don't think Elena had her phone when . . . when we found her."

"She told me they couldn't have phones. She had an idea on how to hide it though. She knew she couldn't walk around taking notes for her project."

"What was she doing?"

Isabel mouthed something at her. "Notes." She held up her own phone and pointed to the icon.

Mia said, "Maybe notes, on the phone. Also maybe a quick voice memo in the bathroom."

Isabel raised her hand, pointing at the ceiling. "Cloud," she mouthed.

Oh yeah! Alice nodded. "Mia, did Elena have an iCloud account?"

"Yes," Mia said. "We all try to store our research in the cloud in case something happens—you lose your phone, your computer gets a virus, someone nabs your backpack. Journalists have to preserve what they learn."

"Do you know her password?"

Silence. "I'm not sure," Mia said. "It might be futuroseguro1." Isabel scribbled it down.

"Thanks," Alice said. "If I hear anything I'll let you know."

"Okay."

Alice called Files, left a message: "What if the dead girl, Elena Ramos, stored her notes in the cloud?"

Isabel stood up. "I just stopped by for a second, to check that the petition got filed and all was well." She grinned, looking at Alice's face. "No, I have no classes this afternoon, since you're about to ask me that."

Alice laughed. "I was indeed. Yes, we filed the petition and the discovery requests. What are you up to?"

"I'm on my way to our ranch where it's quiet, so I can finish my extra credit paper. You know, to make up for that midterm I told you about. Okay, gotta go." And she was out the door.

Well.

Files called back in half an hour. "You know I'm not working this case."

"Your pal Eads won't pass the time of day with me," Alice retorted. "I don't think he even interviewed Elena's friend Mia. If he had, he might have learned where she kept her notes."

"Where?"

"He might have taken a look at the cloud. But he's not letting even her family know what he's found out, if anything. He sure won't tell me. Since she was found under my fence, and since I think she was working on a project that got her killed, and since her brother Tonio is my friend, I want to give you what might be her password so you can get into the cloud and see if she saved anything there."

"I should pass it along to Eads."

"Nothing will happen if you do," Alice said. They argued about that briefly. Alice finally exploded. "George, Eads won't call me, won't call the family, and doesn't seem to have done anything to find Elena's murderer! Come on, tell me that's not true?"

Files gave a long sigh. "We can't pick our relatives, and sometimes we can't pick our co-workers. If you give me this password I will be sure you hear what Elena put in the cloud that may be relevant to her death. If anything. There may be nothing."

Alice examined that promise. Was it enough? "I need a chance to hear what you think is relevant and what's not. Like, where she was and who she was with."

Files examined her amendment to his promise. "Okay. Give me that password."

"And you'll call me as soon as you get the info?"

Another pause. "I'll do my best."

Alice sighed. "Okay. I know." She gave him Elena's password as described by Mia. "Try this."

So far nothing had worked. Dead ends every time. Had Elena had any opportunity to whisper a voice memo into her phone? To tap a short note? To give any indication where she was and what was happening to her?

Chapter Twenty-Seven

You've Done That Before

T he phone rang. Eddie's voice: "Alice?" He cleared his throat. "How about coming out to see the Wine 100? My last tasting ends at four."

Kinsear had invited himself for dinner. He hero-worshipped Eddie. "Well—"

Eddie added, "You can bring that guy along, if you want. Come at five, before sunset."

She called Kinsear.

"Really?" he asked. "Eddie's new vineyard?"

"Future vineyard. Can you get here in time to get out there by five?"

When Alice and Kinsear rolled up, Eddie stood waiting outside his wine tasting building, late sun slanting on his face. Alice thought he still looked tired, with a grimmer set to his mouth.

"How about if we walk," Eddie said. "I need to stretch my legs."

The three followed the road that wound downhill from the wine tasting building, then crossed over onto a faint path that dipped into a small ravine and then led over a hill to meet the dirt driveway belonging to what he now called the Wine 100. "Let's go check out the little house on the creek first," Eddie said. "Then we can climb the slopes, and I'll show you the way I'm thinking the vines will be laid out."

They walked in silence down the driveway, heads lifted to catch the day's last birdsong and the first tangerine tinge of sunset. Ahead, at the end of the driveway, sat a small one-story house with a front porch overlooking the narrow creek.

"Sweet," Kinsear said.

Eddie stopped abruptly. Alice and Kinsear almost ran into him. Eddie spread his arms, hands signaling silence.

Deer? Fox? Alice wondered.

Eddie half turned, whispered. "See the light in the cabin?"

A faint yellow gleam where no gleam should be.

Eddie moved forward, silent as dusk. He pointed left, and the three stepped off the driveway and filed uphill toward the rear of the house. Eddie signaled a halt fifty feet behind the building and pointed. Tucked on the far side of the house, invisible from the driveway, sat a car. A small nondescript sedan with a rental sticker on the bumper.

Eddie started away from them, toward the car, still moving like a wide-shouldered ghost through the dry grass. He motioned Kinsear back downhill toward the nearer side of the house.

"Stay here, Alice," Kinsear whispered, and quietly moved downhill.

She turned toward the back of the house, bouncing softly left and right, just as on the tennis court baseline, ready to move either way.

Kinsear had nearly reached the house when a figure burst out the front door, leaped off the porch, and started running away from them up the driveway.

"Hey!" Kinsear yelled, charging toward the man.

The man veered and started uphill toward Alice. She gave chase.

Eddie crouched behind the car.

The man swerved away from Alice, panting, and turned back across the hillside, flailing through the grass. Kinsear angled uphill below Alice to cut him off, faster than Alice had ever seen him move. The man ran toward the car.

Eddie LaFarge vaulted toward him and executed a flawless open-field tackle. Alice heard the desperate grunt of his victim as he hit the ground. She and Kinsear raced toward Eddie, now sitting atop a plumpish male body emitting gasps of distress. The setting sun on the back of the body's head showed dark hair, white sideburns.

Eddie slowly moved his weight off the body and stood. Eddie looked at Kinsear. "Good D," Eddie said.

"Looks like you've done that before," Kinsear replied, nodding down at the prone victim.

The hit from Eddie had knocked his breath out. The three watched as Brad Gorman slowly lurched up to his hands and knees, then vomited. Alice grimaced and backed away.

After Gorman heaved a few ragged breaths, Kinsear and Eddie hauled him to his feet and marched him downhill to the house, onto the porch, and into the house's main room.

"We're gonna have a little chat," Eddie told Gorman. "Go rinse your mouth out."

While Gorman splashed and groaned at the kitchen sink, Alice surveyed the comfortable space, with its fireplace, rocking chairs and couch, dining area and small kitchen. The house smelled faintly sweet but dusty and empty, a vacation house smell. On the kitchen counter she saw an iPad, a loaf of white bread, a jar of creamy peanut butter, a dirty knife, and two bottles of Raptor Cellars wine. Red wine.

Eddie stared at the bottles, then shoved Gorman, still wet around the face, into a wooden chair. "Okay, buddy. Time to talk. You whacked me with the white wine, locked me in the vat to suffocate, and then waltzed out with two bottles of red?"

Gorman shook his head vigorously, adopting an earnest expression. Alice and Kinsear leaned against the kitchen counter, watching.

"It wasn't me, Eddie. Honest. Sure, I came back in and left the white, picked up a coupla reds off the counter in the tasting room. You know I'm a red wine guy." Weak smile.

"I don't buy it," Eddie said flatly. "You were pissed, you knew exactly where I was, you knew exactly what I was doing. You called, and when I stuck my head out of that concrete tank, you whacked me." Eddie's face was dangerously red. "You lying son of a bitch." He loomed over Gorman, fists clenched. "You scum-sucking pig."

Alice felt the air crackle with fury.

Gorman blanched, shrank back. "I didn't!" he croaked. "It wasn't me!"

Disbelieving looks from Eddie, Alice, Kinsear.

"No, look, Eddie," Gorman tried. "Sure, I was pissed. You've screwed me on this deal, this property. I needed it! I had to…to leave my room and find some cheap digs." He pointed at the ceiling. "This little place seemed…available. At least until closing."

"How'd you get in?" Eddie demanded.

"I, um, forgot to put the realtor's key back in the lockbox. No one was using this place. Nice view."

Eddie, Kinsear, and Alice stared at Gorman.

"You're broke?" Eddie said, disbelief on his face. "What about that cashier's check? Your buyout? One hundred and fifty thousand! Where'd all that go?"

Gorman chewed his lip. "There were some claims on it."

"*All* of it?"

The four fell silent.

"Weren't you expecting a commission if this property went to your client?" Eddie asked. "How bad did you need it?"

Gorman said nothing, eyes darting left, then right, then to his lap.

Eddie's voice dripped ice. "You're flat busted. You figured you'd lock me up in that tank, and I'd run out of air. Permanently. Your clients would get this place, and you'd get the commission."

"No!" Gorman protested. "Eddie, I got bad clausto. I wouldn't lock anyone in a tank! You know I wouldn't do that to you!"

"I don't know that. Tell me everything you did after I offered you that bottle and you took it out to your car." He leaned toward Gorman's uplifted face. "Everything!"

Gorman took a breath, licked his lower lip. "I walked out. Got in the car." He paused. "I decided I wanted red. You kinda disrespected me, Eddie, with the white. Your old partner."

"That's over." Eddie's voice whiplashed the room. "Over. Okay, you're trespassing here. Plenty of fingerprints. I'm calling the cops."

"Wait! What did you do after you got the red wine?" Alice asked.

Gorman swiveled his eyes toward her. "Nothing. I just went back outside and left."

"Did you see anyone else around the winery?" Alice asked.

Gorman started to speak, then shook his head no.

"What?" Eddie leaned toward him.

"There was a guy on a motorcycle coming up the hill when I left. Only person I saw on this godforsaken road."

"Then what?" Alice asked. She was waiting to hear about that taco order.

"I stopped at this joint on the highway. Flores. Bought some tacos."

"What time?" she pressed.

"I dunno. Twelve thirty?"

"Which tacos?"

"Hey, what is this?" Gorman asked. "I mean, some tacos!"

Alice lifted an eyebrow. "I'm waiting."

"Oh hell. Flour tortilla. Beef. Guacamole maybe? Whatever the special was."

"You don't remember? Probably because you were busy jamming the vat door shut on me," Eddie growled.

"Eddie! Who ya gonna believe?"

"Brad!" mocked Eddie. "Based on our recent dealings, that's obvious. When your lips move, you're lying. Who's your client?"

"Huh?"

Eddie moved his clenched fist closer to Gorman's nose. "Who was backing you on this deal? Who wanted this property? Who wanted Eddie LaFarge not to get it?"

"Me," Gorman blustered.

"No," Alice said. "Not when you're flat broke. Who's your client?"

"That's private," he muttered. "Look, guys, let me sleep here. I got no place to go. I'll leave tomorrow."

"Not yet," Alice said. Eddie and Kinsear turned to her.

"First tell us why you sent the fraudulent email telling the media company to send Holly Dougal's money to a Florida bank account," she said.

"What?" Eddie asked, brow furrowed in surprise.

Well, of course, he doesn't know about that. Alice kept her eyes on Gorman who looked at her like a rabbit at a snake.

"I told the feds already. I had nothing to do with any email like that."

"But it was sent from your internet account, right?"

"No! I mean, that's what the feds said, but I have no idea what they're talking about! Somebody musta hacked me, that's all I know." He looked up at Alice. "I swear, missy—I mean, ma'am—the cops asked me the same thing. I never even heard of that woman."

"Didn't you talk to her husband, Russ Vay, about buying their ranch?"

Gorman's eyes wavered. He frowned. "I mighta talked to him once or twice. Nothing came of it."

"Russ Vay wasn't interested?" Alice asked. She very definitely wanted to hear his answer.

"He said *she* wasn't. His wife."

"And you wanted to buy it to use as a wedding venue?" Alice pressed again.

"Well, maybe just the Cowboy Action part. Even just lease it. But no dice."

"But you say you're broke," Alice said. "You yourself couldn't have bought a piece of Full House Ranch either. Or leased it. Again, who's your principal?"

"None of your business. Like I say, it's private."

"Wrong. It is my business. I'm Holly's executor. I'm looking for every asset she has. Or had. Who are you acting for?"

Kinsear said, "I'd answer that question if I were you."

"I—it's worth my life. Haven't you heard of client confidentiality?"

"Yes, for lawyers, not for land deals," Alice said. "Especially land deals that the police will want to know about, as part of investigating Holly's murder."

Gorman sat silent.

"Okay, we'll call Coffee County and get you booked for breaking and entering," Eddie said. "And, of course, for attempted murder. You'll be safe there."

Gorman shook his head. "No one's safe in jail, Eddie. You heard about those famous, uh, snitches in jail? I mean, you heard about that rich guy in New York, in the tender hands of the feds?" He leaned forward, looked at each of them in turn. "C'mon, guys, I'm down on my luck. I didn't bash you, Eddie. Honest!"

Eddie shook his head and took his phone from his pocket. "Brad, you're in some deep shit. I'm turning you in." He looked at Alice. "What do you think, counselor? Want me to call Conroy, get him to bring over the truck and some of those long plastic ties? Secure the prisoner?"

Alice wondered what George Files would want?

He'd want to hear more about the attack on Eddie and why Brad Gorman was hiding and from whom. He'd want to know where the $150,000 partnership buyout had gone. He'd want to know more about the email to the media company and whether Brad's email had been hacked, if indeed he was innocent. He'd want that iPad.

"The truth's not in him," Eddie said, echoing her thoughts.

"We've made a citizen's arrest," Alice said, "for trespassing on the Graves property, which is under contract to Eddie here. I think we call Coffee County."

"Agree," Kinsear said. Eddie nodded.

Alice picked up her phone and speed-dialed Files.

"Alice?" he said.

"Aren't you guys looking for Brad Gorman?"

"We are," he answered.

"He broke into the Graves property next to Eddie LaFarge's place, and we caught him."

"We?"

"Um, here's Eddie." She handed the phone to Eddie, who gave Files directions to the house.

Beads of sweat glowed on Gorman's brow and upper lip. He slumped in the wooden chair, glanced at the door, and suddenly shoved his way out of the chair.

Eddie lunged at Gorman, caught him, swung him back in the chair, none too carefully. Gorman groaned.

"Now, now," Eddie said.

Alice stood silent, measuring the fear in Gorman's face.

"You need to level with us," she said. "Who're you so scared of? It's got to be your boss, right? You owed him big-time?"

Gorman's eyes slid left, slid right, and back to Alice.

"I told you, it's worth my life. This is…this property was *my* gig."

"If you're telling the truth about not sending that fraudulent email about Holly's money, you'll be safer in jail, because someone's going to try to shut you up permanently," Alice said. "And that's whoever sent the email using your account. Do you have a guess as to who might have hacked you? If anyone did?"

No answer.

Eddie made some coffee. They waited in silence until Coffee County headlights lit the windows. Files walked in with a warrant followed by a redhaired young man with watchful eyes, nametag Assistant Detective Alan Joske. Files took charge of Gorman's iPad and bagged Gorman's few belongings. Joske cuffed Gorman

"Death sentence," Gorman said mournfully. "That's what you just gave me."

"Let's go, sir." Joske walked him out.

Files looked at Alice. "Call me," he said.

Chapter Twenty-Eight

Bad News and Good News

The next morning Alice groaned at the email Miranda had forwarded from River Road, Marcy's group home. Four thousand dollars overdue. "We would hate to lose Marcy as she seems so happy here. Please let us know when payment can be expected."

She left a message for Files. When will the feds get Holly's money back? So the bank can pay her sister's bills?

You may never get the money back, Files had warned earlier.

Alice decided to proceed on worst-case assumptions: Media Central balks, insurer balks, one of us files suit, funds get tied up, for months, for years. What assets could she tap? She penciled a list: Holly's 401k, with Marcy the beneficiary. Conservatively managed, if it even managed four percent growth she'd be lucky. Optimists might say it could cover, annually, a couple of months of Marcy's expenses, assuming no increase in the group home rates. Trustees could not be optimists. What was Marcy supposed to do for the rest of the year? The ranch? It belonged to Russ. That left a small bank account, and the horse Fancy, some jewels, a car. She could sell assets, but what else?

Memories of Holly at their book club flooded Alice's mind—the rosy face, flushed with joy, talking about her screenplays for the new series, *Dark Song Trilogy*.

Alice had leafed through the first screenplay before she locked it in the office safe, the huge antique bank safe that she'd had bolted to the floor joists in the conference room closet. She was hooked after the first page. Maybe now, with Holly recently dead, reputation shining, was the time to get a deal for *Dark Song* too. But where were Holly's electronic versions?

The feds had returned Holly's laptop to Files who'd returned it to Alice. She asked Silla to get it from the office safe.

She tapped in Holly's password and then searched the documents folder. On first scan she saw nothing promising. Hadn't Holly said, the first night Alice met her at book club, that she'd just finished typing them in herself?

Alice told the laptop to rearrange the documents in chronological order. She carefully read each listing from October, then September, then August. Nothing. In fact, none of the documents had even been modified, much less created, more recently than July. She double-checked. Nope.

Puzzled, she called her criminal law buddy, Tyler Junkin, and explained. "So, Tyler, who's the computer genius who can recover documents? Or at least see if they ever existed on this machine?"

"Roddy Ratliff," he said promptly. "Here's his contact info." Her own computer pinged, and she saw "Roddy Ratliff, Minor Genius." He lived ten minutes away.

Alice called him on Facetime. Minor Genius answered his own phone. To Alice he looked about twelve years old. He asked a few questions, grunted a few times. "Can you bring me the laptop?"

"Yes." She put him on hold, asked Silla to take the laptop to him.

"Right away." Silla was out the door.

Roddy asked, "Do you have the laptop owner's email passwords? She might have sent out a document to someone—maybe even to herself. Writers do that, they get so anxious about losing their work."

"Ah," Alice said. She herself had done that when on the road, sending drafts to the office as an extra safeguard.

Roddy's face stared at her from the screen with his terrier-bright eyes. "Does she also have an iCloud account? Do you have the password? Did she store her data in the cloud?"

"No idea," Alice said. "Can you figure that out?"

"Yep, it'll take me awhile."

*****

Two hours later the Minor Genius called back. "Bad news and good news. First, someone did wipe some documents from July to the present."

"Can you tell what they were? Can you get them back?"

"Working on it. But not yet."

"Can you tell when?"

"Yes. About seventeen days ago. But some documents might have already been deleted."

Seventeen days ago…the day Holly died.

Minor Genius went on. "About five p.m."

After the Cowboy Action competition. After Holly was shot. Who did the wiping? Someone else had been busy at Holly's computer that evening.

At book club, Holly had said, "I handwrite, then polish on the computer." Had Holly deleted the files? Maybe copied them on a thumb drive? If not Holly, who? Someone trying to erase any sign that *Dark Song* was Holly's?

Alice enlisted Silla. "Let's take a walk."

They locked the office and walked down the street to the rent house with the keys to the new lock. As the two approached they saw Sandra's Mini Cooper in the driveway.

Sandra herself stood at the front door. She turned as they walked up.

"My keys don't work," Sandra frowned down at the keys in her hand as if they had leprosy. "I need to find something for Russ."

"Oh, sorry. We changed the locks to protect Holly's materials while we finish the inventory," Alice said. "What do you need to find?"

"Some notebooks with Holly's book expenses," Sandra said. "She didn't always keep receipts, but she usually scribbled the costs down."

"We'll help you," Alice said, moving in front of Sandra and unlocking the door. "Of course, we'll keep a note of anything you need to take for Russ. Just for your protection."

Sandra shot a hard look at Alice. Face cold, she said, "I don't think Russ feels you are helping matters."

"What matters?"

"Just—everything. I'm trying to help him make sense of Holly's business dealings."

"Really?" Alice said. "I'll need any such information as her executor. We'll be preparing the tax and asset information for the probate court. I'd appreciate it if you pass on any information that could help."

Sandra said stiffly, "Russ is relying on me, not you. You're not his lawyer." She added, face growing pitiful, "You're just trying to turn him against me. Why? I loved Holly. I'm trying to help Russ, to honor her memory."

Alice lifted her right hand. "Sandra, wait. I don't get this. Holly appointed me as her executor. I'll be filing her will as well. I'm trying to do exactly what she hired me to do. Russ doesn't have to worry about those tasks. In fact, Holly obviously didn't want him to have to worry. She protected him from that, by not making him act as executor." She paused. "What are these expense notebooks you want? What do they look like?"

"Just...little notebooks," Sandra said shortly. She surveyed the bookshelves. "I don't see them. I'll tell Russ what you said." She strode out the door, leaving a scent of *Coco* in the air. The door closed with a bang.

Alice and Silla looked at each other. "Weird," Silla said. She walked around the office, checking windows.

"What are you doing?"

"We changed the locks. I'm just being sure we locked the windows too," Silla said, twisting shut the old brass lock on a window. "That woman's bad news, Alice."

"I need to talk to Russ again," Alice said. "I dread it though, because I'm still not sure where he's coming from."

Chapter Twenty-Nine

What Would Miss Manners Suggest?

On Thursday, Alice felt at least temporarily cheered by the thought that Kinsear was taking her to an early dinner at a restaurant in Driftwood. She looked forward to dinner somewhere no one would recognize them, no one would interrupt, no one would remind her of unsolved problems. Always good to good to get out of Dodge.

When Kinsear showed up, he agreed. "I want to sit across from you and gaze longingly into your eyes, of course, across a glass of decent red, and talk about anything that doesn't involve either of my daughters, recalcitrant book collectors, or hedge funds trying to merge themselves," he said.

"Tell me again about my eyes."

"Brown and I hope fixed devotedly on me."

Despite best intentions, Alice now sat alone and bored in a booth waiting for Kinsear to return from the restaurant porch, where he was pacing back and forth and gesticulating impatiently on a phone call that had vibrated loudly just as they were finishing their main courses. "Sorry," he mouthed, standing up to leave their booth. "It's that Brit."

At least he'd gone outside. Alice always felt her blood pressure soar when people talked on cell phones in the elevator or at dinner, making others unwilling parties to inane conversations. Kinsear would never do that, thank God. She approved of his phone ethics: no cell phones at the table. He usually turned his off entirely and contracted his brows if she hauled hers out for an emergency peek.

This evening his strategy hadn't worked. At the moment, Alice was left toying with the last of her fish and thinking idly of coffee and dessert.

She glanced up as the restaurant door opened and blinked. Split-second decision required: Should she sit up straight and greet the newcomers or lie low? She stared resolutely down at the dessert menu.

Sandra Sechrest sauntered in, smiling her usual half-smile, followed by a man, a tawny-haired man with a tight long-sleeved athletic tee showing carefully curated muscles, brown leather sneakers, and, Alice was sure, pale eyes behind those aviator sunglasses.

What in God's name was Sandra doing with Narcissus?

Was she really *with* him?

Yes. At that moment a bustling waitress was seating the two in the booth just on the other side of the divider wall from Alice and Kinsear. Alice's bench seat jiggled as the new customers slid into their booth. Only some pots of common coleus atop the divider blocked their views of each other.

Alice found herself longing for Kinsear's call to go on. Now that Sandra and Narcissus were seated, she couldn't see them. But she could hear them. With only a minor twinge of scruple, she gently pulled her notebook and pen from her bag, placing the notebook on her lap. She uncapped the pen. Shameless, she told herself.

Sandra employed several ranges for her voice. Alice had heard her use her purr for Russ; her submissive but "busy" voice for Holly; her "hurt but restrained outrage" tone for Alice; her crisp "in charge" voice for office phone calls.

Now she heard the tone of excited intimacy. "Finally!" breathed Sandra. "I thought we'd never get a meal to ourselves. How'd you get away from the old fart?"

"Doctor appointment," said the other, a light tenor voice, surprisingly high given the speaker's musculature. "The nurse stays with him for those. His doc makes house calls, of course."

"Of course," said Sandra. "As one does, if the patient has more money than God."

The old fart must be Craft.

Their waitress returned to take their orders.

"You first," Sandra said.

Alice wanted to hear the man's voice. He ordered in that high tenor, with a California accent. "Just your mixed greens salad with a few slices of steak, seared rare. Vinaigrette on the side. No dessert," he added.

"None of our spicy sweet potato fries?"

"Nope. Water to drink. No ice."

Sandra's turn. "Asian chicken salad." She paused. "A glass of prosecco."

The waitress thanked them and scurried off.

"Still watching your weight?" Sandra asked. "Not a single sweet potato fry?"

"My body's my temple," he rejoined. "Right now, I've got my body near perfect. Seriously. I'm going to order a new video this week."

"For the studios? Again?" Sandra's voice lost some warmth.

"Gotta do it. All these action flicks today, they need new blood. Meaning, there's gotta be a market for a body like mine."

"How much will it cost, this video?"

"Gotta get someone to film it. Think I'll do it outside. Nature boy theme, maybe. What do you think about outdoor lighting? Would that show my body enough? I don't want to underlight."

The waitress returned with Sandra's prosecco. As she left, Alice heard the man say softly, "Celebrating, are we?"

Silence from Sandra. Then: "You about gave me a heart attack. I thought we agreed on Sunday. Instead, we're right in the middle of the stupid cowboy action mess!"

"Hey, I get style points! El Gato!"

El Gato?

Sandra said, "We're not looking for style points."

"You're speaking to the invisible man!"

Invisible man? What did he mean?

"Listen, I might get interested in that cowboy action scene. I'm all about creativity and split-second timing. Those costumes are something. Man, the leather chaps! Those tooled wrist-guards!"

"It's way too expensive."

"You know I love me some good costumes," he said in a dreamy tone. "Those low-slung leather holsters—"

Sandra said in a low flat voice, "You lost us one whole dimension."

"What do you mean?"

"There's nothing self-inflicted about it. Nothing!"

"C'mon, lay off. You're micromanaging again. We can still celebrate, can't we? It's teamwork, Sis! Me elimination, you compensation!"

Sis? Alice almost dropped her notebook. She concentrated on their hushed voices.

"We'll celebrate when it's in the bag," Sandra said.

"In the bag? Not 'in the bank'?" he asked. "When's that happening?"

"Maybe never. It's complicated."

In what bank? Palmetto? The Caymans? But the feds had told Files that they'd checked Sandra's email accounts and found no connection with the fraudulent email to the media company.

"Here you are." The waitress returned with their salads. Conversation on the other side of the booth paused. Cutlery rattled. Alice strained her ears, not wanting to miss a word. Finally, the man spoke softly. "I wish you and I could get together every day or at least talk every day," he said. "I worry when I don't hear from you."

"It won't be long now," Sandra said, her voice soothing.

Another pause. "I need me some cash," he said. "Gotta get that video made. Then we're off to the races. Maybe we two could get a place in the Hollywood Hills? Or maybe Santa Monica. What do you think?" Another pause. Forks clinked gently against plates. He went on. "I've been thinking, after the accident, maybe I could capitalize on the missing fingers. You know, use them to build a new image? I mean a real deformity…these days, why wouldn't that sell? Tough guy takes some blows, keeps on trucking?"

"It's not a deformity." Sandra's cool voice. "It's a work injury. Stunt men lead dangerous lives, I mean, they court danger. But face it, baby bro. Sure, the film industry's trying to be PC, they use more actors with disabilities these days, but I don't think they plan to show hands with actual missing digits. Or parts of."

He grunted.

"Still," her voice softened, "it's a damn shame that car door did what it did to your hand. They should have paid more than just hospital."

She switched topics. "A new vid's a good plan, though. Tell me more."

Kinsear chose that moment to return. "Sorry," he said, sliding back down into the booth. "That's the Englishman with the Texiana collection. He's on a religious retreat at a monastery in the south of France. Meditating. No cell service until now, he claims."

Alice put her finger to her lips, tilting her head toward the adjacent booth. She tugged a page from her notebook, scribbled "Sandra!" and drew an arrow toward Sandra's booth. Kinsear raised one eyebrow fractionally. "Plus Narcissus! Her bro!" Alice scribbled. Kinsear sat motionless, until the penny dropped, and he mouthed across the table, "You're kidding."

Their waitress materialized next to Kinsear. "Anything else?" she asked.

Kinsear glanced at Alice, then said softly, "Two macchiatos. And the check." The waitress nodded and left. Silent, Alice waited, desperate to hear.

Conversation had resumed beyond the coleus plants. "Wish you could've seen the old fart lay into Gorman," the tenor voice went on. "It was hilarious."

Alice's eyes widened, staring at Kinsear. He raised his eyebrows. Gorman?

Alice saw the waitress bustling back toward Sandra's booth with the check. "If that'll be all—"

"Here," Sandra said. "Use this card." The waitress left. No Dutch treat. Maybe Sandra always paid.

The man's voice resumed. "Pretty soon we'll be flush, though. I've got this idea for the video. You can front it, right?"

The waitress scurried back with the check before Sandra responded. "Here you are, Ms. Sechrest."

"Gotta run," Narcissus said to Sandra. "Gotta be there for bed check."

Bed check?

The booth creaked. Alice's seat rocked slightly as the adjacent booth emptied. She suddenly felt she should confront the two siblings. She started to slide out of the booth.

Kinsear's hand covered hers firmly. His face assumed a warning look.

The waitress brought their check.

At that moment a voice rang out, off to her right. "Alice Greer! Hey! I've been meaning to call you!"

Waddling toward their booth, leather vest and all, came Horace Kielbas, a retired Czech sausage master, head of the Coffee County Master Naturalists Chapter. Alice introduced Kinsear; he and Horace shook hands. Horace turned to Alice. "How about coming to talk to the Naturalists again? About water rights and property? Would April work?"

"I think so," Alice said. "Call the office so I can get it on the calendar."

Out of the corner of her eye she saw Narcissus leaving the restaurant. At the door, he half turned and sent an extravagant air kiss to Sandra, lips curled in a mocking smooch. But Sandra wasn't responding. She'd turned back, staring directly at Alice.

"Great," Horace boomed. "We need a professional presentation so this batch of naturalists can get their advanced training."

"Glad to do it," Alice said.

Horace hustled away. Behind him appeared Sandra, sailing directly toward their booth. Sandra bestowed a tight smile on Kinsear, then turned to Alice. "Have you been here long?" she blurted.

Alice watched Sandra's face, watched her eyes change as she mentally reviewed her conversation with her bro, assessing whether any damage control was advisable. "We've had a delightful dinner," Alice said. "And you?"

Sandra looked momentarily speechless.

It was an interesting moment. What would Miss Manners suggest that Sandra say? Maybe, "You deliberately eavesdropped…you should have announced your presence so I could sit somewhere else, so I could edit my conversation"?

Instead, Sandra said, "I like the salads here."

"Is that young man your brother?" Alice asked. "I thought he was in LA."

"Why would you think that? He's got work here."

"I had the impression from something Russ said that he was in Hollywood, aiming at movie work."

"Well, at the moment he's enjoying what he does." Sandra smiled at Kinsear (but not at Alice, as Alice noted). "I must go." She spun on her heel and walked briskly away.

Kinsear laid some bills on their table and stood.

Alice grabbed her own bag. "I need to see Narcissus again. Let's hurry."

From the restaurant porch she and Kinsear scanned the parking lot. Car windows glinted in the late sun. A black pickup, matte trim, backed partway out of a space, then paused. The driver turned his sunglasses toward the restaurant. Then he looked down at his lap. Four spaces away Sandra had made it to her brown and cream Mini Cooper.

She too was looking at her lap, probably texting. Narcissus turned his head again and stared directly at Alice, then roared out of the parking lot.

Kinsear repeated the license number into his phone.

He put his arm around Alice, held her close. "Damn," he said. "Here we go again."

"What do you mean?"

"She knows you know…more than you did. And her bro? Bad news."

"Narcissus," Alice said. "Remember what happened to him in the myth? Drowned, looking at his own reflection?"

Kinsear had laughed uproariously when she'd told the story of her faux fly-fishing venture. He'd said, "I admire your verisimilitude, with the special fly for the Guadalupe River smallmouth bass." Now he wasn't laughing.

"Now he knows exactly who you are," he said. "And where you live."

"How do you figure that? Not from those pleadings I sent his boss, Mr. Craft? He's just muscle, he wouldn't get to see legal papers."

Alice generally felt a sense of security at home, even though she lived alone, because she believed people couldn't easily find her home address. The county appraisal records only included a metes and bounds description of the ranch, with no street address, and only listed her post office box as the billing address. Her website, her pleadings, used only the office address. She knew someone might dig up a street address from the internet, but she generally felt fairly secure alone at home.

"Before, if your Narcissus even saw the documents you sent Craft," Kinsear said, "he knew which lawyer filed the trailer lawsuit, but not where the lawyer lived. After your fly-fishing foray, he may have thought you were just some ditzy neighbor. Now he can put it all together. You're the lawyer who's causing problems for Sandra, and you're the lawyer who sued his boss, and you live just down the creek."

"Umm," Alice responded. She hadn't quite realized.

Driving back to her office, Kinsear was quiet. "I wish I didn't have to go back to Fredericksburg tonight," he said finally. "I'd rather stay with you."

She looked at him, the graying black curls, the new lines around his mouth. "That new bull?"

"Yes. Jaime's driven the new one back to the ranch, and I told him to wait on me before he tries to unload him from the truck. You remember what happened last time he tried to handle a bull alone?"

Alice did. "Concussion. Maybe this bull will be more tractable."

They rode in silence back to her office, where she'd left her car. Kinsear said, "Lock up tight. And keep your phone on. I'll call."

She kissed him goodbye.

*****

At the ranch, in early darkness, with the waning moon slipping in and out of the clouds, Alice let herself back into the house. The only noise was the quiet hum of the refrigerator. She opened the sliding door to the deck and stepped out, loving as always the downhill view of the creek at the bottom of the bluff, and the silent valley beyond. A cloud wafted over the moon. Nothing moved below. Somewhere above wings fluttered. A nightjar?

She loved the quiet, the solitude, of her house on the bluff—a sanctuary from road noise and the bright lights of development marching inexorably toward Coffee Creek from greater Austin. She turned on lamps in the living room by the old leather armchair, where she planned to sprawl with a book.

She lit a small fire for comfort. The air grew warm, the fire crackled softly, and the print in her paperback wavered. She shook herself awake. Ten o'clock.

She locked and checked all the doors, even the sliding ones. She often left those open; not tonight. She ran hot water into her tub, added bubble bath, climbed in, then slid down into the warmth. Relax, she told herself. *Nada te turbe, nada te'espante,* nothing can trouble, nothing can frighten, went the Taizé chant. She liked it, but somehow even the fact of saying it made her nervous.

She added more hot water to her bubbles and thought about the cryptic conversation she'd overheard. What did Sandra mean, "you about gave me a heart attack"? What was her brother supposed to wait until Sunday for? Why was he the invisible man? What did he mean, "style points"? What did Sandra mean, "nothing self-inflicted"?

One image stayed in her mind. The air kiss Narcissus sent his sister from the restaurant door, the pouty-lipped smooch. Why was that niggling at her head?

More questions. At the cowboy action site, why was Russ shaking his head no at Gorman? Gorman, who had sent the faux email instructions?

She decided to call Files in the morning, her mind full of unanswered questions. Did he know yet which gun killed Holly? Whose? When? Did Holly's death involve Sandra? Or her brother?

Chapter Thirty

Zero at the Bone

Alice woke, heart thumping. She checked the bedside clock. Four a.m. She slipped out of bed, trying to recall what small noise woke her.

First she tried her bedroom sliding door to the back walkway: firmly locked. Systematically she began checking the house doors, waiting for her heart rate to slow. Guestroom sliding door: locked. Hallway: silent. The kitchen, with its sliding door to the deck: locked. Front entry door: locked. Utility porch, living room French doors, back door: all secure.

Maybe she'd just had a bad dream.

Soon it would be five. Too late to go back to bed. She made a pot of espresso, frothed some hot milk into a puffy comforting cloud, and took her first sip. Usually this ritual, with the coffee's dark richness, restored some hope for the day to come.

She perched on a stool at the kitchen island, drinking coffee, answering emails, checking the news. She poured another cup. She carried it out the sliding door onto the deck so she could examine the stars, confirm they were still there—Orion with his sidekick Sirius and the mysterious nebula in his sword, and, nearby, Capella, Procyon.

By the time she'd finished answering emails and despairing of the online news, the first soft orange of the sun had lit the sky. Her entry door faced east, right into the sun. That meant she could always see every mote of dust on the old Saltillo tiles that covered her floor. This morning was no different; the sun sparkled through the caliche dust that made its way through the front door.

This morning she also saw mud. By the front door, she saw one footprint, a large footprint, just past the door mat. Had she missed it yesterday? Whose footprint? She took two steps toward it and saw a flash of red, a flash of gold. Moving. Under the old cherry breakfront by the front door.

So fast, a whiplash. Red and yellow, making gold. A snake in the house. Zero at the bone. Alice backed slowly out of the room, turned and raced to her closet, wriggled her feet into her cowgirl boots. She crept back down the hall, clutching Jordie's binoculars. She twirled the focus knob, aiming under the breakfront.

The snake was long but slender, encircled with black scales, then yellow, then red, then yellow, then black. Alice swallowed. "Red and yellow, kill a fellow; red and black, friend of Jack." Great. A lethal coral snake. Not a friendly trespassing scarlet kingsnake.

Her key task: to keep the snake where it was. The last thing she wanted was an escaped coral snake hidden between couch cushions, curled beneath her bathtub. She needed to trap it under the breakfront, prevent its escape under the breakfront's arched baseboards at the floor.

She remembered four rectangular glass vases stored in the linen closet. She moved quietly to the closet, found the vases, tiptoed across the tiles. She gently placed one in front of the opening at each end of the breakfront and two across the front, then backed away. Sudden movement sent Alice jumping backward. Peering through the glass, she saw the coral snake swish into a coil and lift one end of its narrow self. She refocused the binoculars on the coil. Yep, the snake had erected its tail, not its head. She'd read that coral snakes used that peculiar defense.

But it could still uncoil and exit the back of the breakfront. She slipped out of the living room and hurried to find the tall mirror leaning against her bedroom wall, just long and tall enough to block the back opening at the base of the breakfront. She slid the glass flush with the back of the breakfront, then stacked books against the mirror to hold it tight.

Whew! She knelt a yard in front of the breakfront and peered through the vases.

The tail stared back.

She called Kinsear.

"Are you okay, Alice? You sound funny."

She began giggling. Finally, she managed, "I'm fine. Sorry to call so early, but I need advice."

"I'm strong on advice. Any topic. Just ask," Kinsear said. "I do better with coffee, though. Hang on, I'm pouring a cup."

She heard the sound of coffee flowing into his cup and looked at her own empty mug.

"There's a coffee snake…I mean, a coral snake, under the old breakfront in the living room, by the front door."

"Well, put your boots on!"

"I did. I've got it blocked under there. Who should I call to get it out?"

"I like the way you're thinking. I'd subcontract that job. You could call the sheriff's department? They'll know who can handle it. But if you'll wait for me, I'll pick up a snake trap and come on over. I could be there in less than an hour."

"Excellent," Alice said. She paused for effect. "You can help identify the footprint inside my front door."

Silence. "Inside?" She almost heard him thinking. "You're saying someone stepped in and dumped a coral snake?"

"I think so." Alice told him about waking up early, feeling some sound had roused her, but finding nothing amiss. "All the doors were still locked, but…when the sun came up I could see this one footprint."

"I knew I should have stayed with you last night," Kinsear said in disgust. "I knew it."

"Did the bull behave?" she asked.

"Non sequitur. Don't distract me. He was very gentlemanly. Okay, Alice. I'll be there pretty quick."

He hung up. Alice stared through the glass vases along the base of the breakfront. No gold flash currently visible. Just a silent pile of gems. Onyx, ruby, topaz, not moving. She found her phone and crouched over the footprint. She hadn't seen one quite like it: a fine herringbone pattern, with a distinctive wave-like design incised into the sole across the heel. She took pictures from different angles, then turned an empty plastic laundry tub over the footprint. But what if she dislodged the laundry tub and smeared the footprint? She cast her eye around, grabbed the tallest books from the bookcase, propped them all around the upturned lip of the laundry tub.

Then she felt blank, numb, like her brain was malfunctioning.

How about more coffee?

*****

When Kinsear stalked down the stone steps into her fenced yard, carrying a snake trap, he offered no smile, no kiss. He was all business, demanding first to see the snake's location and the footprint. Alice closed the rusty wrought-iron gate behind him and led him around the deck to the sliding doors to the kitchen, and then back to the entry door. "So we won't mess up the footprint," she said over her shoulder.

As he followed her he began laughing.

"Nightgown, robe, and boots. Great outfit. You know what I'm gonna get for you? One of those bumper stickers that reads 'Texas women kill their own snakes.'"

Alice grinned. "Red's got one." Her friend Red indeed sported one on the bumper of her red truck. "But I don't kill coral snakes. I, um, relocate them. Rattlers, that would be a different matter."

Kinsear took his time looking at the coral snake, then gently lifted the books off the laundry tub and placed the tub carefully behind him. "I'd say size 12 running or sport shoe, maybe a pretty fancy one," he said. "Looks like Snake Man stepped inside with his right foot—see this mud here?" (pointing to the doormat) "—then turned slightly to his right while planting his left foot here" (pointing to the footprint on the tile), "then leaned forward and let the snake out?"

The two heads, bent toward the floor, considered Kinsear's analysis. "Sounds right," Alice said.

Kinsear replaced the laundry tub over the print, then glanced toward the kitchen. "You have any coffee?"

She nodded. Why hadn't she already offered? Where was her brain? She stared out the front door. Something about the gate…

"Ben…" she said. "I just realized. The gate was open when you got here."

"Yes," he said. "Did you close it last night?"

"Of course," she said. "I always do. Otherwise the damn donkeys get in the yard and munch my roses."

He looked at her again.

"You mean…whoever it was opened the gate, then got your door unlocked, and then didn't close your gate?"

She nodded. "I think what woke me up was the gate. You know how it squeaks? But whoever it was never closed it."

"Precisely because he'd figured out it squeaks."

She shivered. "Somehow that's even scarier."

Then she was in his arms, clutching the canvas ranch coat he wore, burying her face in his flannel shirt.

"You call the sheriff yet?" he asked.

"No." She nodded, slowly. "Yeah, I should. But I wanted to get the snake dealt with first."

"I'm only mildly flattered, Alice, that you called me as your preferred snake retriever."

"I'm sure you're much more attractive than whoever Parks and Wildlife might have sent."

"I'm mad at myself for not being here last night." He breathed into her hair. "Should we go ahead and trap the snake or wait for the sheriff? Do you want to point at it in situ, for evidence?"

"Well, we've got the footprint, don't we? And what if that snake gets loose?"

He pointed to the landline. "Call the sheriff about the break-in. Ask if they want the snake as evidence."

She did.

"Just stay far away from the snake, and we'll be there, ma'am," said the disembodied voice at the sheriff's department. "Don't try to move it."

Alice went to change. No way was she reporting to the sheriff in her nightie.

Two hours later, she'd given her statement to a deputy, watched the deft removal of the coral snake, watched the crime scene operators measure and document the footprint including sampling some of the mud, and told them she had not seen the intruder, and could not say who the intruder was.

But she had a possible candidate.

C h a p t e r   T h i r t y - O n e

Uh-oh!

"Uh-oh!" Silla called from the workroom. She materialized in Alice's doorway, waving a legal-sized envelope and some papers. "This just came. Here's your copy. Hope you didn't have anything scheduled for Monday."

Alice looked at the transmittal letter: Craft's response to Ham and Julie's lawsuit, with Motion for Temporary Restraining Order; Motion for Protective Order; Motion to Dismiss, etc.

Alice flipped the pages, scanning. Craft's lawyers wanted her at the courthouse at ten a.m. Monday for a temporary restraining order hearing, a TRO. They'd asked the judge to require Alice's clients to stop harassing Mr. Craft and to declare void the covenants against his trailers. They also wanted a protective order against having to answer Alice's discovery requests.

"We need to send this to our clients."

"Already did!" Silla said.

Alice called Julie, told her about the hearing Monday, and said, "We'll have to be ready. I'll want you there. Sorry, but he's making you spend some money." Julie asked what Alice thought. "I don't think the court will be impressed," Alice said. "This makes Craft look like…the kind of neighbor you don't want."

"Go ahead," Julie said. "We'll be there."

Alice called Isabel and explained the TRO process. "Can you help us get ready? Like tomorrow or Sunday afternoon?"

Isabel paused. "I've got to write a paper tomorrow, but I'm all yours on Sunday."

"Deal."

*****

All hands on board. Three o'clock on a soggy Sunday afternoon. "Whew! I think we're done," Alice said to Isabel and Silla. "Did we miss anything?"

On the conference room table lay Alice's response to Craft's motion for a TRO, including Julie's photos of the trailers. Silla had already emailed Craft's lawyers a copy and had the original ready to file with the court clerk first thing Monday. Silla patted the stack of hearing exhibits, safely in their folders. Isabel had assembled Alice's trial note-book, her security blanket for court.

"Strong work, Isabel!" Alice said after leafing through the note-book. Isabel had sat in while Alice talked with Ham and Julie about their testimony in case Alice had to call them as witnesses. Isabel had then drafted questions for the clients.

Isabel surprised Alice. "Um, could I…how about if I come to the courthouse with you tomorrow morning? I could help with the documents. Or whatever you need."

"What about your classes at UT?" The last thing Alice wanted was for Isabel's "internship" with Alice to hurt her classwork.

"My big paper's finished, and I don't have any classes until Monday afternoon."

Alice studied the young face. "Okay. But if the court docket's too long and we get bumped to the afternoon, you'll have to head to Austin."

"No problem."

The conference room lit up with a blue-white flash, followed by an enormous crash of thunder.

"That was close!" Silla said.

Rain pelted down, battering the conference room windows. The backyard pecan tree thrashed, sending late leaves across the grass.

Silla thumbed her phone. "Whooee! We're under a storm warning. Look at this radar."

Alice and Isabel looked at the green and orange and red blobs on Silla's phone. Silla put the radar map in motion.

"Gosh, that's enormous!" Alice said. The storm path on the radar map showed heavy rain stretching from Corpus Christi on the Gulf Coast north toward Austin, with the heaviest rain heading directly to-ward Coffee Creek.

"We'd already got three inches when I came in this morning," Silla said. "The ground can't soak up much more."

Alice looked at Isabel. "You'd better get moving. Don't drive over any low-water bridges either."

Isabel grabbed her raincoat and bag. "See you tomorrow!"

Alice loaded the cumbersome trial briefcase with her trial notebook and exhibits. "Taking these home to study. Listen, Silla, thanks for spending your Sunday at the office."

"Hey, you be careful out there. You don't have any low-water crossings to worry about, do you?"

"No," Alice said. "Unless the water along the creek road gets out of its banks."

* * * * *

Just as she left Kinsear called to announce he was bringing oysters and boudin sausage to grill.

"The forecast's dreadful," Alice said. "What if we can't grill?"

"Stop by the grocery on the way home and grab some filé powder, would you? And fresh thyme and some okra? If we can't grill we'll make jambalaya. Then, *ma chère, ma douce,* we can *laisser les bons temps rouler,* etcetera!"

His "etcetera" sounded even better than oysters and boudin to Alice. So, yes, despite the rain, she'd stopped for Kinsear's grocery list. The parking lot bustled. She grabbed the last basket, and ran into her friend Miranda. Her cart held beer, wine, and bottled water. "Gotta stock up," she said. "My friends from Corpus are heading up here to stay with me. They said Corpus is about to get hit by a hundred-year storm. No telling what we'll get here."

Alice picked up extra charcoal and candles—the shelves were emptying fast—and sat in line to put gas in the car. But she didn't plan to travel; she planned to stay warm and cozy with Kinsear.

He had the touch, the gift to make her laugh, relax, misbehave. Thinking of *les bons temps*, and the etcetera, she found Beausoleil on the car radio, sang along to the irresistible zydeco beat. Michel Doucet's fiddle, she found, made her accelerate. She tapped the brakes trying not to hydroplane on the accumulated sheets of water covering the winding road. When she finally turned onto the sodden caliche road leading to her gate she had to slow to a crawl.

Kinsear's Land Cruiser rolled in just as she finished unloading groceries. Alice felt a strange sensation—as if her heart had relaxed. She looked up at him as rain bounced loudly on the carport's tin roof.

"What's that smile about?" he asked.

"I'm just thinking how extremely glad I am to have you here before this storm hits!"

"That's because I'm going to help you get the porch furniture stashed," he said. "Come on, the wind's really starting to gust."

She and Kinsear lugged the porch furniture into a corner, secured anything that might blow away, carried in the outdoor pillows, brought in boxes of bottled water. She lit some candles. "Just in case the power goes," she said.

Kinsear waggled his eyebrows. "Okay, let's get down to business about this storm."

"Isn't that what we've been doing?" Alice asked.

"Think, Alice! What's the very first order of business for tomorrow morning? It is to grind coffee. If the power goes out tonight I don't want to be freezing in your kitchen in my pajamas, if any, mashing coffee beans with a mortar and pestle. We can always boil water on the grill if we have to. Where's that grinder?"

Alice felt warm all over, thinking about the hours ahead, alone with Kinsear.

His cell phone dinged. "That's Isabel," he said. "Hey, honey. Where are you?"

"On her way back to Austin, I think," Alice mouthed.

He listened to the phone, then frowned. "You can't drive out to Fredericksburg tonight! The low-water crossings are already flooded!"

He listened again, then said, "Hold on. No, hold on. Listen to me! You can't get there! The ranch has already had nearly eight inches. You'll never make it across the low-water dam. Hear me?"

He paused, listening. "You're closer to Alice's than the ranch. Turn around and come straight here. You don't have to cross any low-water bridge to get to Alice's. You can leave in the morning." He paused again. Alice could hear Isabel's high voice coming from his phone.

"Plenty of room," he said. "Your own bathroom." Pause. "You've got no choice. Come on, sweetie. I don't want to hear you've drowned somewhere. No, seriously." Pause. "Isabel, we're having oysters. Barbecued. And boudin." Pause. "Yes, you can have chimichurri sauce on yours. Okay. See you soon."

The etcetera would have to wait. Kinsear looked at Alice, eyebrows asking if he'd done right. She nodded. "Of course." Holy cow! Isabel would be under her roof? With her dad here?

*****

Her own phone rang. George Files, on a stormy Sunday afternoon?

"I didn't think this should wait until Monday," he said. "Two interesting developments. First, on our dead writer, Holly Dougal. The techie people have confirmed what I told you: the fraudulent email did indeed come from Brad Gorman's email account. He acts mystified, keeps swearing he never heard anything, never knew anything about Holly's business, much less any Cayman's account. But his iPad says different. Just in case, the techies are checking to see if he was hacked."

Gorman? Seriously? Alice shook her head. She still couldn't see the connection to Holly.

"Second, about Elena Ramos," Files said, "the young woman found under your fence." Alice shook her head, hating the way he'd said that. "You were right about the cloud. I—we took you up on that issue of whether she'd used her phone. I—we talked to Mia and found Elena's account. Elena was using an app, keeping notes there. She also saved some voice memos. They stop the afternoon before you found her."

"Where was she when she was making those notes?" Alice broke in. "Can you tell?"

"Techies are working on that. Looks like she was no more than twenty minutes from that shopping center she mentioned to Mia, the one where she expected to be picked up."

"What did she say? What was she doing?" Alice said. Then, "George, can you talk louder? The rain is hitting the roof so hard it sounds like a jackhammer."

"We'll get a transcript, but here's what I've got in my notes." He was almost shouting. "She says she and five other women and six men were picked up in two SUVs. After they were picked up they had to wear hoods with no eyeholes. Here she put an exclamation point in her notes. They were driven to a location where they were locked in a trailer. She says she could hear water outside. She thinks it took about twenty minutes to get from the shopping center on Highway 290 to the trailer location, but she has no idea where the trailer is. She says the men were put in a different trailer. The women and the men were driven in two separate SUVs to work wedding venues on Friday and Saturday and to clean up the same venues on Sunday afternoon. She's hiding her phone in her underwear. Phones are forbidden."

Two trailers…

"The last thing she says, Alice, is that she thinks Monday is the day she and the other the women will be driven out toward El Paso, supposedly so they can get permanent jobs in the U.S. Then Elena switches from notes to a quick voice memo. She says she's going to try to escape before they get taken anywhere else. She says something garbled then—the voice memo's messed up—something about a cat. A *gato*. And a bad dog. *Perro malo*." Pause. "That's it."

"Sounds like she was scared."

"Yeah."

"I knew Eads wouldn't look," Alice said.

Files didn't respond.

"But thank goodness you did," Alice went on. "I'd like to see the transcripts." Silence: no promise from Files. "But the issue is, where was Elena? Can't you pinpoint her from a cell tower?"

"We're trying."

"But George," she exclaimed, heart pounding. "George, a place with two trailers—I think I know the place! It's just upstream from me. There are two trailers on Waterfall Road, the south side!"

Silence for a moment. "I can't get there," Files said, at last. "Just checked. That low-water bridge is closed."

"It's Sunday night! There may still be people in those trailers! Locked in!" she cried.

"Alice, I'll try to get someone there as soon as I can, but it's bad right now. I've got no one to send and don't know how they'd get there. We're stretched thin—emergencies all over the county, wrecks, water rescues. We'd need a chopper to get to Waterfall Road, and the only one we have is in the air taking an emergency case to Brackenridge Hospital in Austin. The low-water bridge is the only way in to Waterfall Road, right?"

"Right," she said.

"If I find a warm body I'll try to get someone out there. But listen, don't do anything crazy. You need to stay safe. We're in for a bad night. I've got to go." He hung up.

She looked for Kinsear, then heard voices at her front door. Isabel came into the kitchen, carrying her backpack. She and Alice stared at each other for a moment, then both broke into giggles. Kinsear looked from one to the other.

"Sitcom land," Isabel burst out, laughing.

"Yup," said Alice.

Kinsear rolled his eyes. "Don't mind me. I'm just the...uh...father? No, wait...widower dad? No, let's see, I'm being played by Brad Pitt, I believe. The irresistible...um...hero?"

Rain thundered on Alice's metal roof. Water sluiced off the gutters.

Alice sobered up and told them what she'd learned from Files. "He says the county responders are jammed. But there may be people locked in those trailers, like Elena was."

"How bad is the creek?" Kinsear asked.

They grabbed umbrellas and walked out on the deck. The roar of water deafened them. The creek, a foamy mass the color of café au lait, had already covered Alice's landing.

"You can actually see it rising as we stand here," he said.

Across the creek a sycamore, uprooted by rising water, crashed into the creek and disappeared downstream.

A child's pink innertube sped by.

Alice stared down at this vast brown creature, the once peaceful creek. The noise was overpowering. In her mind, she saw the view from her neighbor's stairs up the bluff: the Hermit's stone wall, iron gates, the trailers sitting on cinder blocks.

With locked doors. With barred windows.

"We've got to get them out," she said. "If we go right now we can shelter at Ham and Julie's if the water gets too high."

"I'll get tools." Kinsear left for his Land Cruiser.

"What about a rope?" Isabel called after him.

Alice phoned Ham and Julie to explain. They were only a quarter mile away, but she had to yell over the static. Yes, they said, they'd carry a ladder to the wall.

Kinsear was back carrying a tire iron, some rope, some carabiners, and a massive bolt cutter.

"You've got a bolt cutter? In your car?"

"As one does. Don't you?" He turned to Isabel. "You stay here. We'll be back."

"Nope," she said. "You need three. Including a translator."

"But—"

"There's no time to argue. Let's go," she said.

C h a p t e r   T h i r t y - T w o

Vamonos!

The sky was almost dark. Alice grabbed flashlights for all. They pulled on slickers and boots and began picking their way down the bluff, on the slick wet stairs below the house, toward Alice's landing, now half a foot under water. Lightning lit the sky; thunder rumbled. Occasionally the roar increased as a bank broke loose, a tree let go, and the water rose higher.

Kinsear lashed one end of the rope to the last big tree above the landing. He tied a shorter piece of rope around Alice's waist and knotted one end to a carabiner. He did the same for Isabel. "You two need to hook the carabiners on the rope before you start across," he warned.

He started down into the water, paying out the rope. Alice watched the water swirl above his knees. When he reached the other bank, he wound the rope around an oak on the other side, tugging at the knots to be sure they would hold. Alice, then Isabel, inched down the bank into the swirling brown water, each holding to the main rope. "Attach those carabiners! Hold tight!" yelled Kinsear. "Plant your feet!"

Water filled Alice's boots, then rose well above her knees and higher. The force of the water on her body astounded her. She clung to the rope, moving hand over hand, and kept both feet on the rocky stream bottom, shuffling her boots along. She was sure that if she raised her foot the water would grab her. She was nearly to Kinsear. Finally, he caught her hand and hauled her up onto the muddy bank.

Isabel was right behind Alice. Kinsear hovered, ready to grab her. "I got it, Dad!" she said, reaching the bank. She unclipped the carabiner, untied the rope around her waist, pulled her boots off, emptied them, and stomped them back onto her feet.

Alice pointed upstream, yelling into the wind. "We get to my fence, then cross the next lot, then we're at Ham and Julie's."

Kinsear turned. "Look at that." Broken planks careened down the creek. Brown froth blew off the water. The wind, blowing straight downstream from the west, rose to a dull roar. Alice heard something else.

"Holy cow!"

A wave, a tidal wave, rose upstream, at least a foot above the rushing water.

"Must have been a rain bomb, up one of those feeder creeks!"

Kinsear yelled. "Come on! Let's move!"

Blinded by rain, wind full in their faces, the three stumbled toward Alice's fence line. They moved farther inland as water licked higher and higher up the banks. The rattle of rain on their slickers with the wind and the roaring water made speech difficult.

Alice pointed. "My fence!" She could barely hear herself.

She held apart the strands of barbed wire while Kinsear, then Isabel, crawled through. Kinsear helped Alice through.

She pointed down the fence line toward the creek. "That's where we found Elena."

They staggered across the vacant property, then through the barbed wire fence that bounded Ham and Julie's pasture. Alice fumbled for her phone, tried to keep it dry beneath her hood, called Julie. "It's Alice!"

"Where are you?"

"In your pasture. Can you meet us by the stone wall?"

"What?" Julie yelled.

"By the Hermit's wall!" Alice shouted. "We're almost there!"

The Hermit had built his stone wall a foot from Ham's barbed wire fence, making a sort of no-man's land between his property and Ham and Julie's. Through the rain they saw Ham and Julie, staggering down the pasture carrying two sections of an extension ladder.

"We need a ladder on each side!" Julie said, setting up one piece of the ladder by the stone wall. "The pecan tree they cut down was on the other side, about here."

The creek was now about forty feet away. Water had already reached the section of stone wall the Hermit had built along the creek. Alice began to wonder how long that wall could withstand the water.

Ham held the ladder while Kinsear climbed up and sat astride the top of the wall. The ladder's feet sank into the mud. Panting, Ham hoisted the second extension of the ladder up to Kinsear, who pulled it up and over, and, leaning sideways, planted it on the other side of the wall. He turned back to face them. "The water's coming up through the gate," he yelled. "I don't think that trailer's tied down very well. Can you pass me the bolt cutter? And the tire iron?" He peered behind him, then turned back around. "Water's coming up fast. After Alice gets down, let's move both these ladders about ten feet farther uphill, or we'll lose them in the water."

Ham held the ladder while Alice climbed up with both tools. She stood on the top rung while Kinsear climbed backward down the second ladder. He held the second ladder while Alice crawled over the top and got her feet planted. She passed the tools down, one at a time, and cautiously descended the wet rungs of the ladder, clinging tight to the sides.

Alice watched as Ham, on one side, and Kinsear, on the other, tugged the two ladders out of the mud and planted them farther up the wall. She looked uphill toward the second trailer. Beyond sat the Craft garage wing. Between the garage and the house, a tall safety lamp lit the asphalt drive and a black SUV sitting there. She blinked rainwater from her eyes and squinted at the license plate: "MYWAY."

She could see the second story of the house above the fence that divided the trailer property from the Hermit's elegant back yard. No face in any window. Was no one watching the creek? The rising water? The trailers?

Were they empty?

Isabel's face appeared at the top of the wall, and down she climbed, splashing into the rising water.

Kinsear reached the door of the trailer. Rain pouring down his face, he angled the bolt-cutter into the padlock on the door. The wet bolt-cutter slipped several times before, with a loud crack, the lock broke open. Kinsear pocketed it. Then he pushed open the door, calling *"Hola!"*

A frightened woman peered out. Other faces crowded around her.

"Hurry!" called Kinsear. "We need to go! *Vamonos!*"

They stood frozen.

Isabel splashed up to the door. "*Somos amigos!* Friends!" In rapid Spanish she explained, as best Alice could tell, that the water was rising and they had to escape. The women disappeared, trying to grab their belongings.

The water had other plans. With a groan and a thump, the downhill corner of the trailer closest to the door slipped off the two cinder blocks that propped it up. Alice heard women screaming inside. Another wave of water hit the rear of the trailer. The long white metal oblong toppled slowly over onto its front. The door was pinned underneath.

Desperate, Alice grabbed the ladder from the wall and propped it on the trailer. Kinsear scrambled up. "Tire iron!" he yelled. She passed it up, then followed him onto the side—now the top—of the trailer. Both tried not to slip on the treacherous wet metal siding.

Kinsear pried at the bars on the window that now faced the sky. Frightened faces watched from inside the trailer. One bar was free, but water was shifting the trailer. Alice crouched, holding the folds in the siding. Isabel climbed the ladder and crawled quickly to the window. "Wait, Dad!" She yelled in Spanish to the women staring up through the window, who nodded and moved back, covering their eyes. Isabel yelled, "Now!" Kinsear broke the window with the tire iron and pried up the last two bars.

The women below lifted and pushed up the first of their group to emerge. Alice and Kinsear pulled her through the window. Isabel helped her down the ladder and pointed to the wall. Five more women squeezed through the window and then down the ladder. Alice and Kinsear climbed down and returned the ladder to the wall. "*Son todas?* Everyone?" Isabel asked.

"*Sí. Pero los hombres!*" They pointed uphill at the men's trailer.

Kinsear was already halfway there with Alice. At least this trailer was not yet in the water.

"Señor! Sir!" A short, dark-haired middle-aged woman wearing a uniform and an apron trotted downhill from Craft's parking area, waving at them. She stopped to catch her breath, then held her hand out to Kinsear. "Hurry!" she said, wiping rain from her face. "Mr. Craft will kill me if he knows I brought you the key."

"Are you the cook?" Alice asked. The woman nodded. "What's your name?"

Kinsear had the key in the lock.

"Rosa Saenz. Hurry, please! I have to take it back before he knows!"

Kinsear pulled open the door and thrust the key at the cook. "Thank you!" he said. She ran back uphill toward the house.

Soon six men were stumbling through the water toward the ladder, with Isabel issuing a patter of explanations in her swift Spanish.

Alice looked at the first trailer, now partially afloat as the brown water rose higher. She got out her phone and took pictures of the scene: the trailer floating sideways in flood water, the other trailer, the men climbing up the ladder and over the wall, and, finally, Kinsear holding up the padlocks and the bolt cutter and tire iron. In the darkness she had to use her flash: night was falling.

She considered adding Kinsear to her witness list.

She looked back uphill. Yes, indeed, the first day he invaded Alice's office, Gorman was driving that black Jeep. Why was it parked at Craft's? Why had Gorman hidden out at the Wine 100 with a cheapo rental? Where was the Hermit? Where was Narcissus?

"Alice! For the Lord's sake! Hurry up!"

She turned. Kinsear, atop the wall, yelled at her to get to the ladder. "Watch out! The trailer's moving!"

Alice scrambled to the top of the ladder and looked back. She heard, rather than saw, a roaring mass of water hit the Hermit's stone wall along the creek. Like a slow-moving trail of dominos, the wall collapsed, causing the central fence between the trailer lot and the Hermit's private yard to fall slowly to the ground.

As Alice watched, hypnotized, the onrushing water lifted the women's trailer which slowly revolved, heading toward the stone wall she sat on.

Alice pulled up the ladder, flung it to Ham and Julie's side, and scrambled down the other ladder. She, Kinsear, Ham, Julie, Isabel, and twelve men and women raced uphill as the waterborne trailer hit the stone wall and brought it tumbling down in a long, slow, rumbling crash. Like the walls of Jericho.

Chapter Thirty-Three

What Do We Do Now?

H am, Julie, Alice, Kinsear, and Isabel, trailed by twelve silent men and women, climbed the hill and past the front of the house, with its deck facing the roaring creek, to the covered back porch by the driveway. All seventeen removed their muddy footwear and stepped into the kitchen. Ham and Julie's children, ten-year-old Beth and eight-year-old Sam, stared wide-eyed at the visitors.

The twelve huddled together, faces uncertain. Julie welcomed them, indicated the supper waiting on the kitchen counter, pointed down the hallway toward the bathrooms, and then to the adjacent dining room. A slim man with a lined face and intelligent eyes—wary eyes—stepped forward and nodded to Ham and Julie. Alice judged him to be over forty. "*Gracias. Muchas gracias.*" He must be the informal *jefe*, the leader. A quiet chorus of "*Sí, gracias!*" followed from bowed heads, lowered eyes.

Covertly scanning the group, Alice realized that except for the man who'd first spoken, the visitors looked to be in their twenties. Even in their current state, tired faces, somber eyes, all were attractive—pretty girls, handsome boys. She'd worried about panicked parents with children trapped in the trailers, but this group included no children.

Julie had left Beth and Sam with instructions to create a big hot supper as fast as they could. They'd raided Julie's emergency food stash and filled her biggest pot with canned ranchero beans, the 52-ounce size. Alice had never seen cans that big. The pot simmered, filling the air with the aromas of chili and cumin. The kids sprinkled grated cheese and jalapeño slices on cookie sheets spread with tortilla chips. "Nachos, Mom!" said Beth. She pointed proudly to the kitchen counter, with opened packs of more tortilla chips and jars of salsa, and with paper plates and napkins, forks and spoons.

Ham and Kinsear scoured the house and brought more chairs to the six already at the dining room table. Julie filled and passed out plates and pointed the visitors toward the dining room. They sat, visibly uncomfortable, glancing at each other.

Julie, standing in the doorway with Alice, took charge. "*Para ustedes!*" she said, smiling and gesturing at the plates before them. "For you!" A soft buzz of Spanish filled the dining room, followed by the silence of the hungry.

"I don't think those folks have eaten all day," Julie said, turning back into the kitchen.

"Maybe two days," Ham said.

Alice barely heard them. She had other things on her mind. "Isabel," she said softly, "could you ask a couple of questions?" She needed Isabel's fearless fluency.

"Wait a sec." Isabel pulled out her phone. "Okay, ready."

"Can you ask about this *'El Gato'* and the *'malo perro'* that one of them mentioned? Where is he? And his dog?" Alice was mystified why Narcissus—she thought, given the "bad dog" reference, that he could be "El Gato"—hadn't charged downhill to stop them from finding what was in the trailers.

Isabel tapped notes into the phone.

"Also, do they know anything about Elena, the young woman who was shot? Of course, they may not have heard her name."

"Sure."

"Plus, did they ever see Richard Craft, the guy who owns the place? What's he like? Who else works there? We know there are two SUVs; who's the other driver? Besides the cook we saw, does Craft have a housekeeper? Or a nurse?"

"What about where and how they got picked up in the first place?" Kinsear suggested.

Alice nodded. This didn't appear to be a random group of asylum seekers; they were too similar in age and attractiveness. Preselected and prepackaged for…party work?

"No problem," Isabel said. "I'll also ask where these guys were taken to work and for how long. And whether they've been paid. Joke, I'll bet." Isabel grabbed another chair and dragged it next to the *jefe*. Peeking from the kitchen, Alice watched Isabel smile at him, her eyes intent on his face. Soon they were in deep conversation. Periodically he raised his head, asked the group a question, then turned again to Isabel.

Alice noted the other eleven kept their heads down, glancing at each other below lowered eyelids, giving monosyllabic answers to the spokesman. They were probably scared to death. With a shock she realized that their visitors might still feel like captives, might think they'd escaped from one trap merely to be placed under new management.

Julie made coffee and put mugs and cream and sugar on a tray. "Let's go into the living room. Ham's building a fire in the fireplace."

The crackling fire, with the tang of cedar smoke, created such a sense of warmth and comfort that when Alice and Kinsear sank together onto the couch they sighed in unison.

"I'm whipped," Kinsear admitted.

"Me too," Ham sighed.

"It's hard work, wrestling ladders, climbing on trailers and banging in the windows, and hauling people up," Alice said.

"But what happens next?" Julie had a worried frown on her face.

"Yeah, what do we do now?" Ham asked.

Silence. They looked at one another.

Alice debated whether they should call the sheriff. She wanted law enforcement to see the wealthy Craft's vicious economic swindle, his jake-leg trailers and cold-eyed enforcers. For the twelve, though, wouldn't it mean the end of the road? Jail? Detention facilities? Deportation?

For her or Kinsear or Ham or Julie to drive the group somewhere else offered no solution, no sanctuary. Where? Back to the border? Into El Paso, Sonora, Amarillo, to try to disappear into the crowds and find work?

Isabel joined them. "Here's the scoop," she said. "They only got here a few days ago. You're right"—she nodded at Kinsear—"a man they've never seen again picked them out down at the border, where a coyote brought them from Ciudad Acuña. That man drove them up here crammed in a horse trailer, dropped them off at a storefront on the highway. That's where the two SUVs picked them up. Since then, they've worked a big rehearsal party Friday night, the wedding on Saturday, and then cleanup this morning. Zero pay. They were promised that tomorrow they'd be driven out to El Paso for paying jobs."

Ham raised an eyebrow. "More likely dumped somewhere in the desert to die."

Isabel went on: "About Elena. They weren't here, of course, but one of the SUV drivers threatened them. 'You try to run, you die. El Gato will take care of you like he did that girl last week. Yeah, he shot her. No second chance. Hear me?'"

Kinsear broke in. "Where is this second guy?"

"He left. Hours ago. In one of the SUVs."

"And El Gato?" asked Alice.

Isabel shook her head. "They saw him this afternoon, out the little trailer window. Then—no more."

"Damn," said Kinsear. "I kinda wanted to have a little talk with El Gato."

Isabel looked at her dad, then Ham and Julie, then Alice. "So, what's the plan?"

"We're just trying to figure that out," Alice said.

A log fell in the fireplace, wood crackling, sparks flying, followed by silence. Alice realized she heard no soft whispers from the dining room. She rose from the couch just as the *jefe* appeared in the living room doorway, holding his muddy shoes.

"Gracias, señores, señoras, señorita," he said. *"Hasta luego."* He gave them a little smile, then disappeared back down the hallway and into the kitchen. Alice hurried after him, glancing into the dining room on her way. Empty plates, empty chairs. The *jefe* finished tying his second shoe, nodded at Alice, opened the back door and left.

Alice, followed by Isabel and Kinsear, then Ham and Julie, crowded outside onto the back porch. Ham and Julie's two kids stole out to join them. The rain had changed to a persistent light sprinkle; the sky was dark, thick, and damp. Was the creek's roar just a little softer? They caught a last glimpse of the *jefe* before he vanished east, into the darkness. Faintly in the distance they glimpsed movement as he joined the others.

Julie burst into tears. Ham put his arm around her shoulder. The kids hugged her.

"They are so courteous. They have nothing, nowhere to go, but they've taken any responsibility off our shoulders," Julie sobbed. "They just made their own decision. They didn't saddle us with it."

Isabel, face stark, looked into the darkness. "Where'd they go?"

Ham said, "They're probably already through the fence and heading across the old Calico ranch. What's left of it runs all the way to the creek road." He stopped, pursed his mouth. "We lost a baby goat last week. I don't know what kind of predator got it. Anyway, with twelve of them, if they stick together they should be okay."

Kinsear added, "If they get to the creek road, they could try to make Highway 290, then the interstate. Maybe get to Sonora or El Paso. Or they could try their luck going north, up Highway 281 toward Abilene or Amarillo. And then who knows? New Mexico? Colorado?"

"Or dry up in the desert," Isabel interjected. "No money, no map, no water, no food, no nothing."

Julie groped for a tissue, wiped her eyes, blew her nose. "What a world."

"I gave the *jefe* my card," Isabel said.

"Card?" said Kinsear, startled.

"I'll show you one, Dad. Just my name and contact info."

O Lord! Wait until ICE sees that.

She remembered she still had a hearing in the morning. How would she get there? "Let's go look at the creek," she said.

They walked around the house and downhill to the muddy banks. Light misty rain was still falling. In the darkness white-capped waves rolled downstream. Behind the continual roar of unleashed waters, they heard the crash of branches hitting rocks, hitting banks.

"It's gone down a bit, but no way can we get back across tonight," Kinsear said.

"We've got twin beds in the guestroom," Julie said.

Kinsear sighed. "I'll take the couch."

No grilled boudin tonight, and no etcetera, Alice concluded.

"Let's finish the beans and nachos," Ham said. "And a beer or two."

*****

Before slipping into a solitary twin bed, with Isabel across the room looking at her phone, Alice sent Silla copies of the pictures she'd taken: the women's trailer on its side, the men exiting the uphill trailer, flood waters everywhere. She drafted a terse amendment to her response to Craft's motion to dismiss. She wanted the judge to know, even before the hearing began, that this case no longer involved a minimal violation of covenants. Craft hadn't just brought in trailers; he was running a business onsite, further violating the covenants. Not only that, his "business" constituted illegal trafficking in undocumented people, whom he'd left to die in the floods.

She emailed Silla: "First thing tomorrow, file this amendment, with the pictures as exhibits. When I get in I'll sign an affidavit about taking those pictures. Then we need deposition notices for Craft, his nurse, and Standifer Sechrest, also known as El Gato. Let's serve the papers on Craft's lawyers as soon as possible. If we can cross the low-water bridge I'll get to that hearing."

Maybe if she couldn't cross the bridge Ham would let her borrow his truck to cross the Calico ranch.

*****

Alice tossed and turned all night. Just at midnight both kids texted: "Mama! We saw about the flood! Are you all right?" "Everything's fine," she texted back. "Talk later. Love you!"

With the sky beginning to lighten she gave up on sleep and by five thirty was outside in her muddy clothes, sucking down coffee, watching the creek. As the sun came up, turning the sky blue, she heard tires on the driveway and turned to see Ham's truck.

"I went down to check out the low-water bridge," he said. "It's going down pretty fast now that it's quit raining, but it's still too high to cross. I talked to a county employee on the other side of the bridge, putting up more barricades. He heard some fool tried to cross it yesterday and didn't make it."

Julie came outside, followed by Kinsear, clutching his coffee cup. "Ham?" she said. "Ed Fischer just called. He said to come up to their house. They think they see a truck in the water."

The Fischers lived just beyond Craft's place.

"Well, let's go," Ham said. Kinsear and Alice hurried to the truck.

Ed Fischer stood in front of his house twenty feet from the water. He shook hands with Ham, said, "Glad to see my lawyer," to Alice, and was introduced to Kinsear.

He pointed, but there was no need. In mid-creek, one taillight angled up above the water. "I think the front of the truck must've hit a dip in the creek bed," he said. "I can't think anyone's still alive in there."

"What time did it leave the bridge?" Ham asked.

"Pretty sure it was late afternoon yesterday. There was at least a foot of water over the bridge by then and whoever it was moved the barricades and tried to gun it across the bridge." Fischer sighed. "Doesn't matter how many 'turn around, don't drown' signs you put up, some people are too dumb to live."

"Does the sheriff know?" Alice asked.

"Yes. They're trying to get a wrecker crew out here. The county's short on wreckers and winches at the moment, what with all the other idiots who wanted to see if their vehicle could waterski."

"I can't tell if that truck's black or dark blue," Alice said.

"We'll know soon." Ham glanced at the sky. The rain had stopped; the few clouds were a rosy apricot in the sunrise.

Alice's phone buzzed. Silla, already at the office. "I've got the amendment and deposition notices served on Mr. Craft's lawyers. They'd already left messages saying their client can't get to the hearing and they want an extension. When they read your amendment they'll call back with their hair on fire. Can I say 'their hair'? Is that proper English? You know they'll need time to respond."

"Tell them I'm planning to make the hearing, they don't need their client present to proceed, and I'll call them about an extension." Alice wanted to get the court's attention focused on Mr. Craft as soon as possible. Still, they were entitled to more time to respond to new allegations. She'd look better agreeing to an extension and could probably get a shorter response time that way.

She looked down at her muddy pants and boots. What the hell could she wear to a hearing? She kept a suit and shoes in a bag on the back of her office door. What about that route across the Calico ranch?

Just then a wrecker lurched slowly down the opposite bank, engine grinding, brake lights on, yellow lights flashing. A sheriff's department SUV followed. A brown-shirted deputy climbed out, waved at them. "You folks know anything about this truck? Is there anyone in there?"

"We don't know!" Ham yelled back. "I heard one went off the bridge late yesterday."

The deputy rubbed his eyes, heaved his shoulders. "I'd rather go after the live ones, but let's see what we got."

The wrecker driver, sturdy, balding, wearing waders, assessed the truck. "Looks stuck in a dip," he said. "It's gonna be hard to get the chain on the front. Let's try the back."

The deputy called across the creek, "Did anyone walk down to see if a body's downstream? Maybe caught in a tree snag?"

Ham and Kinsear and Alice looked at each other.

"Not yet," Ham called back.

The three looked at each other again, and without a word started downstream, walking ten feet apart along the creek bank. Alice took the uphill end, feeling a cloud of foreboding.

Chapter   Thirty - Four

Red in Tooth
and Claw

Alice's boots, still sodden from the day before, squelched with every step. She envied Ham's dry footwear as he made his way along the bank, scanning the opposite side of the creek. Kinsear helped her cross the collapsed barbed wire fence, now covered with branches and debris, that separated Ham and Julie's property from the section of Calico Ranch that lay between their place and Alice's.

"This brings back memories of the Wimberley flood," Kinsear said.

In May a few years earlier the Blanco River rose forty feet in an hour and a half, flooding the nearby town of Wimberley, sweeping away river houses, snapping age-old cypress trees. At least thirteen people died. The town of Coffee Creek had flooded too, but not like Wimberley. Alice had patrolled her own property, watching her creek rise higher than she'd ever seen it, leaving flood trash thirteen feet high in trees along the bank.

The three walked across the Calico property. "I wonder if our visitors took this path last night," Alice said.

"And whether they made it somewhere and picked up a ride," Kinsear said. "They seemed pretty resourceful. At least *el jefe* did."

He looked across the creek and farther downstream. "Hey, Alice, I see your stairs, going up the bluff across the creek. We must be almost to your fence."

"If it's still there." She knew where her fence should end, just above the creek. Instead, where her fence should be, the water had hurled a forest of tattered branches like Birnam Wood come to Dunsinane, and just as grim. The water-flung forest—cedar, sycamore, dried grass—had flattened her fence. One part of her brain calculated the cost: Tonio, new metal posts, barbed wire. Another part of her brain thought it might not be just branches caught in her fence.

Ham stopped at the water's edge. "Lord, look at the debris. Look how high up the bank the water came." He pointed to a clump of sycamores not far from the water. "Look at the trash caught in the branches."

Kinsear and Alice worked their way uphill. They'd almost reached the point where the tangled forest ended.

"Alice." Kinsear pointed. A pair of sneakered feet stuck out below the branches, splayed on the ground—bare white ankles, brown leather sneakers with white soles.

"Oh, man." Alice felt sick. Before her flashed Elena's lifeless body, caught under her fence, almost exactly where this new body lay.

A broken sycamore, the lower end of its trunk shattered, lay across where Alice thought the knees should be. Flood trash and branches obscured any view of a body. Traces of mud on the sneakers set into relief the herringbone pattern on the soles, with the incised wave close to the heel.

"Let's get around these branches," Kinsear said. At the high point of the debris pile—the point where the raging water dropped its cargo—they climbed across the downed fence. On this side of the pile they saw the head of a man pinioned beneath the broken sycamore tree. His upturned face formed a rictus of such horror as Alice had never seen.

"It's him," Alice whispered. "Narcissus." The body's pale eyes stared at heaven. "Oh God. What happened, to make his face like that?"

Kinsear shook his head. "Bad."

"Did you see the soles of his sneakers?" Alice asked.

"Same as your Snake Man, right? They're pretty distinctive. But what the hell did that?" he said, pointing at the deep jagged wound on the side of the man's neck. Kinsear stepped closer. Using a stick, he lifted part of the burden of branches atop the man. "Oh, Lord."

"What?" Alice asked.

He shook his head. "Come look. I don't want to mess up these branches too much."

She moved closer, peering through the leaves at the man's torso. "I've never…" Her stomach turned.

"Once, on a hunting lease in south Texas—" Kinsear paused, and his voice changed. "Look at the color of the dirt, Alice." She leaned over to look. The dirt around the body was maroon. The man had bled out.

Kinsear dropped the branches back. "On that hunting lease, we came across a big cat kill. The cat took down a deer, pulled out the stomach, ate the liver and heart, then buried the carcass in leaves and branches, like lunch for the next day. I wonder…"

Belatedly he and Alice looked at each other and then down at the mud and sand surrounding the pile of branches. Now they saw multiple prints: toes and pad but no visible claw marks. Carefully they stepped away.

"Mountain lion prints. Agreed?" Alice said, trying to stay calm. Her stomach was still heaving.

"I say yes," Kinsear said. "But this guy—Narcissus—you said he worked out all the time, right? He seemed like a cocky son of a bitch, at the restaurant. Strong, too. You'd try to fight, right?" He turned a quizzical face toward her.

"I'd sure try." But if the cat jumped you, bit your neck, what could you do?

Kinsear turned, put two fingers to his lips, and sent a sharp whistle upstream toward the deputy.

Ham joined them. They cautioned him about the footprints. Kinsear hefted the branches again. "Take a look."

Ham whistled. "What a way to go." He studied the face. "Listen, I'm almost positive that's the dog guy," he said. "The one with the black truck and the dog that scared my Sam. Of course, that day he had on a ballcap and a cocky expression. Looks like he lost them both."

Kinsear took another long look, then lowered the branches. Alice knew he was chewing over something. She waited.

"Did you look at his forearms, his hands?"

Ham and Alice both nodded. "Well, his right hand—his pinkie and ring finger are just stubs," Ham said. "Otherwise, I didn't see anything."

"That's the point," Kinsear said. "Why not?"

"Hey!" The three turned to face the deputy, huffing toward them across the Calico property.

*****

The deputy stared at the sneakers. "Found him?"

"Yes. Hey, your pants are dry. How'd you get across the creek?"

asked Ham.

"Drove a high-centered county truck over the bridge. The water's going down fast. Okay, lemme see what you got down here."

Alice watched as Kinsear and Ham pointed to the cat prints. "Don't step there," Kinsear advised. "Evidence." He and Ham used sticks to lift the lighter branches on top of the pile. They and the deputy stared at the body.

Alice was thinking about the sneakers. She heard Kinsear say, "You better ask her."

She found herself answering for the dead man.

Name? "Standifer Sechrest. Stage name, Stan Sechrest."

Job? "Former stuntman, now working for Richard Craft, owner of the place upstream with the two white trailers in the back."

Next of kin? "Sandra Sechrest. Here's her contact info." She pulled out her phone and sent the info to him. She was glad no one had asked her to call Sandra. She was still debating whether to tell the deputy what Isabel learned, that a fellow employee claimed Stan Sechrest had shot one of the trailer prisoners. She decided to wait for George Files.

The deputy turned away and called the sheriff's department. Alice heard "Crime scene?"

Her pocket buzzed: text from Silla: "Call Craft's lawyers! Here's # for Piers Wisenthorpe." Was that really his name? Alice looked down at her own muddy self and realized she needed to start hiking across Calico Ranch if she meant to make the hearing. But she had a better idea. She punched in his number.

"Piers Alan Wisenthorpe speaking."

Heavens, he uses all his syllables. "Hi, Alice Greer here. My secretary said you called about an extension on today's hearing?"

"Yes. I mean, your so-called amendment just arrived with these ridiculous allegations about Mr. Craft."

"They're hardly ridiculous. They're true. Your client's running an illegal business using undocumented people. He nearly killed a dozen he'd locked in illegal trailers right next to my clients' property."

"What possible proof can you have?" he scoffed.

"You mean, beyond five witnesses and pictures showing a harrowing rescue from your client's trailers during this flood?"

He blustered. "You're not giving the proper context."

"I'm eager for the judge to see these pictures and hear our witnesses," she said.

"How can you expect us to respond today?"

"You got my deposition notice for Craft and his employees?"

"Yes."

"Tell you what," Alice said. "If you'll present Craft for deposition this Thursday—that's plenty of time to prepare—we'll agree to postpone the hearing for fourteen days. Provided you request no further extensions. And provided you also present his cook, Rosa Saenz, for deposition on Thursday."

"That's not nearly enough time!"

"The sooner we get these depositions, the sooner you and I can resolve this little covenant dispute."

"But the cook? Why in the world do you want her?"

"She has knowledge of the trailers."

Silence while Wisenthorne weighed his options.

"Or I'll just head on into town," Alice said. "With my witnesses." Well, maybe.

"But I need to depose them too!"

"Here's what we'll do. I'll take Mr. Craft and Rosa Saenz this Thursday. Shouldn't take long. Then you can take my clients' depositions next week, assuming you still want to. I can't see why you would; we ought to settle this. But let me know now, because otherwise I'll head straight to the courthouse."

Wisenthorne protested, "My client can't come to the hearing! He can't cross the low-water bridge—it's flooded."

"Nor can I," Alice said, "since I'm practically next door, but I plan to show up for the hearing anyway. The judge'll get a kick out of my appearance, given how muddy we got rescuing the people trapped in your client's trailers. Unless we're agreed? Depositions on Thursday? Two-week hearing extension, but no more? I'll send a draft Rule 11 letter to confirm our agreement—good provided you agree within fifteen minutes. After that I'll be on my way in."

She heard a sulky "Hmmph." "Is that a yes?" she pressed.

"Yes."

She emailed him the Rule 11 letter. She could march into court and enforce a lawyers' Rule 11 agreement the same as a court order. Wisenthorpe had to deliver his client, Dickie Craft, for deposition. She could hardly wait to get Craft under oath.

By then she'd have George Files poking his nose into Craft's business, big time.

But first she wanted to confirm with Kinsear about Narcissus's hands.

Chapter Thirty - Five

They Disappeared

The creek was too high to wade across, so Ham drove Isabel, Kinsear, and Alice back to Alice's house. He slowed to a crawl, inching across the low-water bridge, through four inches of fast-moving muddy water. On the other side of the creek, the tow truck shuddered and strained, gears grinding, ready to pull the rear of a black pickup out of the creek.

Alice called George Files.

"I'm already on my way." He was hoarse. "Been up all night. I hear you found the guy you think might have shot Elena?"

"Yes. He also put a coral snake in my house."

"He what?"

"The crazy thing is, his sister is Sandra Sechrest. She was Holly Dougal's secretary. She's still working for Holly's husband, Russ Vay. You're still working Holly's death, right?"

A long silence. "Alice. You're going to have to start at the top. Wait till I get there."

"I'll meet you by the tow truck." She hung up before he could tell her no.

"I'm coming too," Kinsear warned.

At Alice's they changed into dry clothes for the first time in what felt like weeks. Alice's feet were white and wrinkly from her wet boots. She sighed with relief at the miracle of dry socks.

Isabel stood by the front door, backpack in hand.

"Remember, if you go down the creek road to Coffee Creek and get on Highway 290, you can get back to Austin without having to cross any low-water bridges," her dad said. "You know that, of course."

"Of course." She paused. "I want to stay too."

"You've got classes!" Kinsear said.

She sighed. "I know. Promise you'll tell me absolutely everything."

"Absolutely," Alice said. "George Files will need to talk to you."

Isabel looked at Alice and started laughing. Alice felt herself beginning to giggle.

"I was going to ask if I could come back tonight," Isabel shook her head, lifted her eyebrows.

"Of course," Alice said.

"I can't, but tell Files I'll come out tomorrow if he wants to talk."
She kissed Kinsear on the cheek and then, to Alice's surprise, hugged
her and ran out the door.

Alice lifted her eyebrows and grinned at Kinsear. "She's smart,
she's strong, she's funny."

Kinsear enfolded Alice in a hug that lifted her off her feet and
smushed her face into his shirt. He exhaled a sigh of relief. "Parent-
hood."

"I've got to see that truck!" Alice wriggled free.

"Okay, I'll bring my own car, then head to the ranch. Javier says
we've got some marooned cows."

She kissed him.

*****

Files climbed out of his Coffee County Sheriff's Department SUV
just as Alice, then Kinsear, pulled up. Files looked first at Alice, then
Kinsear.

"I never could get a chopper," Files said. "Want to fill me in on
what happened at Craft's place?"

They told him a condensed version, ending with the floating
trailer colliding with the stone wall.

"Then what?"

Alice shrugged. "Julie Dupree fed everybody, and they disappeared."

"Disappeared?"

"Literally. One minute they were eating nachos in her dining
room. The next minute—gone."

He nodded slowly, brown eyes moving from Alice to Kinsear and
back. "Tell me again about the cook who brought the key to you."

"Rosa Saenz. She said Craft would kill her if he knew what she
was doing," Alice said. "She kept saying 'hurry,' then raced back up to
the house as soon as we gave her back the key."

"Craft knew about the trailers, knew people were locked up,"
Files mused. "That's helpful. I can't get testimony from disappeared
people."

"Yeah, but she's an employee. And we're witnesses. Mr. Tire Iron here"—she pointed at Kinsear—"got those women out of a locked trailer sitting on cinder blocks, before the flood sent it crashing over on its side."

Files asked questions, made notes.

Below on the creek bank the tow truck groaned and whined. Finally, the engine accelerated, tires crunched forward up the stony bank, and the black truck, smeared with mud, emerged tailgate first out of the creek. The driver's side door swung open. The window was down or missing.

Water trickled out of the truck bed, out of the interior, onto the bank.

Files walked down, peered in. Alice and Kinsear followed.

"I see luggage wedged in the back, behind the driver's seat," he said. "Two suitcases and a long soggy box." He turned away, pulling his phone out of his pocket.

Alice heard him say, "Crime scene investigator. Yeah, asap. I need to see what's in the luggage, but I want crime scene to see it first."

He turned to Alice. "Looks like your guy was running out on his boss, doesn't it?"

"Along with the other SUV driver," Alice said. "Isabel asked the, um, rescued people. They said both guys left Craft's place before we got there."

"Isabel?"

"My daughter," Kinsear said. "She helped with the rescue. She speaks Spanish."

"I'll need to talk to her." Files took her contact info. His phone beeped. He checked the screen. "Crime scene people are on their way."

"What about"—she started to say "El Gato"—"Stan Sechrest? Has anyone looked at his body yet?"

"Based on the deputy's report I asked for an autopsy."

"The driver's door is open," Kinsear said. "Is the seatbelt unfastened too?"

"Yes."

Kinsear gave his card to Files, said he'd be available if needed, and hugged Alice. At the same moment each said to the other, "Call me!" He left.

A county crime scene team arrived. Like Files, they looked worn, exhausted. Files gave them instructions. Alice heard, "I want a complete inventory of the truck." The team began suiting up.

Files turned back to Alice. "Let's talk about how this Stan Sechrest connects to Holly. If he does."

Alice retrieved her notebook from her car, the notebook in which she'd covertly scribbled while eavesdropping on the two Sechrests. "Sandra criticized her brother for somehow getting them 'in the middle of' the cowboy action scene. She criticized him for eliminating anything 'self-inflicted.' It's cryptic, but what if he was out at that shooting competition? And killed Holly?"

"Those volunteers made everyone who came in the gate sign a release. I'm pretty sure his name wasn't on that list."

Files's phone beeped again. He lifted a hand to her, climbed into his SUV, listening.

Alice looked at the sky. Empty, blue, chilly, but sunny. She felt the need to run, felt desperate for the open road.

She drove home, tugged on running pants, running shoes. She wanted to clear her head of the memories of Sechrest's body under the branches, of desperate upturned faces trying to climb out of the trailer, of the furious tug of the flood waters as she and Kinsear and Isabel crossed the creek.

She was, for the moment, free. She declined to feel responsible for the world. She planned to hit the road, with earphones and strong music, watching the pastures to see if any bluebonnets planned to bloom in this too wet spring. Alice had in mind a three-and-a-half-mile run, from her drive and then out the Old Hays Road, a two-lane blacktop that led west past the turnoff to Full House Ranch and all the way to Johnson City. She wanted a run that would let her feel safe, feel in charge of herself, surround herself with air, sun, sky, beauty. Well, what passed for beauty at the end of winter, beginning of spring.

At the last minute she realized she'd forgotten her phone. But what the hell? Off she ran.

Chapter Thirty-Six

Saved by Old Seabed

Once she was on Old Hays Road, the wind hit her. She wished she'd brought gloves. She pulled her sleeves down over her hands, stuck her thumbs through the openings at the cuffs, felt a little warmer.

The sight of her thumbs sticking out made her think of the dead man's hands, white, still, with stubs where the rest of his pinkie and ring finger should be.

The man who'd never send another mocking smooch, lips pursed, to his sister Sandra.

She stopped dead on the side of the road as it all came back to her, the images clear as could be: the tall red-booted blonde in the women's restroom, applying bright red lipstick and giving a kissy face to the reflection in the mirror, whose red gloves, holding the lipstick, had a pinky finger slightly askew…as if stuffed with tissue…and whose red boots, she'd seen below the divider in the cubicle next to hers, stood planted and pointed toward the toilet. Not away. Who didn't speak, but swaggered off with that sassy walk…and whom Alice later saw by the parking lot.

"Style points"? "The invisible man"? She thought about the comments she'd heard Sechrest make to his sister at the Driftwood restaurant.

Alice started running again, staring west at the horizon. Was it possible? Files said no one reported seeing Stan Sechrest at the cowboy action event. But was he tricked out in blonde curls and Chanel sunglasses?

She picked up the pace, thinking, pounding along the narrow grassy shoulder. If she'd brought her phone she could've called Files. She wanted these miles, though. Some sort of release, after holding too much fear in her body. Elena, snake, flood, death. Run instead. There was no traffic. She breathed the cool almost-spring air as she crossed the drive leading into the old Jamison ranch. Next to the driveway stood a steel pipe holding the keypad for the gate, and next to the road stood the ranch mailbox, sitting on a block of solid limestone. The Jamisons had high-fenced their ranch for exotics. Were those wildebeest out in the pasture? Or could they be a herd of gnu? Who knew? She would try that out on Kinsear.

She reached the end of the Jamison spread and turned back, staying on the same side of the road. Here she had to watch her footing between the narrow shoulder and the small swale between the road and the high game fence with its stout green metal poles. Why would someone keep wildebeest instead of, say, donkeys?

She pounded on, feeling strong. Okay, think it through. Why would Narcissus kill Holly?

She heard an engine behind her, glanced over her shoulder. An old blue truck, slowing. No worry. Suddenly the engine revved. Startled, she swung around. The truck raced straight at her, sun glaring off the windshield. No way to climb the fence; her only hope was that the truck was too big to fit between the mailbox and the steel gate post. Lungs bursting, running faster than she knew possible, she hurtled through the gap between the mailbox and post.

Out of the corner of her eye she saw the truck hit the limestone block of the mailbox and careen back onto the asphalt, tires screeching. The left rear bumper bore what looked like the tattered Full House bumper sticker. She could see the driver's head silhouetted in the sun— too short for Russ? The truck disappeared over the hill. She stood, holding onto the gate and catching her breath, fearing the truck might turn around and roar back for more. Silence.

Hands on her hips, gasping, Alice crossed the drive to the limestone block. Saved by old seabed, she thought. Fresh white chips and limestone dust speckled the grass. The truck had taken out one corner of the stone pillar. She bet that left a big scratch on the truck's right fender. She saw a smidge of blue paint on the rock.

But who at Full House? And why?

Still shaken, she trotted home, anxious when she heard a vehicle approaching, relieved when she turned into her own drive, and even calmer when she saw no strange car or truck waiting.

Once inside she grabbed her phone. The screen showed two calls from Files. She called him.

"I'm still alive," she said, "but barely." She told him about the careening truck.

"From Full House? You're sure?"

"I can't absolutely swear to it but it looked like the bumper sticker

I've seen."

Files sighed. "I called to tell you something. You know we'd notified Sandra Sechrest about her brother's death."

"Yes. I gave the deputy her contact info."

"He might have mentioned to her where he got it. Anyway, as next of kin she had to identify the body. I scheduled it so I could be there. She seemed . . . kind of resigned. No tears. She asked where his effects were, wanted to take everything home. She got very upset when I told her we couldn't release them yet; we were looking at them in connection with two deaths. She wanted to know which deaths. I told her Elena Ramos and Holly Dougal."

"What did she say?"

"'Who's Elena Ramos? And what possible connection could my brother have to Holly Dougal?'"

"Did you ask her if her brother came to the cowboy action event?" Alice broke in. "Because I've got this idea."

"I asked her that. She said she hadn't seen him."

"Funny response," Alice said. "She didn't answer your question. Why didn't she say 'absolutely not' or 'I would have told you if he was there'? She kind of left the door open to be able to say she knew he was there but didn't see him. But, listen, about my idea—"

"Wait, I'm not through. Here's why I called. Sandra Sechrest sniffled some, dabbing with a tissue, and said, 'Is this because of Alice Greer? I don't know why she hates me so much. She'd do anything to interfere. She's the one who screwed up Holly's trust account.'"

Alice digested that. "That's a weird reaction to identifying your brother."

"I told her there's no evidence you or your office had anything to do with the fake email instructions. Then I said, 'What do you mean by interfere?' She said you tried to turn Russ and Holly against her. Kept dabbing her eyes. She'd just had to identify her brother's body, so her focus on you surprised me. Usually people want to know what happened to their loved one, like, did he suffer. She didn't even ask about that neck wound."

"Huh. It's true she dislikes me. She told Russ I'd mistreated her, asking about whether she had access to Holly's email accounts, suggesting I was hostile to her." Alice knew inside she'd always felt some vague distance, some barrier, with Sandra. "But if you want to talk about hostile? How about whoever was driving that truck straight at me!"

"You couldn't identify the driver?"

"No, not with the sun reflecting the way it did. I saw just enough to think the driver looked a little too small for Russ."

"Well, here's some, um, colorful info. In the dead guy's suitcases in the truck, we found a blonde wig, a red satin jacket, red leather gloves, and red and white boots."

"That's what I wanted to tell you!" Alice began.

"Also a Ruger New Vaquero pistol, which we've sent over for ballistics examination, against the bullet that killed Holly Dougal."

"Ah!" Alice thought about the autopsy, the medical examiner's forceps tugging the bullet from Holly's heart, tried to brush that thought away. "Let me tell you about the women's restroom." She described her bathroom encounter with Red Boots, the smoochy mouth, the lipstick, the skewed pinkie, and the boots' orientation in the bathroom cubicle.

"Boots pointing toward the toilet? Is that definitive evidence?" First chuckle she'd heard from him in days. "I'd enjoy hearing a defense attorney question you about that, but I guess we won't get the chance. Assuming Sechrest is Red Boots."

"Maybe it's not proof, but it's suggestive," Alice retorted.

"Even better, the crime scene team reported someone had stuffed tissue into the right glove pinkie."

That felt gratifying. "But assuming my Red Boots in the women's restroom—blonde hair, red gloves—was indeed Narcissus—I mean Stan Sechrest—wouldn't he have had to sign a release at the cowboy action site? Even if he used a fake name? Did you actually check with everyone who was there?"

"Eads told me he contacted everyone who signed a release."

"Including Red Boots? I saw her—him—standing by the parking lot, close to the time Holly was shot. I didn't see him or her after that. Do we know when Red Boots left?"

He grunted. That meant no. "Maybe that won't matter if we get positive ballistics evidence on the pistol."

"I've also been wondering about the guy in the black truck who picked up the trash," Alice said. "There was no trash in the trash container I saw. At the restaurant Sechrest said he loves a good costume. And termed himself the 'invisible man.'"

After a moment Files said, "Maybe he's played his last two parts. One more thing. The long box in the truck held a rifle. Ballistics has it as well. But since we never found the bullet that hit Elena, that may be no help in solving her death."

"Supposedly the guy who told our…our rescued people about Elena getting shot is one of Craft's SUV drivers. Supposedly he left the afternoon of the flood, before Sechrest. Did anyone ask Craft's cook about him? Rosa Saenz, she's the one who brought us the key?"

"I'll tell Joske."

Alice felt relief. Not Eads.

"Also, I'll send someone out to take a look at the Full House ranch truck. What time did the truck send you scampering behind the Jamison mailbox?"

She knew she should have taken her phone. "I wasn't scampering, I was running for my life. Maybe forty minutes ago."

"I'll let you know what we find. Meanwhile, I'm asking you not to mess with Sandra Sechrest. Obviously we've now got more questions we need to ask her once we've got ballistics back. The reason I'm sending someone out to Full House even though we have our hands full? It's so you won't go yourself. Got it?"

"I'll be careful. When will you have the ballistics results from that Ruger pistol?"

"Maybe Thursday or Friday. But seriously, don't go talk to Sandra Sechrest."

"I'm Holly's executor. I still might have to talk to her about Holly's assets."

"Oh, hell. Couldn't you at least hold off for a couple of days?" He hung up.

Chapter Thirty-Seven

I'll Save Your Life Any Time

Her phone pinged: "Prepare for Craft depos."

A much-needed reminder that she earned her living by achieving results for her paying clients. Files, not Alice, should be tracking down Holly's murderer, Elena's murderer. Alice should be working on the task Ham and Julie were paying her for: making Craft abide by the covenants that protected their land values. And if Holly, after death, still paid a whit of attention to this planet from wherever she'd gone, she'd point out that Alice should also be working to secure Marcy's future in the group home. Finding that money was key.

Alice pulled on pants and a jacket that could go to court if needed and drove down the creek road to the office. Propelled by anger after the blue truck attack, she slammed her car door and strode straight to her desk.

Silla poked her head around Alice's office door. "Someone made us mad?"

Alice described playing keep-away with the truck. Silla shook her head. "Honestly, you could find a safer way to exercise. Yoga? Barrel racing? Want to come ride with me?"

"Nope."

"What about the dead guy I heard you and Kinsear found this morning? Julie Dupree called to tell me."

Alice was shocked. Was it only this morning? She'd tried so hard to get the images out of her head: the white face, naked hands, terrible neck wound. The white ankles in expensive sneakers, trapped beneath a sycamore branch. But Silla deserved to know, so she leaned against the wall and described finding the body and the cat prints and watching the pickup get winched up out of the creek.

"Those low-water crossings." Silla shook her head. "You can tell people a hundred times and they still think they can get their truck across. That's weird about the cat, though. I read a book about a killer cat, out here in the Hill Country." She shivered. "Cat bites you on the neck, that's it."

Maybe that's what Kinsear meant. Paralyzed. You couldn't raise your hands to fight. Hence…Stan Sechrest's bare white hands.

Instead she said, "Let's get ready for those depositions."

Under her agreement with Craft's lawyer, Wisenthorpe had to produce both Craft and the cook, Rosa Saenz. Alice had debated which order to specify in the deposition notice—whether to put Rosa or Craft first. Initially she'd thought she'd take Rosa first, fearing Craft might intimidate his cook. Then she decided that Rosa might be a better follow-up, since she could contradict Craft if he lied. As she expected he would. Alice was also betting Wisenthorpe wouldn't have prepped Rosa for some of Alice's questions. Craft would be the first to go.

Alice focused on two goals in a deposition. First, get testimony supporting each element she had to prove: Craft knew the trailers were on his property, he'd authorized or permitted them to be there, and he knew they violated the applicable covenants. Bonus points if she could establish the second violation, that Craft used his property for nonresidential business purposes. Her deposition notice required Wisenthorpe to produce Craft's documents about the money he'd earned from the party venue business, built on the backs of locked-up workers. She might find some goodies in the documents.

Silla brought in a stack of printouts. "Everything I found online about our Dickie Craft. Also tax docs from Coffee County, and his deed and the covenants."

"See what you can learn about Rosa Saenz. Anything that affects her credibility." Silla knew the drill: arrests, convictions, other issues.

Alice glued herself to the keyboard, hammered out deposition questions, stewed about exhibit order, thought about Rosa. She wanted to get the name of the second SUV driver. With Sechrest dead, Craft might think he could deny everything. Isabel had followed two SUVs to a wedding venue, Bluff Wines; she intended to ask Craft what he made from that gig.

*****

Toward the end of the day Files called back. "I sent Joske out to Full House Ranch. He talked to Russ Vay and Sandra, separately. Russ told him that he'd been out riding all morning, first on his horse, then Holly's, and as far as he knew the truck had been there all day."

"What about Sandra?"

"She said she'd been there all morning. Then she volunteered that she'd used the truck to move some plants from the greenhouse. She said she'd thought she'd put it in park but it was in neutral and rolled into a tree. She showed him where the right fender hit the tree."

"Seriously?"

"Yeah, he looked at the fender, and it was dented."

"And the tree?"

"Had lost some bark. I can't say he was completely satisfied, but that's what he got."

"George, I saw blue paint on that limestone mailbox."

"I don't doubt it."

"Hey," Alice said. "Assistant Detective Joske didn't mention my name out there, did he?"

"No, Joske told them we'd had a report from a runner on Old Hays Road about almost being hit by a truck and that the runner thought the truck had a Full House bumper sticker. People know that brand around here, so that didn't sound too crazy. Joske was a little surprised that neither Sandra nor Russ Vay asked who the runner was or whether the runner was okay."

She wasn't surprised that Sandra didn't ask; she was surprised about Russ.

*****

"Eddie's closing on his new vineyard property is this Friday," Silla reminded her. "Jane Ann sent over the closing documents. I've emailed a set to Eddie."

Alice had only seen Eddie once since he got out of the hospital after being concussed and locked in his own wine vat. On that day she'd looked out the office window to see him lumbering up the sidewalk with a case of wine.

"It's half viognier," he'd said, laying the case gently atop her desk. "The other half's my new sangiovese, the one I aged in Hungarian oak. Aren't you more of a red wine girl?"

"Thank you!"

"Well, it's only for saving my life. I should've brought you the whole cask. But I've got to sell some so I can keep paying my lawyer."

She couldn't help it. She hugged him. "I'll save your life any time."

He gave her a classic unblinking Eddie look. "I know." And he left.

Now she studied the closing documents. Everything looked in order. She called Eddie. "All you have to do is show up Friday at Jane Ann Olson's, ready to sign. You're about to get your new vineyard."

"Right," he said. "Hey, I called the jail. Ol' Gorman's in the lockup."

"I guess he couldn't post bail this time."

"Or didn't want to," Eddie replied. "He may think he's safer inside."

Chapter Thirty-Eight

The Whole Truth and Nothing But

On Thursday at nine a.m., the court reporter and her videographer arrived with their equipment. Silla took them to the large conference room at the rear of the house to set up for the video depositions of Richard R. Craft and Rosa Saenz.

Ham and Julie came next. "I can't wait to see the guy who locked up those people," growled Ham. Silla led them to the kitchen, showed them where to get soft drinks and coffee.

Then Alice walked them to the conference room and showed them where the witness would sit, at the end opposite the videographer. "You two sit here, next to me." Her notebook and exhibit folders lay ready on the table. She handed them each a sticky pad and a pencil. "If you have a suggestion or think we need a break, just pass me a note. I'll be back shortly." Alice wanted a few uninterrupted moments at her desk to think.

Promptly at nine-thirty, Piers Alan Wisenthorpe parked his sedan in front of Alice's office. He looked just like his picture on his firm's website: navy suit, red tie, a little pudgy, thinning hair. Alice, still at her desk reviewing the pleadings file, watched from her window as he extracted a walker from the back seat and set it up on her sidewalk. He opened the front passenger door and for the first time she saw Richard Craft.

Craft was a tall man, hunched, with heavy frown lines and wispy white hair. He didn't thank Wisenthorpe, just put big-knuckled hands on the walker handlebars. He focused malevolent eyes on Alice's front door and stood glaring while Wisenthorpe grabbed his briefcase and a stack of documents from the car.

Silla opened the front door. "Can I help you up the—"

"Out of my way, girl." Craft almost hit Silla with the walker. Silla gave him The Look and pointed Wisenthorpe and his client toward the conference room.

Whoops! Silla won't be bringing you any coffee, Mr. Craft.

She heard Silla ask Wisenthorpe, "Where's Ms. Saenz?"

"She had an errand to run and wanted to drive herself. She'll be here in a few minutes." He followed Craft down the hall.

Alice mentally raised an eyebrow. The cook was showing inde-

284

pendence. She glanced outside to see a small Toyota parked at the curb. Rosa Saenz climbed out, wearing a navy dress instead of the uniform Alice had seen during the flood.

Alice came out of her office to greet her. Rosa Saenz levelled a direct gaze at her. "Thank you for coming," she said. "Please call me Alice. May I call you Rosa?"

"Yes."

"Rosa, what's the other driver's name? Not Stan Sechrest, the other?"

"Edgar Berry."

Aha! "Thanks."

Silla took her to the conference room.

Okay, curtain's going up. Alice made her last notes, scanned her desk to be sure she hadn't forgotten anything, picked up her laptop, squared her shoulders, and entered the conference room. Rosa sat by a window, away from the table. Craft sat in the witness's chair, opposite the videographer and next to Wisenthorpe. The court reporter, a woman who took most of Alice's depositions, sat next to the witness's chair.

Wisenthorpe rose as Alice came in. She smiled, shook his hand, then introduced herself and held out her hand to Craft. He did not extend a hand, did not say a word, just glared. Wisenthorpe's face pinkened. Alice introduced her clients, Ham and Julie, who nodded. Craft gave them a long look, turned his head, and stared out the window.

"You've got the documents I asked for?" Alice asked Wisenthorpe.

He picked up his stack and handed them to Alice. "Um, could we speak for a moment?"

Alice walked him back to her office, clutching the documents. She leaned against her desk, waiting.

"Can't we settle this now, Alice? I mean, maybe he could agree to take the trailers off his property. You could withdraw the lawsuit and let these neighbors, ah, act like neighbors."

"Sorry," Alice said. "My clients need a written agreement, enforceable, that neither he nor any later owner will violate any covenant. Plus, my clients need their costs."

"Costs? Come on, Alice."

"I mean it. We sent a letter, one neighbor to another, asking Mr. Craft to comply voluntarily. Your firm stonewalled. If he'd been reasonable, my clients wouldn't have had to file suit."

His face fell. "I don't think he'll go for this."

"Well, then, let's not waste time." She stood up and headed for the door.

Isabel had arrived. She stood in the entry, hugging Silla. Alice took them both to the kitchen and handed over the documents Wisenthorpe had brought. "See if you find anything showing Craft owned the trailers, knew about the workers and trailers, Bluff Wines, and so on. I'll need them after the break. I'm gonna get started."

The videographer adjusted the microphone on Craft's collar while Craft heaved an impatient sigh. Alice settled herself next to the court reporter, with Julie on her other side.

The court reporter read the oath, made Craft raise his hand, asked Craft if he swore or affirmed that the evidence that he would give "shall be the truth, the whole truth and nothing but the truth." He grudgingly agreed.

Alice started with background, age, education, work history. He snorted impatiently at each question. She thanked him for each answer. She passed him his deed and the covenants. He agreed he owned the property next to Ham and Julie. She made him read aloud the covenant clauses prohibiting trailers and business use. He did so, then said, "These are ridiculous. Completely out of date."

"Objection, nonresponsive. Sir, whether you approve of the covenants or not, you agree that they prohibit mobile homes on your property?"

"That's what this paper says."

"And prohibit business use other than agricultural?"

"Yes, but that's not fair." Craft glared at the exhibit.

"Objection, nonresponsive. You knew of these covenants when you bought your property, right?"

"I knew about them."

"Sir, you walked into my office under your own power today, correct?"

"You saw me."

"Please answer."

He snorted. "Yes."

"You're aware that as of the flood just days ago two white trailers were on your property."

"It's possible Sechrest might have put something out there by that time," he said. He added, "I don't go outside much." He furrowed his brow. "I don't get around too well."

"You don't deny there were trailers on your property as of the flood?"

"There might have been, but I have no knowledge."

"When you received our lawsuit, it included a photo of two trailers on your property, correct?"

"It looked like it but could've been faked."

"You've taken no action to require removal of any mobile home on your property, correct?"

His face reddened. "I thought your letter was ridiculous. I didn't care what you said."

"Objection, nonresponsive." The court wouldn't like his response. She switched gears. "Is Rosa Saenz your cook?"

"Yes. You already know that."

"She's your employee?"

"Yes." He rolled his eyes. Alice saw Wisenthorpe frown. At a video deposition lawyers didn't want clients to roll their eyes. Alice could swear Wisenthorpe tried to nudge him under the table.

"You've also employed Stan or Standifer Sechrest?"

He furrowed his brow and turned to Wisenthrope, who looked confused.

"Yes. I hired Sechrest to drive."

"You had him live onsite, correct?"

"Yes."

"You also employed Brad Gorman?"

Craft shrugged. "I let him stay a couple of weeks."

"What was his job for you?"

" Supposed to find real estate deals, but he was worthless."

"When did you kick him out?"

"Objection, form," Wisenthorpe said. "Form" was the only objection Wisenthorpe could make. The witness still had to answer.

"You can answer," Alice said to Craft.

"Two or three weeks ago."

"That's correct, that you made him leave your property?"

"I did. Worthless so and so."

"You also employed a second driver, Edgar Berry. Correct?"

"Yes."

Thank you, Rosa!

"Berry picked up workers and drove them to your property, correct?"

"I don't know."

"Berry locked workers in the trailers on your property, didn't he?" She heard the hard edge in her voice.

Wisenthorpe blinked, then tried to control his face. His role was to defend the deposition; whatever he might deplore about his client, he couldn't let his face show his true feelings, especially if he felt surprise, horror, revulsion. Alice felt only slightly sorry for him.

"Locked? I don't know anything about that," Craft said.

"Sechrest kept workers locked in the trailers, correct?"

"Told you, I don't know about workers in the trailers. You'd have to ask Sechrest." He smirked. "Of course, he's dead."

"He died in the flood this past Sunday, didn't he?"

"Yeah."

Wisenthorpe's forehead wrinkled, and he shot a glance at Craft. Had Craft not told him about Sechrest?

"Your employees Berry and Sechrest drove these workers from your property to local sites to work events such as weddings, correct?" Wisenthorpe's eyes widened. He glanced again at Craft, who ignored him.

"I don't know," muttered Craft.

"Mr. Craft, you're well aware, aren't you, that your employees Berry and Sechrest drove workers from the trailers to Bluff Wines to work an event within the past six weeks?"

Wisenthorpe interrupted. "Alice, we need a break."

"Shortly," Alice said. "Mr. Craft, answer the question."

"Bluff Wines, I don't know anything about that."

"Nothing at all?"

"Right. Nothing."

He'd regret that. "Back to the trailers," Alice said. "Did you tell your employees, like Rosa Saenz, that they must keep the trailers on your property locked at all times?"

"Of course not," Craft said. His forehead looked faintly damp.

Alice saw Wisenthorpe glance at Rosa, who didn't look at him. She continued watching Craft, her face unreadable.

"When the floods came last Sunday, you knew people were locked inside the trailers, correct?"

"I did not!" Craft said.

"Windows in your bedroom at the Waterfall Road house face the creek, correct?"

Craft narrowed his eyes at Alice. "You have no business asking about my bedroom."

"Objection, nonresponsive. Answer the question."

Craft turned to Wisenthorpe, who said, "Yes, you have to answer." His mouth was set.

"You can see the creek from your bedroom window, correct?"

He scowled.

"Answer the question, please," she said.

"Yes."

"At any time during last weekend's rains did you watch the rising water from your bedroom?"

A pause. "No."

"You were aware the creek was flooding, correct?"

"Somebody in the house said something about it. Maybe her." Craft nodded toward Rosa.

"You're referring to your cook, Rosa Saenz?"

"Yeah."

Alice looked him square in the eyes. "You know that one of the trailers came unmoored in the flood and knocked down your stone wall, don't you?"

"Someone told me. Later."

She leaned forward. "Is it your sworn testimony today that you never came to your bedroom window during the flooding and saw water threatening the trailers?"

Craft's face had darkened to a dangerous red. "I've told you over and over I saw nothing! No trailers, no people!"

Alice said, "Objection, nonresponsive."

Wisenthorpe sat hunched over his legal pad, pencil tapping the paper. "Alice, I think it's time for a break."

"We can take a break shortly," she said. "First, I've got a couple more exhibits to show the witness." She placed in front of Craft and Wisenthorpe the Coffee County tax records where Craft had assessed two trailers at his address as his personal property.

Craft looked at the records for a full minute. "I paid my taxes. But the county's wrong, this is a mistake." He pointed at the signature line. "That's not my signature."

"Does the tax firm Dudley Taxes prepare your tax filings?"

"Yes."

"Dudley Taxes is shown as authorized representative on this filing with the county for your annual rendering of business personal property for your location, correct?"

He looked at the document.

"It says Sid Dudley of Dudley Taxes."

"Do you authorize Dudley to sign tax filings for you?"

"Yes."

"Now, Mr. Craft, you're using workers whom you house in these trailers, which you acknowledge are your personal property, to staff local events like weddings, correct?"

"No. Unless maybe Berry or Sechrest did that."

"You're saying under oath that you have no knowledge that workers in the trailers on your property are being made to work local events like weddings?"

"No, I told you!"

She handed him the next exhibit: a blown-up photograph of the uphill trailer with men climbing out, Craft's parking area visible behind. Craft grudgingly agreed the trailer appeared to be on his property. "If the photo isn't faked."

"This was taken the night of the flood last Sunday," Alice said.

"You've said you knew the water was rising."

He nodded; she made him answer aloud. "Yes," angrily.

"You knew these men were kept locked in the trailer," she said.

"I had no idea."

"You told your employees to keep them locked in."

"Never!"

"You knew the trailer keys were kept in the kitchen."

At this he furrowed his brow. "I've said I don't know anything about keys and locks."

"Alice, how about that break?" Wisenthorpe said.

"Almost there. Here's the next exhibit." She handed Craft the photo of the women's trailer, on its side, floating toward the wall, and the women climbing the wall. He and Wisenthorpe stared down at the picture.

"You knew these women were locked in the trailer during the flood," she said.

"No!"

"Let's take a break," Alice said, not hiding the disgust in her voice, and went to her office.

Chapter   Thirty - Nine

Now for a
Little
Lagniappe

Silla and Isabel waited inside, both excited. Alice closed the door. Across her desk lay neat groups of Wisenthorpe's documents.

"Look, here's an invoice to Bluff Wines." Isabel pointed to the first group. "'Pay Craft Work three thousand dollars for catering, serving, and cleanup'!"

"Plus more invoices—all these blue-tagged ones," Silla said. "All invoices from Craft Work, address Waterfall Road. Also, take a look at what's in the mobile home ownership records. The orange tabs."

"Wow!" Alice said. Right there, two pages titled Statement of Ownership, each to Richard Craft for a white single-wide trailer, dated just months ago. Location: Coffee County.

"Before you ask, the dba, the doing business name, for Craft Work belongs to our Mr. Craft," Silla said. "Pink tab."

Alice grinned at both of them. Isabel's face glowed. "Great! If you want you can come watch Rosa's deposition," she told Isabel. "That'll keep her honest. Not that she's not."

Alice reconvened the deposition. "Mr. Craft, do you use the do-ing-business-as name Craft Work?"

"I don't recall. Maybe sometimes." She could see his mind work-ing, deciding how much to admit. How much to lie.

"Did you charge Bluff Wines three thousand dollars for workers doing catering, serving, and cleanup?"

"I don't recall."

She plopped the invoice before him and his lawyer. "Next exhibit. Do you recall having this invoice sent?"

Craft stared at the invoice. "I've never seen it."

"Objection, nonresponsive. Do you recall having this invoice sent?"

Slowly he nodded; she made him answer yes aloud. She put the other invoices in front of him, asked the same question. He slowly leafed through the invoices and said yes.

"These invoices, like the one you sent Bluff Wines, are for work done by people you took to the site, right?"

"I—it's for work done."

"Objection, nonresponsive. Answer the question. You sent these invoices for work done at these sites by people you sent to the sites?"

"Yes," he growled.

Alice turned to Wisenthorpe. "You didn't produce the requested documents showing these invoices were paid."

His mouth was set. "We'll take another look for those."

Next Alice laid the mobile home Statements of Ownership on the conference table before Craft. He and Wisenthorpe stared glumly at the two documents.

"You own these two mobile homes, correct?"

He turned to his lawyer. "I need some water." Wisenthorpe walked over to the conference room credenza and poured a glass of water for his client. Alice was enjoying Wisenthorpe's discomfiture. And Craft's.

"Please reread the question for the witness," Alice told the court reporter.

"I can't tell if they're the same ones as you're talking about on my property," Craft grumbled.

"If we look at the manufacturer's serial numbers on the trailers on the exhibits, and the serial numbers on the trailers currently at your property, we'll be able to learn that, won't we?"

"Maybe so."

Alice requested access to check the serial numbers. Wisenthorpe said he'd look into providing access.

"One last time, Mr. Craft. Do you agree that mobile homes, trailers, were on your property when you got our letter, when you got our lawsuit, and last weekend during the flood? Yes or no."

"Objection, form," Wisenthorpe said. "You can answer."

"I—yes."

"And you've agreed the covenants prohibit that?"

"Yes, but—" For the first time Craft looked uneasy.

"Thank you." Alice quickly assessed: Craft finally admitted trailers were on his property at key times, in violation of the covenants; he'd dodged and evaded about locked-up workers, but admitted authorizing the Craft Work invoices for work done by workers he'd sent; and she'd make Wisenthorpe provide the payment documents. She'd gotten what Ham and Julie needed for their lawsuit, and she felt grim satisfaction. Now for a little lagniappe.

She requested a quick break and checked with Ham and Julie outside the conference room—any more questions? They looked jaunty. "Nope."

She went back in. "Back on the record. No further questions. I offer all of plaintiffs' exhibits." Alice pushed the stack of numbered exhibits to the court reporter.

"No questions from me," Wisenthorpe said flatly.

"Are we ready for Rosa Saenz?" chirped the court reporter.

"Can we please have another break?" Wisenthorpe asked.

"Sure," Alice said. "You two can use the small conference room next door. We'll wait here."

Isabel entered the conference room, waved at Ham and Julie, smiled at Rosa. Rosa smiled back.

Wisenthorpe and Craft returned. The videographer clipped the mike to the collar of Rosa's navy dress, the court reporter swore her in, and Alice walked Rosa briskly through routine questions about name, age, education, work history. Then Alice leaned forward.

"Ms. Saenz, you're employed by Richard Craft as a cook at his house on Waterfall Road?"

"Yes, for a little more than four months."

"Do you stay there full-time?"

"Yes, I have a room."

"Can you give me the names of other employees working for Mr. Craft while you've been there?"

"Edgar Berry and Stan Sechrest. I think 'Standifer' is his full name."

"What job duties did you see Stan Sechrest carry out?"

"He drove workers from the house to the events. He made them stay inside the trailers. He checked the locks were locked, door and windows."

"Is that everything?"

"He worked out, exercised his muscles, trained his dog." Rosa stopped. "He used the dog to make the workers get in the trailers."

"What do you mean, he used the dog to make the workers get in the trailers?"

Ham and Julie both sat at attention, eyes riveted on Rosa.

"That dog, people were very afraid of it. Sechrest would have the dog on a leash but let it jump up at people, snarl at them."

"You personally saw this?" Alice couldn't help letting emotion into her voice.

"Many times. I wouldn't let him bring that dog in my kitchen."

Wisenthorpe glanced furtively at Craft. Alice would bet money that Wisenthorpe knew nada about the dog. Craft narrowed his eyes at Rosa, ignoring Wisenthorpe.

"Did you hear people call his dog the 'malo perro'?"

"Oh yes. That dog attacked workers when they were too slow into the trailers."

Alice slowed her voice. "Did Mr. Craft know how Sechrest used the dog to intimidate the workers?"

"Yes. He laughed about it. In my kitchen."

Wisenthorpe shut his eyes.

Alice continued. "Did Sechrest, what, guard Mr. Craft's property?"

"Yes. He patroled, you call it. With the dog." Rosa added, lip curled in scorn, "Sechrest liked to call himself El Gato. He was…a strange man."

"Objection, nonresponsive," Wisenthorpe interjected.

Alice had a flash. "Did Sechrest keep snakes?"

Rosa all but rolled her eyes. "He did. He wanted to keep mice for the snakes in my kitchen. I said no way. Mr. Craft made him keep them in the garage."

"How do you know Sechrest kept the workers locked in the trailers?"

"Anyone could see that by looking out the window. Sechrest would go out and unlock the trailers before the workers went to the events, and afterward he locked them back in."

"You yourself saw this?"

"Yes, from the kitchen."

"Were the keys kept in the kitchen?"

"Yes, by the door."

"Did Mr. Craft know there were workers in the trailers?" Alice leaned forward on the edge of her chair.

"Of course."

Wisenthorpe stirred, ready to object.

"How do you know?"

"Every time a new group came in, Berry and Sechrest had to report to Mr. Craft. How many, were they good, what events were scheduled, things like that."

"Did you actually hear the reports being made to Mr. Craft?"

"Yes. When I took him a breakfast or lunch tray upstairs, I would hear."

"Did you hear Mr. Craft tell them to be sure the trailers were locked?"

"Practically every day."

Alice stole a look at her notepad, then glanced at Wisenthorpe. He looked sick. He'd edged his chair away from Craft.

"Last weekend, where were you when the creek was rising?"

"In the house, mainly in the kitchen. I took lunch and supper up to Mr. Craft."

Alice had been taught, never ask a question if you don't know the answer. She broke her own rule. "Was Mr. Craft in his room when you took him supper?"

"Yes." Rosa looked straight at the videographer. "He was standing by his window, looking at the creek."

"Could he see the trailers from his bedroom?"

"Of course. When I stood by the window, I could too."

"What, if anything, was said between you?" Still breaking her rule, but the room sat spellbound.

"I said, 'What about the people in the trailers? The water's getting too close to them!'"

"Did he respond?"

"He said, 'Mind your own business.'"

All eyes turned to Craft. He sat stone-faced, eyes boring into Rosa.

"What did you do after that?"

"I was worried sick. I took those people their meals, those people in the trailers. I knew they'd be helpless, locked in like they were. I kept looking out the kitchen window downstairs. Then I saw one trailer had turned over on its side. The water was rising so fast. I knew I had to do something. Some people were trying to help the women inside climb out a window. I grabbed the keys and ran out and gave them to the man trying to open the door to the men's trailer. I had to tell him to hurry and give them back. I knew if Mr. Craft saw me out his window he'd be furious."

The court reporter's flying fingers stopped. She looked at Alice, eyes wide. Usually she was impervious to deposition horror.

Alice thought for a moment. She kept waiting for Wisenthorpe to object to her questions as irrelevant. She had what she needed for Ham and Julie but here was Rosa, under oath, on videotape. This was about murder. Alice forged ahead.

"When you brought the keys out, were you afraid Berry or Sechrest would stop you?"

"No, they'd gone," Rosa said. "I saw Berry drive off before the low-water bridge closed. He came to the kitchen, told me Craft said he could go check on his family. He only took a backpack with him. Sechrest, though, he carried down suitcases from the apartment over the garage, where he and Berry stayed. He loaded them in his truck. Didn't load his motorcycle, but he took his dog."

"He had a motorcycle?"

"Yes. A red Yamaha. He kept it in the garage under a tarp."

"What time did Sechrest leave?"

"About five."

Alice shifted gears. "Do you remember Brad Gorman?"

"Yes. For a while, at least a month, Mr. Craft let him stay in the garage apartment. Then he got rid of him."

"When?"

"A couple of weeks ago."

"Tell me what you know about that."

"They had an argument out on the terrace by the kitchen. Really loud. Mr. Gorman didn't get some real estate deals Mr. Craft wanted, especially one with a vineyard. I heard Mr. Craft say Gorman needed to pay him back, that he couldn't keep sponging off him. He made Gorman leave, made him leave his clothes and his car at the house. Berry shoved him into one of those SUVs, and I don't know where he took him."

"Alice, where's the relevance?" Wisenthorpe asked. "I object to this line of questioning."

Alice's mind had moved to Elena's bloody body. "One more question. Did you hear anything about Sechrest shooting, killing, one of the women workers?" Across the table Craft shot her an evil look.

Rosa took a long breath. "No. Berry might know. I did see Sechrest patrolling one night with that long gun, and Berry was with him."

Hmm. Alice had hoped Rosa had heard about the shooting. She had another flash. "Do you recall when someone cut down a large pecan tree by one of the trailers?"

"Yes. I saw that tree come down."

"Who cut it down?"

"Sechrest and Berry."

"Why?"

"Berry told me it was so no other workers could climb it and escape over the wall."

"Did he say someone had escaped?"

"Yes. A young woman. A little over a month ago."

Elena.

"You confirm Mr. Craft's your employer?"

"Until noon today."

Craft suddenly opened his hooded eyes.

Rosa added, "I'm quitting as of noon today. I've got another job."

Alice, surprised, said, "Let's take a break, so I can talk to my clients, see if we're through. Piers, you and Mr. Craft can stay in here." She needed to check whether her clients had more questions. She thought she had plenty: Rosa had confirmed that Craft directed his employees to keep workers locked in the trailers onsite. Rosa confirmed Gorman was kicked out without his belongings. What about that motorcycle? Hadn't Gorman said he saw one when he was leaving Eddie's? She wanted to get this transcript to George Files as soon as possible.

She gave a "follow me" nod to Ham, Julie. She asked Rosa if she'd like a restroom break. "Isabel can show you where it is." Rosa unclipped the mike and followed Isabel. Alice didn't want Wisenthorpe quizzing Rosa outside the deposition.

Ham, Julie, and Alice stood inside Alice's office. "What do you think?" Julie asked.

"I think we've got what we need. Can you two think of anything else?"

"Nope."

"I need more coffee." Alice sped to the kitchen where Silla was handing a glass of water to Rosa.

"Rosa, thank you again for coming today. Where's your new job?"

"Dripping Springs. My sister lives there. I'm going in with her on a catering business."

"Can you give your contact information to Silla here? Email, cell, everything?"

"Sure."

"And listen, Rosa, after what you've said today, I'm worried Mr. Craft might try to shut you up."

Rosa stuck her chin in the air. "Just let him try."

Alice knocked on the conference room door, then stuck her head in. The court reporter was checking Alice's numbered exhibits. The videographer was repacking his equipment.

Wisenthorpe stood at the table, "We're done," he said, stuffing tablets and notebooks in his briefcase. "No more questions."

The court reporter looked inquiringly at Alice. "I offer the rest of our exhibits. No more questions," Alice said. "And yes, I need a rush on these transcripts."

Wisenthorpe brought Craft his walker.

"Goodbye, Mr. Craft," Alice said.

He turned angry eyes on her. "You're gonna regret this."

"Just doing my job." She held his eyes. He grabbed the walker and stalked out.

Wisenthorpe followed, stone-faced. He said nothing about getting dates to depose Alice's clients. What could he possibly ask Ham and Julie after this? He'd just be giving them another opportunity to tell the truth about his client.

Alice didn't envy Wisenthorpe, having to drive Richard Craft back to his house on Waterfall Road. She shivered. The embodiment of evil. Maybe Silla would burn a bundle of sage in the conference room. But her job was merely to enforce those covenants. She'd call Wisenthorpe tomorrow about getting those trailers off the property.

Chapter Forty

Nested Russian Dolls

Friday midmorning: The draft deposition transcript pinged in her email. Bless the court reporter, she'd turned it around overnight. Alice found and highlighted the testimony she was after, then emailed a copy of the entire transcript to George Files with a note: "See reference to Gorman, p 24, and Berry, p 26." Then she picked up the phone.

To her amazement Files answered his phone on the first ring.

"What's up?"

Alice heard road noise. She plunged in. "You probably aren't reading emails."

"Yeah, I am. Sitting on the side of the highway."

"Did you see the depo transcript from Richard Craft's cook, Rosa Saenz? I highlighted the part in the depo where she describes how our friend Brad Gorman lived at Craft's for a while."

"Hang on, let me look." Then he said, "Yeah, we knew that. When we picked him up out there next to LaFarge's vineyard he didn't want to say where he'd been living, but we found out."

"But don't you see? There he was, living in the same apartment as two other guys who worked for Craft...and one of them is Stan Sechrest!"

"Our flood vic. Keep going."

"Gorman's iPad was right there in the same apartment as Sechrest."

"You mean Sechrest could have hacked it? But why?"

"Because his big sister told him to!"

She could hear Files breathing.

Slowly he said, "The financial crimes unit cleared her email account."

"That's what Hooks said."

You're saying Stan Sechrest sent the fake instruction email to Media Central."

"Yes," Alice said. "I think he hacked Gorman's account and sent that email."

"And that's the connection between Sechrest and Holly Dougal? He and his bright big sister were working together on the money grab?"

"Yes!" Alice said. "That's why, at dinner in Driftwood, they were talking where in California they might move, once the deal was 'in the bank.'"

"Was Stan Sechrest smart enough to do that? Hack Gorman and send a convincing fake email?"

"I don't know about Stan. Sandra was smart enough to concoct the email herself. Sandra had ready access to the Media Central files in Holly's desk, the ones you picked up. I'm sure she could also see Holly's email, literally see it, on Holly's office laptop, with that magnifier screen. And what about Holly's phone? You remember how simple Holly's phone code was. Sandra could've called her brother and told him exactly how to hack an account, and what to say in the email. But more likely she sent him the wording, via email or message. I'll bet the financial crimes unit wasn't looking that direction, wasn't looking for her communications with her brother when they cleared her account."

"You may be right. But this makes no sense unless either Sandra or Stan owns the Palmetto Bank account."

"Right," Alice acknowledged. "My money's on Sandra. She was on the spot when the trust account was created. She's worked before as a corporate law paralegal. She knows how to gin up limited liability companies, how to handle filings with the secretary of state."

"Okay, thanks."

"Wait!" Alice said, before he could hang up. "Also, see in the deposition where I ask Rosa about Edgar Berry, Craft's other driver, about the shooting?" She waited for him to catch up. "See? Edgar Berry might confirm who shot Elena."

Again, the pause while Files scanned the transcript. "We'll see if we can find him. Otherwise...We're nowhere on Elena. No witnesses and maybe no live killer."

Alice's mind made a connection. "But if Craft ordered it?"

"We'll talk to Berry. If we can find him."

"When you do, ask him about Stan Sechrest's motorcycle in Craft's garage. Rosa described it."

"Remind me?"

"Remember, Gorman said he saw a motorcycle coming up McElrath Road when he left Eddie's. There might be prints. Will you let me know about Sandra and the email, George?"

"I've started wondering how long she plans to stay around Coffee Creek, with Holly dead. Maybe she's only waiting until his body's released."

"Maybe she's waiting to see if the financial crimes unit finally runs out of time and has to unfreeze the account."

"Okay, I'll try to see if we can get more information." He didn't elaborate.

She wanted to say, but didn't: "Tell the financial crimes unit to check her emails to her baby bro! Check her calls and messages! Find Berry! Find the motorcycle! Take prints!"

His voice changed. "Meanwhile, Alice, I'm dead serious. I don't want you mixed up with her. You understand?"

Alice felt resistance. "Hey, remember, I'm Holly's executor. How do you expect me to do my job if I can't communicate with Holly's secretary?"

"Stay clear of this investigation," he warned. "I'd be damn careful."

After Files hung up, Alice zeroed in on what bothered her about his request. Holly's executor should be pursuing a deal for the *Dark Song* screenplays as alternate funding for Marcy's trust account. With the Media Central money still out of her reach, Sandra might also be thinking those screenplays could fund her own retirement, somewhere on an island with palm trees. So even if Alice steered clear of Sandra, Sandra might have a head-on collision with Alice.

What had Holly said about the Austin law firm? Young whatever? Maybe she meant Young Elder Young, a name that tickled Alice. Alice had worked with Ginny Young on a women lawyers event when they were both associates. According to the firm website Ginny had made partner, focusing on entertainment law. Alice called her.

After the requisite pleasantries Alice asked if she remembered an employee named Sandra Sechrest. Ginny's voice changed immediately to lawyerly caution. "Let me touch base with our personnel manager and call you back."

When she called back, Ginny's first question was, "Are you planning to hire her?"

"No." Alice explained about the Media Central wire transfer.

"So, this is completely off the record. We let her go, without a reference."

"Okay."

"Five years ago, I represented an Austin film writer who came up with a great series idea, great script, great title. We needed a domain name for a new website, needed to design media ads and trailers for the series and merch, all that. But we found various forms of our proposed domain name had been reserved by an LLC, owned by some LLC, owned by another LLC. In intellectual property work you grow suspicious. Sandra worked for my associate. One night I searched our document management system and found those LLC documents were created in our very own office. Thank you, Sandra Sechrest."

"What'd you do?"

"She wanted money for the domain names. We threatened suit. Made her assign all rights to our client. And leave."

Chapter Forty-One

A Safe Place

Friday at noon, Silla returned to the office with two greasy paper bags. The aroma of tacos filled the air.

Files called on Alice's cell. She grabbed the phone and answered with her mouth full.

"Thought you'd want to know. The ballistics report came through."

"Sechrest's Ruger New Vaquero?" she asked.

"Ballistics says it's a match for the bullet that killed Holly."

Holy cow. It was all piling up on the Sechrest siblings. But Alice was chained to her desk until she finished her executor's report.

*****

"You've got less than a week to file that report with the probate court!" Silla called.

"I've got a draft!" Alice yelled back. Well, a draft list with question marks. The deadline approached for Alice as executor to file her record of Holly's assets.

By three she had a decent document, with a few blanks and question marks. Questions for Russ. He emailed her: "I've found most of those papers you asked for."

"I think I'll cut to the chase," she told Silla. "I'll go get the missing info from Russ."

*****

On her way out the Old Hays Highway Alice sang along to every song on Sun Radio until she turned down the Full House Ranch drive. Then her voice stuck in her throat. She reminded herself of her mantra for difficult conversations: stand up, stand straight, stay calm. She usually found "stay calm" the toughest.

Russ opened the door for her. No smile, but he briefly put his arm around her shoulder. That felt encouraging. "Let's go to the study." He took the key from his pocket, unlocked the door.

He was still in guard mode.

He settled Alice in a chair facing Holly's desk. He pulled up a chair beside her, sat down with a sigh, and flipped open a folder on Holly's desk. "I went down to the bank and opened the safety deposit box. Here's the deed to the ranch. Also, some insurance papers on Holly's personal property. 'Personal property'—that's a weird term, isn't it? We'd insured some of her jewelry, like the pearls and the squash-blossom necklace, and also her piano, in the living room. You already got the car title info, right?"

Alice nodded. "Thank you. I'll get copies and bring these originals back." She showed him the asset list. "Can you think of anything else to add?" She pointed to two penciled question marks and turned to face him.

His eyes bored into hers. "Listen. Detective Files came out to tell me they got a ballistics match on the gun used to kill my wife. Did you know about this?"

"I just heard."

"He said she was shot by a pistol belonging to Stan Sechrest."

Alice nodded.

"And that he's Sandra's brother."

Alice stared back.

"Alice, you knew? Did you know this guy?"

"I've seen him. I never talked to him." She added, "My friend Kinsear and I found his body."

His face turned red. "Well, dammit, I feel like a complete idiot! I've got this woman working here and her brother's gun killed Holly? What about him—*was* he the shooter?"

Alice turned her head to check that the door was closed, then faced Russ. "That's my guess. What did Files tell you?"

"He's looking at it as a possibility." Russ shook his head, eyes toward the window. "Here I am in front of Holly's desk. She should be sitting right on the other side. What the hell?"

"I know," Alice said. She did, too. Death left vast emptiness.

After a moment she said, "I think I've got about everything I need. One blank we'll have to fudge, though—whatever we can get for her *Dark Song* trilogy."

After a short pause, he said, "You did find those screenplays?"

"Yes." She took a chance. "But something weird, Russ. Someone wiped Holly's laptop."

"What do you mean?"

"Everything she wrote on that laptop from July on—it's gone. All her writing."

Russ knit his brows, stared in disbelief at her. "That's impossible. Holly would never do that."

"She didn't. It happened after she was shot." She watched his face change. "I haven't told Files yet, but I will."

"You've got those screenplays, though?"

"Yes. They're in a safe place."

Alice felt a draft and turned. Sandra stood at the study door, smiling at Russ. "Oh! You two are still meeting. I . . . I just had one question, Russ, about that plumbing bill."

"I'll be out in a bit," Russ said shortly.

Sandra smiled again and softly pulled the door to.

Alice stood, heartrate a little faster, and picked up the folder. How long had Sandra been there?

"Thanks, Russ. I'll get these originals back to you and send the revised list."

She did not want to talk to Sandra. She thought Russ might. As they left Holly's study Russ locked the door behind him, then walked Alice to the front door. She got a distracted goodbye. He turned away.

*****

From the car Alice called Red. "Still on for dinner at the Beer Barn?

"Wild horses couldn't stop me."

Solace, pure solace: her best friend and a cold beer, though Alice was really a wine girl.

When she pulled open the door to the Beer Barn, Red had already claimed their favorite barstools, in the corner where they could see the stage and the dancefloor. No one was playing yet.

History, the bartender, greeted them. "Ladies, Jaime's trying out his chile relleno recipe tonight. First time. He's a little nervous."

"Pecans or raisins?" Alice asked.

"Both," History said.

"Sour cream?" Red asked.

"Definitely," History replied.

Red and Alice glanced at each other, then nodded. "I'm in," Red said.

"Same."

"Plus my Dos Equis," Red added.

"And my Modelo Especial, draft."

Alice leaned both elbows on the bar and sighed in relief, gazing into the golden bubbles.

Red said, "Tell me where things stand on Holly. I still can't believe she's gone."

"On Holly." She realized with shock that Red knew virtually nothing about this saga. Her best friend, and they hadn't talked since before the flood. Where to start? "Well...first, we found Elena."

"I remember, that was the day Holly came to book club," Red said. "But what does that have to do with Holly?"

"Elena was shot trying to escape from what was really slave labor, at Richard Craft's house on Waterfall Road."

"You're kidding. Who shot her?"

"Maybe the same guy who shot Holly. He worked for Craft, keeping the undocumented workers locked up. He wouldn't want Elena to get away and spill the beans. But we didn't find out about that until the flood." She tried some of her draft beer. "After Holly was killed at the cowboy action event, Eddie LaFarge got bonked on the head and locked in his new concrete wine tank. He could've died."

Red asked, "Who did that?"

"We thought it must be Brad Gorman, Eddie's former partner, who tried to talk Eddie out of buying some land Gorman wanted to buy. He's a jackass, but maybe not a killer."

"Who locked up Eddie?"

"Well, it turns out Gorman was living at Craft's and supposed to be signing up real estate deals for him. If not Gorman, it's possible that the guy who shot Holly also locked up Eddie so Eddie couldn't get that real estate deal Gorman wanted. For his boss."

History brought them each a platter. "Ooh," said Red. "Looky here!" The chiles rellenos, golden, fragrant, sat regally in a mélange of beans and salsa, with sour cream and guacamole decorating the platter. For a few moments only the sounds of satisfaction could be heard.

Red finally put her fork down for a moment. "I'm completely lost," she said. "What does Eddie getting locked in a tank have to do with Holly getting shot at the cowboy action event?"

"Nothing really, except I forgot to mention the fake email. Do you remember Holly was hoping for a TV series deal on her *Tales of the Road?*"

"Vaguely."

"She got the deal, and money was supposed to come to her new trust account that she set up for her sister."

"Sister?"

Alice realized explaining everything was hopeless. "Oh, Red, it's too complicated, and I'm talking out of school, because there's still not enough proof of some of this. Plus she was hoping for another deal." No, way too complicated. Alice applied some sour cream to her chile relleno. "Tell me what's going on with your horses."

"I still love this rescue business," Red said. "When an abused horse gets to a safe place, it's always beautiful, watching that horse relax."

A safe place. Alice thought about the safe in the conference room closet where she had stashed the *Dark Song* original screenplays.

She and Red told History to kiss the cook for them. "Maybe not," he said. "You two drive safely."

"Always," Red said.

Alice lifted an eyebrow. Maybe not always.

A thunderbolt struck as she opened the car door. "Who is it?" That's what Sandra said as the trail boss ran toward the Swingin' Doors Saloon. Why "who," not "what"? Did she already know?

*****

The office was on her way home, more or less. She thought she'd just check on that "safe place," though Silla had made sure the office was wired, with motion detector lights around the eaves, both front yard and back, and an electronic alarm system for the doors and windows.

Alice sped out the one-way street from the Beer Barn, then turned left just before she reached the courthouse, and turned left again onto Live Oak, a block from her office. She slowed.

This stretch of Live Oak consisted mainly of small houses turned into offices, like Alice's and the dentist's office next door. At night, after hours, Live Oak was usually dark.

She drove slowly along. No lights at the dentist's, but lights ahead on the right—at her office. She braked and dowsed her headlights. She reached under the seat for her flare gun and loaded a flare into it, scolding herself. Why didn't she have something better?

She rolled forward slowly, headlights off, staring intently out the open passenger window, and braked softly to a stop just past the dentist's office but just ahead of her driveway. No lights shone inside her office but all the outdoor motion detector lights were on. Then they flickered out in the back yard. After a few seconds the front lights flickered out.

Was someone still there, lurking motionless in the bushes by the front door? She lifted the flare gun, pointing it out the passenger's window.

She glimpsed sudden movement on her left, and turned just in time to see Sandra, five feet from her window, pull back the hammer of a large silver revolver and fire at the driver's side window.

Glass shattered. Alice felt fine slivers prick her face and neck. Terrified and furious, she ducked her head, stomped the accelerator and raced forward. At the next intersection she braked and skidded into a U-turn and roared back toward her office. In her headlights she saw the old blue ranch truck pulling away from the curb across from the dentist's office and gaining speed as she closed in.

Must have been parked under that big tree across the street, and she'd missed it.

A siren whooped. Two blocks ahead at the courthouse a black and white SUV, lights flashing, stopped dead in the middle of Live Oak.

Oh hell! Alice realized the truck was going to try to make the next right turn before the courthouse. Yes, truck brake lights, screeching brakes. She stood on her own brakes and slid partway into the intersection. With a grinding noise the blue truck reversed at high speed and crashed into Alice's left front fender, then screeched forward and slewed right at the intersection.

Furious, Alice floored her accelerator. Her car was already dented, so what the hell. She sped past the truck and hit her brakes.

Behind her the blue truck swerved left onto the courthouse lawn, then passed her and veered back toward the street, smashing directly into the fire hydrant next to the sidewalk. Water spurted into the sky. The truck backed off the hydrant and turned sharply toward the street, but the county SUV, red and blue lights flashing, blocked it in.

Alice squinted out her windshield, turned on the wipers, looked at the SUV number. She could see the officer in the SUV talking into his mike. Just as she found her phone, it rang. Files.

"Listen," he said. "I just got a call from Russ Vay—"

"Wait," Alice said. "Tell your guy in unit 323 Sandra's armed. She's got a revolver." In a moment she saw the guy talking in the SUV turn and stare at her, then pick up his mike.

Files was back. "And you're where?"

"Courthouse."

Two more sheriff's department SUVs with flashing lights pulled up and flanked the blue truck.

A fire department truck pulled up, followed by a city water department truck.

Alice watched from a relatively dry distance as armed deputies advanced on the blue truck under a curtain of falling water. She saw them drag Sandra from the truck, handcuff her. Time seemed to speed, to crawl, at the same time. She looked up to see Files and Joske approaching. Files opened the driver's side door while Alice climbed out. He peered at her front seat and raised an eyebrow. "Didn't try your flare gun this time?"

She ignored him.

Joske nodded. "Ma'am."

"Let's go to my office," Files said.

Alice didn't move. Coming down the sidewalk was Sandra, handcuffed, hair streaming, clothes soaked, a soaking wet deputy holding each elbow. Two other deputies walked behind, hands on holsters. Alice heard her protesting, "But officers!" Then she saw Alice.

Sandra stopped dead on the sidewalk next to Alice's dented car, shrieking, "This is her fault, not mine! She rammed my truck!"

Alice felt a wave of fury so strong she thought she'd explode. "Murderer! You got your brother to do your dirty work so you could kill Holly and steal her life!"

The mask of Medusa. Alice had never seen such hate in a face.

"Come on, miss," growled the deputy, tugging Sandra, her high heels clicking, down the sidewalk toward the sheriff's annex.

When Alice gave her statement, she told Files and Joske about Holly's wiped laptop. "I think she heard me talking to Russ, at Full House. I'd told him I had the original *Dark Song* screenplays in a safe place. Plus, she heard me say I was going to tell you about the wiped laptop. She didn't want that."

"Because?" Files asked.

"She thought she already had the only electronic drafts of the *Dark Song* screenplays. If she could also get the only hard copies, she could wait awhile and try to pass them off as her own work. Or hold them for hostage."

Files gave Joske a look. "Get a warrant, see if she's got those electronic files somewhere." Joske nodded.

Awhile later, Files was on the phone to the prosecutor. Alice overheard "conspiracy" and "attempted murder." Files walked her out to her battered green Discovery. He shook his head, looking at the shattered driver's side window.

"Well, thank goodness for safety glass," Alice said. For the umpteenth time she dusted tiny fragments off her face and shirt.

Files shook his head again. "That's not what I mean. You know what Russ Vay said when he called me? He said he'd confronted Sandra after you left, asking questions. Later he discovered she'd taken his blue truck. She also took his Ruger New Vaquero and a pouch of bullets. He felt terrible that he'd mentioned to Sandra that you were going to talk to me."

"Whatever she planned, was she trying to put the blame on Russ?"

"Maybe. Who knows how her mind works. But Alice, you're only alive because the ammunition she picked up was his pouch of light-load bullets, for cowboy action."

He pointed at the window. She looked at the crazed spider web in the glass. "See where that bullet hit? Your head was right behind it. If that had been a regular thirty-eight, you'd be dead."

Alice felt blood leave her brain. She felt her knees go and caught herself before she just sat down in the wet grass. She leaned on her car instead. Files, silent, waited with her until she stood straight and pulled out her keys.

One more thing she couldn't tell her children.

Chapter Forty-Two

Maybe None of This Would Come Up

After his client's disastrous deposition, Wisenthorpe speedily agreed to Alice's proposed settlement, which required Craft to affirm the validity of the covenants, remove the trailers on his property within one week, refrain from any commercial operations, and pay the plaintiffs' legal fees and court costs. Alice filed the settlement in court as an agreed order that the plaintiffs could enforce any time Craft violated it and get their fees and costs.

Eddie invited Kinsear and Alice to the groundbreaking for his new petit verdot vineyard.

Conroy was providing barbecued ribs, his recipe. Eddie said, "I'm thinking, Alice, we need a food truck at the vineyard. You know any food truck law?"

Sechrest's dog washed up dead five miles down the creek.

Files, as he'd predicted, found the light-load bullet from Russ's Ruger next to the curb by Alice's office.

Files also found Edgar Berry. He told Alice, "Berry left Craft's SUV at Convict Hill in Austin and caught the bus to Houston. I asked him if Sechrest shot Elena. He said, 'Yeah, Sechrest shot at that girl when she climbed the tree and went over the wall. I made him stop. It was too dark for him to see what he was shooting at anyway. If he hit those horses next door we'd have a real problem.'"

Alice shook her head in despair for the human race.

Tonio told Alice that Files had called to say that the department concluded Stan Sechrest had shot Elena. "I guess that's closure," Alice said. "It's not justice."

Tonio looked at his feet, then back at Alice. "That's okay, the cat did the justice."

Alice thought about that. "I'll be at the service for Elena."

Media Central's funds were in the trust account. Alice hired Holly's agent to negotiate a similar deal for *Dark Song Trilogy*. Even if rates of return stayed low, Marcy could stay in her group home.

"Okay, boss," Silla said. "You can play next week. It's spring break."

Alice would pick up John and Ann at the Austin airport Sunday. She stewed about whether, and if so, how much, to tell them about Elena's death. Or Holly's. Or Stan Sechrest's. Or whether the spiders who'd spun the webs that caught Elena and Holly—Craft? Sandra?—would pay any price for their roles. She didn't want her children to worry, to give up on this fearful world.

She didn't want John and Ann staring off the deck at their family home at the fencepost where Elena died, where Sechrest's body was found.

Maybe none of this would come up.

*****

At five o'clock on the evening before John and Ann would arrive, Alice and Kinsear repaired to the treehouse. Alice climbed up the treehouse ladder with two champagne flutes. Kinsear unwrapped cheese and pears. They sat together looking out through the heavy twisted branches of the venerable live oak toward the edge of Alice's pasture, where the bluff tumbled down to the creek. A soft breeze ruffled Alice's hair. "That's a spring breeze, not a winter breeze," she told Kinsear.

"Bluebonnets." He nodded toward the patches of distinctive grey-green rosettes with their slender fuzzy stems holding spires of bluebonnet blue. "Amazing how they can grow in bare caliche. So beautiful, so tough."

Like the Hill Country. Alice's eyes fell on the three burros, little Big Boy, in front, flanked by Princess and Queenie. Heads high, ears cocked, they trotted slowly toward the edge of the bluff and stopped dead. Big Boy put his ears back, stomped one front hoof.

Alice pointed at the tall grass at the edge of the bluff. "Look. Ears!" she whispered.

"I swear that's a cat," Kinsear breathed.

Big Boy snorted loudly. The ears vanished. Kinsear turned to Alice. "Were those ears…a little big for a bobcat?" They watched the bluff. No ears returned. "Hmm."

He pulled a bottle of Pol Roger champagne from the cooler bag, unwrapped the foil, untwisted the wire, put his bandana over the top to catch the cork. "I've gotten where I really like this one. See what you think." Pop!

A mist of bubbles filled the air. Alice inhaled the sparkle, holding out the two flutes.

They sipped in companionable silence, watching the grass turn gold in the setting sun. The western sky grew pink, apricot.

After a moment Kinsear said, "You may have noticed I've been pretty quiet lately."

"I have," Alice said. Was he okay? "Your quiet is disquieting. Is something bothering you?"

"I'm not sure if you're gonna go for what I've been thinking." His eyes looked worried. "Alice, I want to marry you."

She'd never seen him so serious.

How would they resolve all the questions, the decisions, the…?

"I think yes," she said.

T H E   E N D

ABOUT THE AUTHOR

Helen Currie Foster writes the Alice MacDonald Greer Mystery series. She lives north of Dripping Springs, Texas, supervised by three burros. She is drawn to the compelling landscape and quirky characters of the Texas Hill Country. She's also deeply curious about our human history and how, uninvited, the past keeps crashing the party.

Find her on Facebook or at www.helencurriefoster.com.

HEARING FROM YOU

Thanks for reading *Ghost Cat!* If you enjoyed it, please consider rating it or putting a short review on Amazon. You readers who take the time to review books can and do make a difference in the success of a series.

Comments, questions or suggestions? Drop a note to thealicemysteries@gmail.com.

You can learn more about Alice and her adventures at www.helencurriefoster.com, and subscribe to the mailing list there, for updates and news about upcoming books.

This book would not have taken shape without the collaboration of Larry Foster and Grace Currie Bradshaw, nor hatched without valuable comments from Megan Biesele, Ann Ciccolella, Keith Clemson, the amazing critique group, beloved book group, and Heart of Texas Sisters in Crime. Thanks to Drew Foster for mapping. Many thanks to the Tejas Caballeros for the warm welcome at their cowboy action shooting venue, where Alice learned she liked a trace of gunsmoke in the air, and to David H. Donaldson Jr., John B. McFarland and Prentice Craig, who provided invaluable information about cowboy action shooting. All have my heartfelt thanks. Any errors are mine.

For advice from Jay Hodges and for Bill Carson's cover, design, layout and sheer professional brio, thanks and more thanks.